TRUEHEART

MEL STERLING

Mel Sterling
http://melsterling.com

Cover design by Skyla Dawn Cameron at Indigo Chick Designs.

ISBN-13: 978-0-9971391-0-5 (trade paperback)
ISBN-13: 978-0-9971391-1-2 (ebook)

For Mark, for always.

⮞ Chapter One ⮜

Murder, mayhem. Torture and titillation. Thomas would do, and had done, anything *she* asked.

He bowed his head enough to be respectful, though he kept his eyes on the Queen's. The band circling his left arm below his biceps grew warmer, as it always did in her presence. When she was displeased with him, it burned and throbbed like the stings of a hundred wasps. When she wished him before her, it tightened until he came to her side. As a motivator, it was effective. After two centuries, it was appreciably thinner than it had been when she first wound the filaments of gold-laced bone around his arm. Each strand represented a task, the Queen's bidding to be done. Only when every strand had snapped and curled away like a broken harp string would Thomas be free again.

He had never dared to ask what kind of bone it was. He wasn't sure, even now, that he wanted to know. Knowledge wouldn't change a thing as far as Thomas's bondage was concerned.

"Those are my possessions. I will not have them taken from me."

Thomas knew he could not ask the question the Queen's statements begged. Why was she keeping precious things at the goblin market? Why not somewhere here at court, safe from thieves? The Queen had her reasons, and it was not his place to question them.

But it was appropriate to ask what had been stolen.

"What do they look like, these possessions, my Lady, so I may guard them properly?"

Her lips curved, a smile Thomas remembered well from the decades when his Lady the Queen had kept him for his human beauty and sensual prowess. He clenched his teeth in his closed mouth and stifled the shudder that threatened to fracture the glamour keeping his human form uppermost. He detested his trow form, despite its tremendous strength and endurance. It was hideous and reminded him only of his enslavement. The Queen had set him as her barrowguard, finding him skilled at brawling and protecting valuables and treasure. She called him her knight, but Thomas knew it was merely a glamoured word for "thug."

"Every one is different. Unique and precious to me." The Queen rose from the bone and thistle throne, her shimmering train dragging along the shallow steps of the dais. Her form began to flicker. Thomas could not hide his dislike at the catlike tail-twitch of something hidden beneath the viper green drift of her clothing. Her excited strides brought her to the center of her chamber where he stood.

He swallowed. His armband prickled in the presence of

her eager hunger. She reached out to stroke his cheek with a fingertip whose nail changed from claw to talon and back to nail as it trailed over his skin. He kept his gaze neutral. His Lady was aroused and hungry. Time he left, before she summoned him to her bed. Again he repressed a shudder, straightening to stand tall and thus distance himself from her hungers. She was in no mood to answer his questions about her possessions, either because she was hungry, or perhaps because she wished him to fail in his task.

"Once upon a time I loved you enough to keep you, my Thomas." Her pout was delicious and beautifully sad, but Thomas knew from experience that the edges of her teeth had slit the tender inner flesh of her cheeks and filled her mouth with her own blood. "Young men are not what they were."

But on the other hand, were he to please her—and he knew he could—it would mean one less strand on his armband. Bedding the Queen was less onerous than killing a traitor or criminal, though no less dangerous. He shifted his weight, indecisive, feeling his obsidian blade move at his hip. Behind him, one of the kelpies guarding the door cleared its throat. Thomas heard the irregular plink of water droplets falling from the kelpie's body onto the stone floor.

The Queen's gaze flicked up to the kelpie. "Judge me not, you mess of waterweed."

The kelpie stared at the floor, large horselike teeth bared. "No, my Lady. But I hear your huntsman coming."

Thomas bowed his head once again. "I should go, my Lady."

"Will you not stay and feast, Thomas?" Her tongue flicked out, forked and glistening. "What will Hunter have brought us today? Think on it, meat savory with terror and plump with blood."

Do not show weakness. "The moon is dark and the market is busy. I should return to safeguard your interests."

Her head turned, and though Thomas knew she was thinking about Hunter's prey, her hunger had not yet overwhelmed her control. "See that you do, my Thomas. See that you do."

The kelpies, wearing their glamoured forms of handsome human men, stood one at each side of the tall, narrow wooden doors, so churchlike in form. What would have been crosses of brass or iron in the human world were strange angles of bone and gold, hinges made of the tough cloth of woven nettles. Like mirror images, the kelpies moved as one and flung open the doors.

Through the opening roiled Hunter's hounds, lean, slavering fae beasts yelping with excitement and hunger, their hands and claws flexing. Hungry, always hungry, and frantic with it, eager for scraps from Hunter's spoils. Behind them rode Hunter himself, mounted on a collection of bones and hide and lathered froth that had once been a stallion, before Hunter took it for a mount. Thomas pressed himself against the wall and tried not to look at the bloody, sobbing creature thrown across the saddle in front of Hunter's thorn-spiked knees. Now the Queen had eyes only for the prey—Thomas thought it had been a brownie—and appetite only for its blood and terror.

Thomas turned his head away and waited for the doorway to empty of Hunter's gibbering host. He wondered why the Queen permitted Hunter and his fae beasts in her chambers, but here it was nothing unusual. The tearing sounds of hunger filled the throne room, and the smell of blood rose. The sobbing ceased and Thomas drew a long breath.

He eased past Hunter's horse, halting when a hunk of bloody flesh was shoved before his eyes. He knew the silver gauntlet holding the meat, knew its fabulous smithery and the dried dark blood caked in its fanciful chasings. Fresh crimson marked them now. "You should clean your gloves, Hunter."

"Still squeamish, I see. Will you join us, Half-made?" Hunter's rough voice was like old hinges or the screech of stone on stone. "Be rewarded for your service to our Queen? A taste in friendship and peace."

Thomas tried to ignore Hunter's red-eyed gaze, speculative

from behind the antlered deer-skull mask. A long history lay between Thomas and the Queen's huntsman. Hunter believed the Queen should not admit a human into the world of the fae—humans were amusements and pawns and, occasionally, meals, but never equals. The Queen encouraged their mutual dislike. In two hundred years of interaction, Thomas had never managed to best Hunter, but neither had Hunter quite managed to best Thomas. It was a studied detente.

One day, Thomas knew, that would change, and he wasn't sure an iron-edged blade would turn aside Hunter's ferocity. The more fae Thomas became, the less he was able to tolerate the iron that had won through for him in the past. As Thomas edged around the fist clutching the chunk of flesh, Hunter leaned down and whispered. "Those who will not Hunt will be Hunted in the end, human."

"Vanity ill becomes you," Thomas replied, and put out a hand to deflect the kick Hunter's mount aimed at him as he passed its flank.

The kelpie nearest Thomas gave a wet chuckle like beach stones tumbled by waves. "Coward," it said. "Once a human, always a craven fool."

Thomas smiled as his knife—obsidian fringed with iron— slid from its sheath into his hand. Though the iron made his skin buzz and tingle, it would burn the fully-fae kelpie. Thomas swiftly pinched the kelpie's least finger between blade and thumb, and with a squeeze the digit popped to the floor like a chopped carrot. A rancid-smelling smoke trailed upward. "Judge me not, you mess of waterweed," Thomas mocked softly, and pushed past the bleeding kelpie as it stared dumbfounded. "Make a hoof of that now, if you can."

Likely the Queen would punish him for this, but Thomas couldn't bring himself to care. He'd grown hard and bitter under her brutal tutelage.

A long tunnel led through the rocks and dirt, roots and mud, to the surface. Glowworms lit the way, leaving behind confounding, lacy traceries of luminous slime. A carnivorous pixie fluttered through and pounced on a worm with thin cries.

It seemed the entire mound was ravenous tonight.

At the tunnel's mouth, Thomas nodded to the troll who sealed the entrance with its broad, mossy back. To the humans traveling through Forest Park it looked for all the world like a gray, weather-split boulder. The troll looked over its shoulder to check the area before it grumbled aside, and Thomas stepped into the rainy autumn night.

This particular tunnel exited Portland's Forest Park at its easternmost bulge, a mile upslope from the river and the Burnside Bridge. He settled into his stride, a long-legged human gait. Had he been in more of a hurry, the trow-form would have sped the trip, but tonight he needed time to think. He was to prevent the theft of the Queen's possessions from the market, which meant that at least one had already been taken. But what? Thomas had no idea.

He'd just have to ask around. It was fortunate that most of the vendors and denizens knew him of old. Thomas had built his trow-hold inside the bridge's western pier nearly a hundred years before, as the bridge itself was birthed. The goblin market ran year-round beneath the bridge deck on the western shore of the Willamette River where it flowed through downtown Portland. Everything a fae could want, and some things best left unnamed or unlooked for, was sold in Underbridge.

Once the Queen's Unseelie court settled in Portland, they bewitched and pixie-led countless city fathers and planners until the long series of hills along the western flank of the Willamette was made a park, to be left free of human habitation. As far as Thomas knew, it was the largest fairy mound in existence, and all ruled by his Lady, the Queen. Thomas himself remembered when much of Portland was a wild, wet place, filled with trout streams and moss and the peculiar magical resonance of a land at the confluence of two large rivers and studded with volcanoes both dead and alive. Over decades of human time, the city grew and changed, and under the Queen's unflinching guidance, so did the Unseelie court. The Unseelie were an unquestionable success, living boldly among so many humans, iron, and concrete.

Thomas's feet led him to Burnside Street and the gradual slope toward the river. As he neared the Willamette, he could feel its power inside him, and sense the flow of an underground stream encased in concrete beneath his feet. The Unseelie had their problems with flowing water, but humans had locked most of the water away in culverts and pipes, and made paths across the river. These the Unseelie could travel, though not without a certain discomfort. Thomas, with his human blood and fae senses, fared better than most. The water spoke to him, but did not make him ill.

He passed Chinatown, careful to avoid its borders, marked by its red lampposts, and crossed Burnside to Old Town, where the goblin market clattered and gibbered beneath the bridge at all hours. Thomas had never understood how so large a presence of fae could go unremarked among humans, but the market was even home to a colony of human artisans on the weekends. They sold their bright trinkets and tasty food, unaware of the sulfurous shimmer of goblin taint everywhere.

This was one way the Queen found her human lovers. In the old days, she'd had to seek for them as she had sought out Thomas, whose voice caught her ear in a rowdy midnight tavern, and whose human beauty caught her eye by lantern light. She had beckoned him into the mound of Forest Park and plied him with sweetmeats and sex. Afterward, he had never been the same. Nowadays it was all too easy. The artisans came of their own accord, drawn by the lures of the human market, then slid all unknowing into the world of the fae. Like fish to a worm sheathing a barbed and bloody hook.

He lingered on the fringes of the market, where the Skidmore Fountain played. The human market had closed at sunset, but the goblin market was building to a frenzy. Amongst the fae vendors, a few humans lingered, wandering dazedly. The night was blurred by the rain, but lit by streetlights, headlights of cars, and the spill of fluorescent light from the surrounding buildings.

In the dark it was harder to suppress his trow nature. The bulky, bunchy form wanted to push itself forth, coarsen his fingers and lessen his dexterity. Where his human form was a hand, all deftness and skill, his trow form was a fist. The loose, flapping oilskin coat he wore fit both his bodies and shed much of the wet and dirt of the world. When he was human, as now, he wore it belted snug. But it required much effort to hold his humanity, despite two centuries of practice. Here in the market, though most of the vendors knew him on sight, he would be less remarked if he were fae.

Thomas tugged at the coat's belt and opened a few buttons. Beneath the oilskin, his thin shirt stretched tight as he closed his eyes and gave in to the ever-present itch, the need to relinquish his humanity. He was fortunate that his legs and hips stayed more or less the same length and girth whether man or trow, though his waist thickened. As long as there was a little room in the seat of his jeans and a hole or two left in his belt, he was comfortable enough.

The Queen had once told him if he would only give up his chance at returning to normal—to his former humanity—she would end his servitude then and there. The band around his arm would drop away.

But he would be a trow forever. Broad-shouldered, rough-fingered, with large ears and a nose to match. Hair like the spiky stripe down a hyena's spine and a mouth with almost as many teeth. A tail with a lion's tuft at the end.

It wasn't the looks that bothered Thomas and kept him clinging with bitter desperation to his former life. As the Queen pointed out one chilly midnight, her sharp teeth mouthing and scoring the sensitive places on his body with each word, everyone he'd ever loved was worm's meat by now. None were left to call him Thomas, lover, brother, son.

None but the Queen.

No. He welcomed the power and strength of his trow form,

used it as a tool. But he couldn't set aside the knowledge of what had been taken from him, taken without permission or explanation. He would, one day, be human again, cost what it might.

It was only time, the one thing he had in abundance. Trows lived exceedingly long lives, usually finding death only through murder, misadventure or a particularly noxious meal.

The Queen had reminded him, too, that regaining his human form meant regaining his human lifespan.

Thomas scowled and let his human self fritter away like the dust from a moth's wings. He took a deep breath and shook all over like a wet dog, feeling the trow muscles filling out the spare corners of his flesh and skin, and the cramped coiling of his tail in the back of his jeans. The trow eyes saw the market better, showing him the fae taint that smeared the bricks and concrete and seeped down the plywood of the closed stalls left from the humans' day.

Thomas dunked his hand in the fountain and splashed a palmful of water over his head to slick down the spiky stripe of head-fur, then he strolled into the market. Might as well get a little dinner while he watched for a nobody stealing nothings.

⋟ Chapter Two ⋞

Tess reviewed her notes from the last session with Aaron Eisley. I don't know where I go. I just gotta go, so I do. There's power. Vision. A Green Man, a Wild Man, you know? A Man of the Forest.

It was practically all Aaron had said that session, and she'd only pried it out of him through careful slow questioning and friendly smiles and promises that no one else needed to know his secret. She could hear the capital letters in his voice, the words that were important to him, gravid with meaning. Aaron was all but catatonic these days, declined from the high point she'd seen him at four months ago when he was too blissed-out to resent his family's insistence that he start drug rehabilitation.

Just like Stephen.

Her brother had withered away to a mindless husk with an empty smile. Gone now, buried six months ago. Stephen had been convinced that he, too, was something other. Big brother Stephen, her dark elf. The senselessness of his death still gutted her. Stephen's problems had changed the direction of Tess's life.

Aaron was the fourth such client the rehab center had treated in the past ten months. Four young men, all handsome, all with the world at their feet, steadily decaying from bliss to utter absence of personality, recognition of responsibility or humanity. All of them convinced they were becoming something other than human.

Just like Stephen. While he hadn't been a client at her center, as his sister and only living relative, Tess had been deeply involved with his treatment and eventual hospitalization. Stephen's decline and death had transformed her from a mere counselor to a woman desperate to find a solution. She'd been unable to help any of the young men and unable to determine what drug they'd taken. Its effects were much like heroin, but not one of them had the telltale track marks.

Tess knew that meant it was something they'd swallowed or inhaled, though they all denied doing either.

Her contacts at the police department just shrugged when she asked about new drugs on the street. It wasn't something they'd seen on patrol or on calls. And it was only four young men, decent citizens, no real criminal records except for the occasional oddball behavior—jousting with a sedan on a city street or scaling the sides of buildings only to become stranded on a narrow window ledge four floors up. One of them had ridden an office chair like a skateboard down the steep slope of a neighborhood street, heedless of cross traffic or pedestrians. They weren't stealing or robbing or killing. They wouldn't have blipped cop radar if not for citizen complaints.

But for Tess, it was four people she knew, four souls she

hadn't been able to reach, much less save. There was no methadone treatment for whatever addiction this was. No going cold turkey, no patch. Three of the four lived like vegetables, fed and watered like babies, their noses and asses wiped when necessary.

Which meant Aaron was living on borrowed time. She would do her damnedest to save him. If that meant she had to step outside professional boundaries, so be it. Aaron was someone's beloved brother, too.

Tess sat in her aging Jeep outside Aaron's family's house. The Craftsman bungalow looked warm and welcoming in the noncommittal rain of October, yellow lamplight showing through several windows. She reread Aaron's file by the tiny light on her keychain. All of his counselors and doctors had been baffled by the lack of information provided by testing and interviews. For some time now, it had been in her mind to knock at the door, go in and talk to Aaron's parents, his sister, anyone who could tell her where he'd first found the drug. It was crossing the professional line, and she knew it. So she was still sitting in the chilly car, watching the rain seep along the seams of the Jeep's old tonneau. In another climate, sun rot would have long ago destroyed the canvas, but here in Portland, the wet seemed to preserve it, stretched drum-tight but still snapping into place grommet by grommet each autumn.

She leaned her head back, crushing her brown ponytail

against the headrest, staring at the Eisleys' front door, debating. Go in, violate her client's confidentiality, or stay here like a coward, keeping Aaron's secrets in the dark where they could continue to destroy him.

I'm a Green Man, a Wild Man. She had looked it up, just like she'd looked up Stephen's dark elves, and the redcaps and sprites of other clients. Aaron believed he was a force of nature, a man more than human, a man whose hair was fresh green leaves, whose fertility was vast and relentlessly potent.

Her left hand crept to the door handle and had locked around it when a wedge of light from the front door spilled onto the sidewalk. Aaron himself came out, hunched in his dark hoodie, hands jammed into the kangaroo pouch. He moved down the street as if hypnotized.

He moved like Stephen had, in those last months before Tess was forced to institutionalize him. The same puppet-like pace, jerky and other-guided. He moved with purpose, but not his own. Something compelled him forward in the rainy October darkness.

Tess drew a long breath. She could go in and talk with his family now, and perhaps Aaron would never know…or she could follow him, and maybe figure out what mess he was in and who his pusher was. Somehow, find justice and closure for herself and Stephen.

She waited until he was a block ahead, nearly out of sight in the dimness between streetlights, before she turned the key in the ignition and pulled out of her parking spot. She didn't think he'd be alert enough to notice a Jeep creeping along behind him, but it was best to keep her distance all the same.

Three blocks away, he boarded a bus that took him out of the Alameda neighborhood and down the hill toward the Willamette. Now she didn't have to be as cautious and picked up speed to keep him in sight. The bus crawled through the rainy evening, stopping, starting, but Aaron didn't step off until it had crossed the Burnside Bridge and entered Old Town.

Tess passed him while the bus hid her, turned the Jeep to the right into Chinatown, and stopped just short of the crimson gate guarded by the gold-painted fu dog statues. She parked illegally in a loading zone. It was after business hours and hopefully no one would notice. She grabbed her purse and slung it across her body, locked the Jeep, and hurried to the corner. Aaron had already crossed Burnside Street, headed for the staircase that would take him down to the impromptu market and ersatz camp that formed Sunday nights after the legitimate artisans and vendors had packed up and gone home. This gray market would run in fits and starts between roustings by cops, until the next weekend, when the artisans returned.

She stared, open-mouthed, hardly believing this could be coincidence. Surely Aaron didn't come to the bridge just to visit with the hard-luck cases sheltering there. Boys from the Alameda neighborhood were expected to do better than that. Glancing left and right, she jaywalked, reaching the stairs just as Aaron disappeared under the bridge. Tess followed.

She'd been under the Burnside Bridge a hundred times before, visiting the weekend market with family and friends over the years, and using the market as a shortcut at other times. It had been one of Stephen's favorite places. He loved to prowl the booths and food trucks, always wanting her to share a cinnamon-sugar elephant ear with him. Even in his darker days, as the drugs clawed deeper into him, he'd wanted to go there. Tess still visited on special occasions, but she no longer ate the sweet treat that reminded her so painfully of her brother. She had been thinking of Stephen more and more lately, but sometimes she wished she could leave responsibility and memory behind, cut herself free of that weight, travel more lightly.

For the first time, she began to wonder if Stephen's attachment to the Saturday Market was less about fun and more about hooking up with his pusher. He'd haunted Old Town, too, and seeing Aaron following a path that Stephen had taken gave her a sick feeling in the pit of her stomach. In the months since Stephen had died, Tess had skulked cautiously through Old Town and other seedy parts of Portland at odd hours, trying to spot something, anything, among the hopeless and homeless, that could lead her to a solution for the other young men whose lives were effectively ended. Now she might have a chance at a breakthrough. She'd made the right choice to follow Aaron, rather than confronting his family.

Tonight, the area beneath the bridge sheltered a remarkable crowd of people from the drizzle, more than she would have expected on a gloomy evening. It took her a moment to locate Aaron. He was about fifty feet away, watching a young boy drumming on a collection of overturned cat litter buckets, trashcans and refrigerator drawers. The beat seduced Aaron's feet to a stuttering, hopping dance as he joined a ring of people bobbing and swaying around the drummer. But Aaron lacked grace; the drug, whatever it was, had stolen much of his coordination and sense of timing. Now he looked like any other hopped-up junkie twitching for his next fix, taken over by sensation and stimulation.

Tess tried to be inconspicuous, but her tall frame caught the eye of the vagrants and gray market merchants alike. At the foot of the stairs, she paused next to a man sitting on a blanket with a collection of scavenged books arrayed in front of him. As her gaze passed over the market, he lit a flashlight and shone it over the titles, swiftly flicking the pool of light, watching her face for reactions to the more lurid covers. "You look like an educated woman! I have books for you. Any book, just a dollar!"

Tess shook her head and moved away, keeping her eyes on Aaron, who continued to dance.

Another man spoke. "Hand-rolled smokes here. You know

you want one."

"No, thank you." Her fingers curled more tightly around the strap of her cross-body bag as she tried to look unapproachable, uninterested, fiercely confident, and aware of her surroundings all at the same time. Tonight it was difficult, because she wasn't simply moving through the throng, she was lingering. She couldn't expect to be ignored.

"It's the best, just in from eastern Washington. That high desert grass, you gotta try it!"

Tess glanced at the man, who was moving too close with his cupped handful of joints. They were odd, fat little doobies with twisted ends tied shut with what looked like Christmas tinsel. "I said no thank you." She put an edge in her voice and he backed off, nearly stepping on the offerings of the bookseller behind him.

"Watch it, man," said the bookseller. "Stay outta my space."

"Peace," said the man with the smokes. Tess left them to their argument. She passed another blanket covered with knitted hats, and a street girl with a ferret on a leash. The ferret gave Tess a long, direct look, or perhaps it was her imagination. She shook her head, sidling away, keeping Aaron in her peripheral vision.

A sleepy-looking young man lounged against one of the concrete pillars that held up the Burnside Bridge. "You and me, babe. Meant to be. Fate."

It didn't even provoke a grunt from her. The young man was

almost as handsome as Aaron, but there was something unpleasant about him. A breeze off the Willamette brought with it the familiar weedy stink of the river, even through the moistness of the rainy night. The young man slid a hand down his flat belly to his crotch and licked his lips, laughing when she turned away repulsed.

Sex, drugs and rock-and-roll, Tess thought, continuing to edge through the vendors and loiterers, the city kids out for thrills, stepping out of the way of a skater boy cruising swiftly past on his board. Off to one side, a woman was grilling bits of meat on a hibachi standing on a three-legged card table. She had rigged a golf umbrella to shelter the grill from the weather, and replaced the missing table leg with a dented trash can. The meat smelled both burnt and spoiled.

Perhaps it was her heightened awareness now that she was following Aaron through the market, but the place seemed more inimical than it had in the past. She felt jumpy and nervous. She told herself it was foolish to feel so paranoid. These people couldn't help their situations. They were poor and homeless. What they needed was kindness and understanding, not revulsion. Moving on, Tess carefully avoided the space where two people leaned against each other like herd animals, one keeping watch while the other slept curled and dream-twitching on the pavement. At last she paused near a woman who sat on a paint bucket behind a tiny plastic patio table. Sitting with her back to the chilly concrete of a bridge footing, the woman shuffled ceaselessly through a deck of tarot cards, droning,

"Searching for love,

hungry for fame,

I give you truth

when you give your name."

Though she'd seen the fortuneteller here before, for the first time Tess really looked at the woman, who grinned up at her from a face as glossy and seamed as a walnut shell. In the dimness the woman could have been any age from twenty to eighty, hidden in half a dozen tattered shawls. Tess fumbled in her pocket and came up with a five-dollar bill. The woman stretched out two fingers, and with a flicker the bill was folded and gone.

"Give me your name, pretty girl."

"Julie."

The woman shook her head. "Not your truename, no. Truename, pretty girl."

"It's my name tonight."

"Truename, truename, or the Old Ones, they say nothing you should heed."

Tess slid a glance at Aaron, who had left the circle of dancers, but was still jitterbugging his sleepwalking way through the market. She couldn't follow yet. "I'll take my chances. What fame can five bucks bring me, madam?"

The woman thrust the cards at Tess. "You show me. Shuffle till they feel right to you."

Tess leafed through them absently. The cards felt dusty and sticky, and she wanted to wipe her hands on her jeans. Aaron had paused at a barrel filled with fire. Three men stood back from it a short distance, heads down, caps pulled low, jackets zipped. Could this be it? The men fed a paperback to the fire, page by fluttering page. Each burned with a brief flare, lighting Aaron's blank brown eyes and shadowing his cheeks.

"Pretty Julie."

Tess jerked her gaze back to the tarot reader and put the deck in the woman's waiting palm.

"He's a pretty boy too. Seen him here lots." The woman's chin pointed toward the fire barrel.

"Have you?" Tess tried to control her eagerness.

A slow smile creased the woman's face. "Gave me his truename, so I spoke him true."

"He's a friend of mine. I'm trying to make sure he stays out of trouble."

The shawled head shook. "Too late, too pretty." The cards practically spun down from the deck onto the table.

"Where'd he find this trouble, so I can help keep him out of it from now on?"

The head kept shaking. Her forefinger dithered between two of the cards on the table, and suddenly she swept up all the cards.

The deck vanished in the shawls. "Go away, pretty Julie."

"What about my fame?"

"No truename."

"What about my five bucks, then?"

The woman stood up, folding the table and stuffing its legs into the bucket. "Not my problem. You paid, you lied, I tried, but you lied, you lied..." The singsong continued as she drew her shawls tighter, took the bucket by the handle, and melted away into the shadows.

She didn't move like an old woman. For a moment Tess considered following and continuing to pry for more information about Aaron, but caution stopped her. It was worth the five dollars to know Aaron came here often. If the fortuneteller had seen him, others would have too; Tess just needed to find them. She was turning to check on Aaron when a flutter of ribbon high up in a notch on the concrete bridge footing caught her eye.

Even tall Tess had to stretch to reach it. She tugged at the ribbon, and something small and weighty came away from the hole with it, swinging like a pendulum. She turned to bring it into the light and keep an eye on Aaron, who was moving away from the fire barrel toward the dark, glinting river. The men at the barrel watched him go.

It was too good an opportunity to miss. Tess stuffed the small thing in the side pouch of her purse and meandered up to the barrel.

"Hey," she said.

"Hey, yourself." The men were wary, pulling their caps even lower.

"You know that boy?" She gestured with her chin toward Aaron, tucking her hands deep in the pockets of her sweater jacket.

"What's it to ya?" the tallest of the three asked.

"He's a friend of mine. I'm trying to keep him out of trouble."

They grinned in the dancing light. "Too late, bitch, too late."

She leaned forward a little. "What do you mean, too late?"

"The lady, she ride him. You wanna ride him too, right?"

"Do you mean horse, heroin?" Tess wrinkled her brow. She hadn't heard of a drug called the lady, but maybe it was a new name for something that had been around a while. Still, the man's tone was nothing short of lascivious.

"No, the lady. You wanna keep out of that, you know what's good for you."

"The lady. What lady?"

They tossed in a few pages from the book. Tess blinked watering eyes in the sudden flare of sparks and acrid smoke. In those seconds, the men left her standing alone at the barrel.

Well, she hadn't expected to be able to walk right up and say, "See that young man? He's on some really bad shit, and I need you to take me to his dealer."

Aaron was almost out of sight at the riverbank. Tess hurried after him. She jumped the low chains that separated the marketplace from the roadway. Looking hastily both ways, she jaywalked in the darkness.

⇒ Chapter Three ⇐

Thomas lingered on the periphery of the goblin market, watching without seeming to watch. He recognized most of the fae here, and even several of the humans who were drawn like moths to the dark flicker of glamour. Some were homeless street people, shuffling through the market gleaning crumbs or coins dropped over the day, mumbling to themselves or shouting at invisible demons. Invisible, that is, to most humans roaming the Underbridge. The street people could sometimes see the fae for what they were. Some were junkies, like the kid reeling around the fairy musician thumping at his skin-covered drums.

And some were normal, like the tall woman walking tensely through the market, one hand wrapped around the strap of her sling bag, and the other jammed in a pocket as though to keep her fingers away from temptation. He'd seen her before, and she always caught his eye with her height, the swing of her brown ponytail, and the intent, concerned look on her vaguely pretty face. She didn't belong in the goblin market, yet she came again and again.

Of course, he could say the same of many of the humans here.

Thomas wondered what she saw. She didn't show the same dread some of the streetfolk exhibited, yet each time she singled out someone, it was the fae she approached. Was she fae herself, and if so, why couldn't he see through her glamour? Or was she like him, living in the half-world, with her human form uppermost? Or was she human, with the second sight that permitted her to glimpse the fae world without revealing its deeper bones to her?

He paused at Sharpwit the hob's tiny booth to buy his dinner, a portable lump of fungus and stewed caterpillars and furred moth bodies with lamb's quarters. The whole mess was rolled into a large grape leaf and drizzled with honey squeezed from the comb, bee-parts and all. It would do until he found some bread or shifted back into his human form long enough to consume human food. He did that less and less, since it took increasingly more effort to remain human, and the overly processed foods the humans ate these days sometimes disagreed with his fae-altered digestion.

"Well met, Thomas," murmured Sharpwit, poking skewers through insect pupae and wedges of late apples, and setting them to roast over her tiny brazier. The rising, smoky fragrance, like what Thomas remembered of onions quick-fried in butter, made him feel strangely homesick for the tavern where the Queen had found him.

"What shall I owe you?" He took a bite of his dinner. He

could trust Sharpwit not to take advantage of his open-ended bargain. Underbridge belonged to Thomas, and the fae knew it.

"I want some grubs from the tunnels in Forest Park, next time you can fill a pouch. My herd is thinning. Business has been good."

"Consider it done." Thomas turned back to the market, and again the tall woman caught his eye. She was talking to the redcaps, which wasn't a smart idea if she wanted to get out in one piece. But whatever she said to them made them nervous, because they flitted away soon enough, leaving her standing by their steaming dye vat. The market was filling as dusk came on more fully. The woman moved steadily through the vibrant and humming crowd, heading for an exit at Naito Parkway.

Out of curiosity, Thomas followed, munching. He had to start looking for the thief somewhere, since he had not the slightest idea what nor whom he was looking for. Might as well start with a market regular, human or not.

The woman was tall and girlishly slender, too thin, even to eyes accustomed to the seeming fragility of the fae. She had a neck like a stem, with a clean jaw line that spoke of determination and stubbornness. She wore a dark blue sweater over her jeans, and the evening drizzle beaded like diamonds scattered in the weave. Her brown hair was scraped back into an elastic at the nape of her neck, lank and straight in the damp air. She was no fashion plate, but he liked her stride—focused and serious, her rubber-soled shoes practical in the urban terrain.

When she glanced over her shoulder, he saw her eyes were dark—probably brown, to match her hair—and her mouth looked soft and full as crushed peonies. A moment later she stepped over the low swag of chains that separated the Underbridge from the roadway, and crossed the street.

After a short pause to shove the last of his dinner into his mouth and reestablish his human form, Thomas followed. It wouldn't do for the girl to discover a trow—splayed ears, nose like a potato, hyena hair—trailing behind her. Outside the goblin market, the general glamour that masked everything like smoke or fog wore away.

She crossed the narrow strip of park lawn that bordered the river for a mile and headed north. A hundred feet farther on, she paused, drawing close to a maple tree as if to hide. Thomas's eyebrows rose. Suspicious behavior from her, indeed. Along the path ahead of her, the boy she followed stopped to sit on a lump of concrete and stone, head hanging, hands limp at his sides. After a moment Thomas recognized him as the junkie kid who had been whirling around the drummer in Underbridge. He stepped into the shadow of a nearby statue and waited. He wished for a second snack.

He was content to watch the girl watching the boy until another figure approached from further north. The band around his arm grew warm, and Thomas realized the entrant into the little tableau was the Queen.

Fae glamour was a remarkable thing. Even after two centuries of servitude, and regularly using glamours himself, Thomas was still startled and blinded when he saw the Queen making an effort to charm a human. The ruler of the Unseelie Court was making her way along the walk, hurrying, as if to a rendezvous. She looked young and fresh, in a dreamy, drugging euphoric haze that Thomas remembered like a kick to his gut. Her beauty, when she chose, could make any fae burn with desire, so the effect on humans was devastating. Along with her unhesitating brutality and her total commitment to the Unseelie Court, it was what made—and kept—her the Queen.

Rendezvous it was, because the boy lifted his head, still sluggish, when the Queen drifted up to him, her hair streaming behind her as if lifted by the wind, though the night was still and rainy. The two came together in a ferocious embrace, consuming in its fervor and fury.

The woman in the sweater slumped against the maple and turned her head away from the couple twining on the pathway between streetlights.

Jealous? Thomas looked back to the couple. The Queen was pulling the stumbling human boy along the walkway toward some lair or door she must have near the riverbank. They'd been lovers a while, from the degree the boy seemed drained. Thomas's cheeks burned with the long-ago memory of himself as the

Queen's lovesick toy. The band around his arm cooled noticeably the farther away she moved.

The woman in the sweater straightened and resettled her bag across her body. She ducked her head and walked determinedly away from the path, back toward Underbridge. This time she didn't seem as aware of her surroundings, and it was too easy for Thomas to put himself in her path and let her walk right into him.

"Oh—I'm sorry, I should watch where I'm going," she said, flustered, pushing hair from her face with a nervous gesture.

Thomas grinned. "No harm done. I was a bit distracted myself. That public display of affection caught my eye, I'm embarrassed to say."

Her laugh was breathless and charming, and the crushed-peony lips were amazing when they smiled. "He's a friend of mine. I was trying to catch up with him, but wow, I guess I won't bother now. He'd hardly be interested in anything I had to say after that."

"Not be interested in what you have to say? His loss." Thomas concentrated on his glamour, pouring charm like sunlit honey.

She laughed a little again. "Thank you. I…didn't realize he was meeting someone here."

"You should get out of the rain."

"So should you." She never loosened the death-grip on her

handbag. Now that he was close enough to see them, her eyes were indeed brown, very dark and direct. Her brows were slim and tapered, rising in a swallow's wing arc above her eyes.

"I'm used to it. Been here all my life." With one seeming accord, they were walking toward Underbridge.

"Me too. Born and raised."

"I'm Thomas, by the way." He smiled and gave a tiny half-wave.

"Tess." She looked around alertly, regaining her caution. The dimple that formed next to her lips was as charming as any glamour he could put on, and he reminded himself to stay immune. Fae and human interactions never ended well. The old folk stories were true. "Do you come here often, Thomas?"

"Now, that was…what's the word I want…smooth?"

"That's supposed to be the guy's line, isn't it?" She pushed back her hair again, and he realized it was her tell, the mark of her nervousness.

"You know, I'm not one for pubs and pick-up lines, but yeah, I come here often. I live near here. Coffee…that's my poison."

"Mine, too. In fact, let me buy you a cup. I want to ask you a few questions, if you don't mind."

He slid a glance at her. "You're not a cop, are you?"

"And if I were? You got something to hide?"

Of course I have something to hide. "Not at the moment." The fae didn't lie, but neither did they tell human truths.

"I'm not a cop. Just a concerned friend. I'm scared he's on some bad stuff."

"So you were following him? Trying to catch his dealer?"

"I just want to help him."

And I just want to catch a thief. Addicts are the worst. But if that boy was the thief, the Queen would have known. "I get that. Tell you what, there's a coffee shop I like, up on the Park Blocks, but it's a walk. You okay with that?"

Tess halted under a streetlight and turned to face him. She was utterly up-front, intentions clear, as she looked him over thoroughly.

He knew what the girl saw when she looked at him. Hadn't he spent days, weeks, in front of the mirror in his trow-hold, perfecting the mask he wore to conceal the trow-face from the human world? To his own eyes, he looked as he had always done. Good cheekbones, an easy-smiling mouth. Close-cropped dark hair. Soot-framed eyes that were neither blue nor brown nor gray, but some uncertain color in between. Smallish ears that lay close to his head. A muscular body with a strong frame, cloaked in the belted black oilskin.

Maybe he looked safe enough. He hoped so, because he found himself wanting to go on talking to her. She wasn't pretty in the expected ways, or even attractive in the eyes of the fae. They would find nothing about her beautiful except her large, lucid eyes, which would have appealed to any number of the Unseelie, and not always in a good way. But life as a part-trow, the Queen's bound knight, lacked ordinary human pleasures such as coffee with a woman. Or human friends.

At last, done considering his potential threat, and apparently deciding it was low enough, she nodded. "Lead the way."

But they couldn't take the shortest route, which would be through Underbridge. Too many of the fae knew human Thomas, and he didn't want to attract their attention to the woman at his side until he knew more about her.

"We should stay away from the bridge," he suggested. "This time of night it gets questionable."

"It's mostly the homeless. They just want a dry place to sleep."

"Seems like your faith in people is stronger than mine. I'd rather take the long way around." He looked to the south, considering where the edges of Chinatown and Underbridge were. The *fu* dogs would attack anything fae that came into the territory they guarded and were to be avoided at all costs. On their own turf, they held the power. Only a few scant blocks separated Underbridge from Chinatown. Chinatown's borders were marked by lucky red lampposts. He simply had to guide her beyond them, and if that meant he had to use glamour to do it, he would.

Let her be biddable, he thought, and started to walk.

⇒ Chapter Four ⇐

The man—*Thomas*, Tess corrected herself—led them south along the river. He moved confidently in the darkening evening, head always turning, as alert as she to their surroundings. While they walked, he talked, in a quiet voice that commanded attention even as it soothed. She knew the words were intended to win her trust, and while she remained skeptical and outwardly suspicious, his tactic was working, and she had to smile at herself.

Tess matched his pace along the streets, noting that most of the businesses were closed, leaving only the bars and restaurants open. The streets were steadily emptying of people, and she had a moment's pause in which she considered the wisdom of being out in the dark with a total stranger, desperation over Stephen and Aaron or not. Her fingers traced the lump in the side pocket of her bag, where the pepper spray rested. Thomas didn't make her anxious in that way, but she would be stupid not to be wary.

"So—what do you do for a living?" he asked.

Of course, the proper next conversational gambit in any social minuet. "I'm a counselor at a drug rehabilitation center here in the city."

"Ah." He nodded, his hands in the pockets of his coat. Clearly he would keep them to himself, his body language said.

"So…is that young man really a friend?"

Tess sighed, cover already blown. "He's my client."

"Do counselors always follow their clients through the questionable parts of town?"

She laughed self-consciously. "It's not part of the job description, no. But we're stumped with this case. It's in no way typical." She slid a glance at him as they paused before crossing the street. "We've seen a few other cases like his in the last year or so, and we just can't make sense of them. It's like…it's like there's a new drug out there, one we've never seen, one that doesn't show up in blood tests."

"Huh," said Thomas. They crossed with the light.

"From time to time I've come to Old Town to walk around and see what I could see. Maybe find other people with the same symptoms our clients show. Ask questions. Keep an eye out for drug deals. At least one of our clients came down here a lot." Well, until tonight it had only been Stephen and he'd never been her client, just her beloved lost-boy brother. Now he and Aaron had something in common. It was a start.

Thomas nodded slowly, looking thoughtful.

Encouraged, Tess rushed on. "So when you said you live near here, I wondered…"

"If I knew the dealers or the latest hot drugs." His tone was wry, and Tess felt ashamed. A hot flush rushed over her face.

"I didn't mean it like that."

"I didn't take it like that." He gave her a small smile.

"I'm not usually so tactless. Or so rash as to be out asking these kinds of questions after dark."

"You're concerned for your client. That makes you direct."

"That's it, exactly. I'm worried for him, and for the others like him, the ones we haven't been able to help, the ones who came to us too late."

"Us?"

"The rehab center." Tess started to turn south, a more direct route to the Park Blocks, where he'd said the coffee shop was, but Thomas halted her, and he shook his head.

"Let's go west another block first. That street has too many alleys opening off it."

"Uh, okay," she said, doubtfully. It was Chinatown, and she didn't ordinarily think of it as a troublesome area, but perhaps he knew better. When she came down here at night, she usually drove her Jeep and parked at her destination.

Conversation faltered for a minute or two, and then there were the Park Blocks, and the grass and trees and statues that divided the traffic pattern.

Thomas pointed to a coffee shop she'd never tried: the Park Perks. Warm yellow light pooled on the sidewalk outside its well-lit windows. A few people sat at the cafe tables on the sidewalk, but they were hardcore Portlanders who didn't mind damp hair and wet butts. Tess was glad to get inside, where she was immediately warmer, and the rich smell of fresh espresso and hot milk and the last few pastries in the case soothed her nerves. They'd made it here, by a somewhat circuitous and tense route, but she was safe now, whatever happened next.

They stood regarding the menu. Thomas was breathing in deeply, as if he could eat the fragrance, and she found herself grinning. "My treat, remember," she said. "What would you like?"

"Does the offer extend to a snack, as well? Because that last apple tartlet, there..."

"It spoke to me, too. Shall we split it?"

"Sure. And I'll take the biggest caramel latte they make. Just one shot of espresso, though." He gave a self-mocking laugh. "If I have more than one shot, I'll be up all night."

Tess nodded, and stepped toward the barista staffing the cash register. "Mondo caramel latte with one shot, a grande hazelnut mocha, and that apple tartlet there." She pointed. "Cut it in half, please, two plates."

Thomas chose a table away from the windows and pulled out Tess's chair for her. She thought cynically it was a way of getting his choice of seats—she would rather have been where she could see the door more clearly, but it wasn't worth arguing about, and at least he hadn't chosen one of the gloomy booths that would have made it seem like they were on a more intimate outing.

The barista soon brought their coffees and pastry. Tess

linked her hands around her tall paper cup, warming them. Thomas grasped his fork with his napkin and set it to one side.

"Here, I'll get you another fork, if that one's not clean—" Tess said, rising. Thomas reached out and touched her wrist.

As touches went, it was completely harmless, and devoid of nuance, obligation, or ownership.

And yet.

And yet.

It stopped her in her tracks, causing her to focus on the point where the tips of Thomas's two longest fingers lay gently on her wrist bones, to feel nothing but a pleasant sensation of blurry warmth, and a correspondingly pleasant blurriness in her vision, as everything surrounding Thomas's face seemed to fog over. She gazed at him where he sat in his chair, her attention caught by his eyes. They were a muddled shade of blue-gray-brown, with a beautiful dark ring edging the irises. Thick, short lashes as dark as his hair lifted, opening his eyes to let her see inside him.

At least, that's what it felt like, for the few seconds he touched her.

"The fork is fine," he assured her, his hands folding around his cup. "Thank you." He took a long swallow of his latte, and then another, as though he was very thirsty. Tess stared for a moment, thinking her own drink was far too hot to gulp that way, then sat. He licked his lips, looking so satisfied Tess almost asked,

"Was it good for you?"

But that would be taking things in entirely the wrong direction. Flustered, she picked up her own fork and used the edge to cut a bite of apple pastry.

"You wanted to ask me about the drug scene in Underbridge," Thomas said.

"So I did." She chewed rapidly and swallowed, taking the smallest sip of her mocha to wash down the bite. *Underbridge.* What a peculiar phrasing he used, but it was fitting given the people she had met there this evening. Underbridge, underbelly, misunderstood. "Let me back up a little. The clients we're talking about don't show any medical signs of addiction. Nothing in the blood tests, for example. No heroin, no cocaine. No meth. Usually not even marijuana. The clients swear they're not taking anything. But the behavioral indicators are all there, and more."

Thomas picked up his pastry and bit into it as if it were a slice of pizza. He had strong white teeth that seemed a little large for his mouth, as if he were made for happy grinning. Her gaze drifted back to his eyes. That sensation of falling into him had passed. Tess thought perhaps she was merely overtired and overwhelmed from the fruitless search for the source of Aaron's problems. Thomas's eyes, however, were still some of the most beautiful she had ever seen, eyes like mosaics assembled from a murky blue palette. She caught herself staring into them and lowered her gaze so she wouldn't seem foolish or too forward.

"I guess I'm looking for something else, some drug besides the ones we know how to look for. The police tell us there's nothing new on the streets. If it were deadly, they'd know more, they say there'd be a lot more fatalities in the population."

"So you're asking me if I know what's new and hot?"

"One of the men around that burn barrel under the bridge...he mentioned something about 'the lady,' that the lady was riding my client." She colored a little, remembering the man's implication that Tess wanted to ride Aaron as well. "Have you heard anything like that?"

It took Thomas a long time to answer. He turned his cup on the table, fidgeted with his napkin, unfolding it and refolding it inside-out with deliberate precision. "You shouldn't trust what you hear in...Underbridge." The long pause before he spoke the word gave it too much emphasis. "People there are unreliable."

She found herself believing him. He simply sounded so convincing, so certain. He must have inside information. It took too long to put her thoughts in order. His words filled her brain. "I have to help him. I'm...responsible for him."

Thomas's gaze flicked up. "From what I saw, he's old enough to make his own choices. And it looked to me like he's made them."

Tess gave a loud sigh. While Thomas was pleasant company, he probably didn't have the information she was seeking. "I'm not talking about who he's dating. I'm talking about what he's taking. Maybe I should try to find *her*, and ask her if *she* knows—"

"No."

Thomas's blunt, commanding statement took her aback. Her mouth opened, but she found she had nothing to say.

Thomas grinned. "That came out wrong, and I'm sorry. What I meant to say is your client would have something to say if you got mixed up in his love life. I know I'd be...irritated, if someone started asking my girlfriend about my drug habits. What if she doesn't already know? He can kiss that relationship goodbye, and he won't thank you."

"But what if she's his supplier? A pusher?"

"You can't always save people from their own bad choices." He frowned at his cup. He popped its top, tipping the cup for the last of his latte. He replaced the top, upside down. Tess had barely sipped her own, but now it was cooler, and she swallowed a little. The sugar hit her bloodstream quickly, and the warmth soothed the knots in her stomach.

"It's...it's what I *do*, Thomas. I have a degree in social work and specializations in addiction and recovery. And this puzzle is making me crazy. He's too young to throw his life away like this."

His mouth quirked in a wry smile. "Where were you when I was committing my own youthful indiscretions? I'd give a lot to have been saved by someone as gorgeous as you."

There were those delicious eyes again, faint lines creasing their corners. Tess blushed. "You don't seem to have done so badly for yourself, Thomas." She gestured to his empty cup. "Would you like another?"

"Yes, but I'll get this one. You?"

"Still working on my mocha. One ought to be my limit, or like you, I'll be up all night."

Thomas leaned forward. "Come on, live a little."

She shook her head, smiling. He studied her for a moment, his gaze drifting over her face, lingering at her ears and lips, head tilting slightly to one side. "I know just the thing. Be right back."

"Thomas—"

But he was already heading for the counter.

Tess drank some more of her coffee. This was the oddest conversation she'd ever had, apart from some of the clinical sessions with addicts, where descriptions of hallucinations often took particularly weird turns. When added to the already atypical evening—chasing Aaron through the rainy streets, the daft fortuneteller declining to read her cards, the stranger-than-usual folk under the bridge, she began to wonder if the stress was finally getting to her. It took a lot of emotional energy to treat addictions, and she suspected she had never really gotten over the tragedy of her brother Stephen. *I'm a dark elf. You should see it, Tess. That place. So beautiful. And her. She's like a birch girl, a birch girl, a birch girl, all white and golden and green and beautiful and I am her dark elf.*

She, her. The lady. *The lady, she ride him.*

Stephen's drugged-out comments had never made any sense, yet they were the same sort of drifting, disjointed phrases Aaron used. Tess closed her eyes for a brief moment. Maybe she was just tapped out. She was reaching for her bag, deciding to make her excuses and her escape, when Thomas came back with another giant cup, and a plate with a single chocolate truffle on it.

"It's not the answer to your questions, but I think it could help. I hope you like dark chocolate with raspberry."

Did she ever. She put her bag back down, and when the conversation drifted from Aaron and drugs to more cheery topics, she let it. Why look a gift horse in the mouth? At least something good had come out of this bizarre evening: She had met an interesting, handsome and sensitive man. With magazine cover eyes, no less.

➤ Chapter Five ⬅

The baristas had to chase them out of Park Perks at closing time.

Thomas heard Tess sigh when they got to her Jeep a couple of hours and too many lattes later. A flapping ticket, damp with rain but designed to withstand the persistent wet of a Pacific Northwest autumn, adorned her windshield. "I knew it. I should've moved the car before we went for coffee."

Thomas glanced around them. They were only a block away from one of the city's homeless shelters, and less than twenty feet from the entrance of Chinatown. The *fu* dogs stared and growled at him, scratching their claws on their pedestals, knowing him for what he was even through the human glamour. "Not the best place in the world to leave your vehicle, but it looks like you've been lucky—just the ticket, and not a smash and grab."

Tess patted the lemon-yellow hood of the Jeep. "Nobody bothers my old girl. She looks too tough, all beat-up like this, and every panel a different color." She fumbled in her purse and found her car keys. "Are you sure I can't give you a lift back to your place, Thomas? It's really late. I can't believe we closed down that coffee shop."

He smiled. The trow-form clamored to be released. For two

hours he'd held it in beneath the bright fluorescent tubes of the hole-in-the-wall coffee shop, only a foot or so away from Tess, who looked at him so earnestly as she questioned him about life in Old Town and the streetfolk and their vices and habits. She was confused by the redcaps' comments about her client and "the lady," but he felt he had skirted that delicate issue well. Tess didn't seem to connect the comments and the woman the youth had embraced in the park, except as a potential source of drugs. He was relieved she'd let it go. He would have had to walk away if she'd dug deeper. The fae compulsion to tell the truth—or as much of it as would serve the purpose and satisfy the Unseelie Court's ancient laws—was deeply ingrained after all these decades, and custom demanded that any direct question receive a response.

He could only imagine what would happen if Tess somehow managed to track down the Queen. He hoped he'd diverted her from that path.

"Thanks, but I live just a few blocks away, and I like to walk at night."

She shifted her weight from one foot to the other, and Thomas realized she was about to say her good nights. He decided to save her from the awkwardness.

"I've had a great time. Thanks for the coffee and the conversation."

"I enjoyed it too. I…" For a moment, Thomas wondered if

she would tell him she wanted to see him again. But then she fished in her handbag and pulled out a business card. "Here's my card. If you hear anything else that might be useful, I'd really appreciate a call."

"I don't have a telephone."

"You don't have a..." Tess gaped at him, dumbfounded. "Oh, okay. Um, listen, Thomas..."

Here it comes, the kiss-off, the thanks it was fun and I've got to run now. The trow-form nearly exploded and he had to bite hard on the inside of his lip to hold it in.

Tess spoke rapidly. "Giving you my card was my clumsy way of saying I really had a great time tonight, despite the awkward way we met, and I'd like to see you again some time if that's all right."

Thomas thought she might be blushing, but it was too dark to tell. A savage pleasure flooded him and intensified when she put out a helplessly floundering hand to touch his arm.

"God, I hate being such a dork," she said.

"How about same time next week, the coffee shop?" He held his breath, ignoring the thumping of the trow-heart in his breast. The way he felt, it might burst through his chest and thrash at her feet.

"How about an hour earlier, and we start at the coffee shop, then go for dinner? My treat."

"It's a deal." He took a step back, and her hand slid along his arm to his hand and squeezed gently. He couldn't hide the shiver of pleasure this time, though he did manage to swallow the moan that formed in his throat. How long had it been since he'd been touched except by the Queen? "Gotta run. Good night."

She gave a soft laugh. "Did you know you put your coat on inside out, Thomas? I just now noticed." She patted at the rough seam of the oilcloth.

He'd hoped she wouldn't twig to how he'd turned his coat to shed any fae pursuers. At the coffee shop, he'd had to use a little glamour on her to charm and relax her when she noticed him not touching his fork with his skin, though he felt like a traitor as he did it. He'd folded his napkin inside out as well, to turn away the fae, turned his cup, set the lid on it upside down. All to deflect the notice of the folk of Underbridge. He hoped all the little things had done the job and kept anyone from following them and running to tattle to the Queen. He hadn't seen any fae while they walked to the coffee shop and back, but there were never any guarantees.

"Dazzled by you, I guess," he said, but did not turn it right-side out again. The trow-form was emerging beneath his coat, no matter how hard he struggled to hold the glamour. Observant as she was, he didn't want her noticing his shoulders were broadening, his body thickening. Wouldn't that be the spectacular cap to an already strange evening, bursting into his full, ugly trow self right here on the dark street? He desperately wanted to keep the illusion he had built for her, an ordinary man with an ordinary life, having ordinary coffees with a beautiful woman.

The skin-hunger raged like a kelpie chasing its prey, and Thomas had to turn away hurriedly, waving without looking back, no matter how rude it was. But at the corner he paused, ever so slightly more under control, and looked back to where she was fitting her key in the lock. "One more thing?" If only he could use her name, but he didn't dare.

"Yes?" Her smile lit the entire dark city block.

"Take more care. Stay away from Underbridge. It's not safe there." Thomas didn't wait for the demurral he knew would follow. The trow-form would not be restrained any longer, so he pulled up the tall collar of the oilskin as his ears burst free from the glamour. He rushed into the darkness toward the Burnside Bridge. He could see the *fu* dogs prowling their perimeters only a block away. Their great lion-maned heads turned to watch as he took a corner at a lope, heading east to the concrete pier at the west end of the bridge that he called home.

He bypassed the market altogether, approaching the bridge via the old pumping station beneath it. This time there was no help for it—he had to touch the metal of the fencing as he swung himself up and over, the chain link clattering musically until he slid down the other side and used his big body to mute its vibrations. Aluminum didn't have the bite of iron, but the fence was an obstacle nevertheless. Inside the fenced station yard, he put a foot on a standpipe and launched to reach the sloping girders that formed the bulk of the Burnside's superstructure. This was iron, indeed, strong iron, thick with paint and rivets and the burning powder of rust.

It kept the fae away. It, and the current of the Willamette running strong beneath it. Only the water-fae braved the river, and even they complained of its bitter chemical taste and the human waste and other offal that tainted it with every rainstorm.

Quick and agile for all his trow size and bulk, Thomas moved along the girders to the western pier beneath the bridge operator's tower. There he hooked his claws in the gap between the concrete blocks, pulling open a hidden door and stepping in.

He was home.

He ought to have returned to the market to look for thieves. Question the regulars. Get a clue about what he was supposed to be protecting for the Queen. But instead, shedding his coat and hanging it on a hook made of peeled-up rebar he had wrapped with leather to contain its iron breath, he went to a slit window that overlooked the southern reach of the river. Rosy city night-light dappled the surface, shimmering in soothing movement. Inside, he was guarding a different treasure, the memory of Tess's smile as they said good night, and the touch of her hand on his arm.

Stupid of him, he knew. But too precious to discard so soon.

∋ Chapter Six ∈

Tess sat in the Jeep in her narrow driveway, thinking about the evening. Even though following Aaron had been a bust, she'd had an unexpectedly wonderful time over coffees with Thomas. Just Thomas. She hadn't gotten his last name—it hadn't seemed necessary. No doubt he found her too forward, but at least he'd agreed to see her again. While she had plenty of social human contact in her job at the rehabilitation center, she often lacked stimulating company, and more bluntly, decent companionship. Thomas was intelligent and good-looking, if unconventionally handsome. She liked his quiet eyes and their unusual coloring.

She had forgotten what it was like to have a rambling conversation that touched on anything and everything. Stephen had been particularly good at lightening the load of Tess's too-serious world, and oh, how she missed that. Thomas's sense of humor was shy and quirky. He spoke in a curious mix of old-fashioned courtesy and current street slang. Their conversation had kept Tess rooted in the here and now. While they talked, she hadn't once felt the need to check messages or make notes about a case at work. What a comfort and a delight, to find herself transported from the daily drudgery to a happier, warmer state of mind. Even Thomas's quirks interested her. He didn't have a phone, which could mean anything. Maybe he chose not to participate in the artificial hustle of modern life.

Tess wasn't the sort of person who had flocks of casual friends she could call at the drop of a hat. Her work used up her social energy, leaving her drained and wanting nothing more than a bubble bath or a good book. The spontaneous evening with Thomas might have begun with the deadly serious topic of Aaron and drug addiction, but by the end of the evening, she thought she might at last have made a new friend. He'd even taken her business card and the suggestion of another outing with what seemed like real pleasure.

Smiling, she turned off the ignition and gathered her handbag and the parking ticket, and went inside her half of the duplex that backed onto a greenbelt leading to Forest Park.

In the rear, she stopped at the island separating the kitchen from the living room. She dropped her purse and keys on the counter, stuffed the parking ticket into the basket for her mail, and opened the fridge. She needed a quick and easy snack before bed. The coffee had been warm and sweet, but it sat uncomfortably in her stomach. A little food would balance out the buzz from the caffeine and sugar.

While two slices of bread toasted, Tess fished in the outside pocket of her purse for the object she'd found in the market. Her fingers found the ribbon first, and tugged gently. The little thing swung free in the overhead light.

The size of a golf ball, it looked like a hazelnut still in its shell, with tracings of silver where there would otherwise have been brown markings like wood grain. The ribbon was bound tightly around its equator and its meridian, closing the two halves. Tess studied it, smiling. The fanciful knot at the top proved complicated and too tight to loosen, even when picked at with the point of a toothpick. She was tempted to snip the ribbon in two and see if the nut was made to open, but instead she took it to her curio shelf, and opened the glass door so she could tuck the newest acquisition into an empty space.

Tess was a magpie, collecting all sorts of objects that interested her, but she was most drawn to the items she'd found under the Burnside Bridge in the past year. Her count was up to fifteen, everything from a wooden thistle bristling with bronze spikes, to something like a radiometer, a clear glass bulb with a tiny bead inside that jittered back and forth whenever she held it. Some of the things were interesting enough that she'd taken them to her office for curios. At first she'd tried to find their owners, but since nobody claimed them, she'd given up and kept them for herself. She didn't find a new prize every time she visited the market, but often enough that she kept her eyes open.

The beribboned nut made a nice addition to her collection. Perhaps at Christmastime she would hang it as an ornament on her tree. Still basking in the glow of the evening, she closed the glass door and went to scramble an egg to go with her toast.

Morning came too soon, gray light from the windows waking Tess in her small upstairs bedroom. She had left the window near the bed open an inch or two, loving the fresh air even though the October nights were growing chilly. The window looked out over the green belt into the thickness of the ivy that had escaped from countless city gardens and now threatened to subsume the local ecosystem. Trees rose from a uniform sea of saw-toothed leaves and hairy tan stems. Tess liked the look, though she knew monocultures were often harmful in the long run. It had a certain order to it, a tidy regularity that pleased her. She treasured the glimpses of wildlife—raccoons, deer, opossums, rodents and birds—that were her reward for choosing the duplex on the edge of Forest Park despite its too-high rent. Her tiny slice of country peace just blocks from the pounding mechanical pulse of the city.

"Too much coffee too late. Never again." She sat up, groaning, rubbing her eyes. Her dreams had been filled with confusion and exhausting searches for something she had never quite found. Over and over again, she saw the girl Aaron had met, but each time the girl turned to stare at dream-Tess, with a glare of such open hostility that Tess was taken aback, even in her sleep. Thomas had been there, too, a vague figure on the periphery of the dreams. She bumped into his tall, bulky form when she turned around, but each time he melted away before she could speak. Always, he held out a hand to her, beckoning. The sense of loss at his disappearances saddened her and left her with a melancholy she couldn't quite shake, even after waking.

Today she would visit a long-term care facility on the far slopes of the West Hills. One of her former clients lived there—if sitting in chairs by windows, staring blankly, could be called living—and she wanted to talk to him one more time in the hopes of stirring something. Anything. Maybe if she showed him Aaron's pictures, before the addiction and now, when he was so thin and worn, Rory could give her a clue. She could ask about the lady, too. Maybe it would bring a response.

After her shower and breakfast, Tess dressed in a pair of slacks and a long-sleeved top, and pulled her hair back into a tortoise-shell barrette. She slipped her cell phone in her purse, along with a slim journal for taking notes. As an afterthought, she picked up the silvery hazelnut from the curio shelf and tucked it into the back pouch. It would look interesting in her office. She'd swap it out for something else.

Ridge Manor looked like a large house from the outside. All brick and white pillars and windows. But inside, it was still a hospital, with easy-clean floors and walls, and secured windows that insured the residents stayed inside. Tess signed in at the desk and pinned her visitor badge to her shirt pocket. She followed an attendant to the day room, where one of her former clients was spending his morning in an armchair next to a stack of puzzles and games, which he ignored in favor of staring up at the light fixtures.

"Hi, Rory," Tess said quietly, touching his shoulder. "It's Tess Gordon."

Rory Morris slowly turned his head to look at her, but Tess saw no recognition in his blank brown eyes. Still, it was a response, which was better than some days, when he wouldn't even turn his head.

She pulled up a chair and sat facing him. "Rory, I need your help." She opened a folder and put a picture of Aaron, a happy twenty-year-old at a family barbecue, in Rory's hand. "This guy was just like you, once. Happy, healthy, good-looking."

Rory's gaze drifted slowly to the photo, and then just as slowly lifted ceilingward. Tess touched the top of his head and redirected his attention. "Then something happened to him, just like it happened to you. He started taking something. Losing himself, just like you did." She slipped another photo, taken just a couple of weeks ago, into Rory's hand. Aaron was thin and drawn, his gaze blank and uninterested, unfocused and dull. His dark skin had grayed, looked almost ashy with dust.

"You've got to help me, Rory. I don't want to lose another person to this stuff. Come on." She squeezed his hand where it held the pictures. "Come on. Tell me what you remember. Where you went, who you met. Aaron sneaks out of his house at night. Last night he went underneath the Burnside Bridge—"

Wait. Had she seen Rory's eyes flicker?

"Is it the bridge? Is that where he gets it? I didn't think so, not after last night, because he met a girl there—"

"The lady." Rory's whisper was so faint it could have been an exhalation.

A frisson of excitement and triumph hummed through her. The lady! It was a link, a key. It had to be. Tess felt the tingle of knowledge tantalizing her, just out of reach. The lady. The woman at the riverside. Rory. Drugs. Aaron. It must all fit together, but she could not find the proper pieces and turn them the right way. She fumbled in her bag for her journal, opening it randomly to a blank page. Her pen had come unclipped from the journal, and a quick shake didn't turn it up. She couldn't afford to lose Rory's attention, thready as it was, so she kept talking while she emptied half her purse into her lap. Wallet, keys, the silver hazelnut, old receipts, her phone, a pack of gum, and finally the pen. She grabbed it, clicking the point out, just as Rory leaned forward and snatched the hazelnut, letting the photos of Aaron fall into the space between his chair cushion and arm.

"Rory, Rory...here, let me have that. If you'll just look at Aaron, see how he's fading, like you did..." Tess tried to put the pictures back in one hand while she pried at the other to retrieve the hazelnut. No telling what Rory might do with it, in his strange fugue state. But Rory would not unclench his hand, and Tess was afraid to cause a disturbance. Already a couple of other residents were staring. She repacked her bag except for the journal and pen.

"Tell me more about the lady. Who is she?"

Rory's head fell back against the armchair, and he closed his eyes. His mouth went slack. The photos slid from his fingers again, and Tess, defeated, returned them to the folder. She touched his arm, but he was not responsive. She tried once more to pry open the hand with the silver nut in it, but though the rest of Rory seemed limp and helpless, that hand was rigid and unmovable.

Rory had gone away again, and there was nothing more to be gained by continuing to question him. Tess went to murmur to the attendant that Rory had something of hers in his hand and they should take it away in case it caused problems. The attendant came and talked to Rory gently, taking Rory's clenched fist in his large hand. Finger by finger, he opened the hand, to show Tess Rory's empty palm.

"Nothing here. Maybe he's hidden it. I'll get him to stand up and you can check the chair."

While Tess rummaged beneath the seat cushion and shook out the knitted afghan draped over the arm, the attendant checked Rory's mouth and clothing.

"It was in his hand, I know it was."

"Did you check the floor?" The attendant let Rory sag back into the armchair. "Maybe he dropped it."

But more searching didn't turn up the nut. The attendant asked the other residents if they'd seen it, but no one had. Rory slumped in the chair, more boneless than Tess had ever seen him. In the end, she left her contact information and a description of the silver nut, in case someone should find it. As she walked to the door, she turned for one more glance at Rory. He still lay in the chair, eyes closed and hands loose in his lap, but now a faint smile curved his mouth instead of the slack jaw of the catatonic.

You know more than you're telling. Tess scowled to herself, wondering what in the world Rory could have done with the trinket without leaving the chair. There was no place to hide it that they hadn't searched, and if he'd managed to swallow it, though she couldn't see how, there was no telling what harm it would do him.

⇒ Chapter Seven ⇐

There she was again.

Thomas should have known she wouldn't be able to stay away. She was like a dog with a bone, worrying at it until she got to the marrow. He stood at a slit window of his trowhold and looked out across Underbridge, where Tess was moving determinedly from person to person and fae to fae, meeting with blank faces, rudeness or outright laughter.

A sigh gusted out of him. This couldn't end well, and he'd better go down into the market and stop her before she found a fae who *would* do business with her. Thomas knew that the likes of Sharpwit left the humans alone, but not all fae were so particular or circumspect in their dealings with humans. For a change the redcaps were not tending their cauldron of bloody dye, but there was at least one kelpie dripping about in the rainy evening, and a slender drug rehab counselor would be as tasty as a zonked-out junkie girl, once she'd been drowned in the Willamette.

Thomas slid the narrow chunk of concrete back into place and closed his window on Underbridge. His eagerness to see Tess, a full five days before they were supposed to meet at the coffee shop again, surprised him. Even if it couldn't be under favorable circumstances, he wanted to be with her, hear her voice, maybe even feel her touch again. He hurried up the spiral stairs carved from the solid concrete of the bridge pier to the cavernous, slightly damp room beneath, where he kept his clothes and his kitchen. He shrugged into the oilskin and took a moment to compose himself enough to become Thomas Human again, instead of Thomas Trow. He patted his pockets from the outside, checking for his stone blade and the six large iron spike nails he carried—well wrapped to save himself from the iron—for protection. He grabbed the wooden bucket of grubs he'd collected for Sharpwit, and went up the rest of the stairs to the hidden door that accessed the network of support girders.

In his human form, it was less painful to walk along the iron girders. He hurried along the horizontals, on the lookout for observers, swinging past uprights, until he was able to drop the ten feet to the ground in the fenced area behind the pumping station. A moment or two later he slipped through his secret glamoured gap in the chain link, instead of climbing the fence.

It wasn't difficult finding Tess in the gloom of Underbridge, though she'd moved on from the boggart disguised as a hobo sleeping in a pile of stained blankets, and was heading toward the kelpie. Thomas cursed under his breath as he rushed to Sharpwit's stall and set down the bucket of grubs with a thump, nearly knocking over a pair of brownies waiting for a snack. Tess must really think she was onto something, to come back and be so persistent. He could hear her talking to the kelpie as he approached.

"So I'm looking for some stuff for my friend. He's really sick, but he can't help it, you know? Something called 'the lady.' I promised I'd bring him back some. Just a little hit, you know, to quiet the shakes. Just one."

Bitter bluebell throats and hairy ivy feet, thought Thomas. Did she think the kelpie was a pusher? He strode through a group of hobs who were gaming with knucklebones, disturbing their play but ignoring their shrill cries and their pummeling fists on his shins.

The kelpie stared at Tess hungrily, his eyes hot and intimate. Thomas could see through the glamour to the horse-shape just beneath the surface, a shape running with liquid and clothed in waterweed, teeth harsh as bad dreams and just as vicious. All the kelpie needed was for her to agree to walk away with him. It would take her toward the river, and Tess would not return from that walk.

Thomas broke into a run. His sudden movement caught the attention of half the market—*just what she needs, for me to draw all eyes to her*—including Tess and the kelpie. She turned with a delighted smile.

"Thomas! Fancy meeting you here."

"Yes, fancy," drawled the kelpie, not looking away from Tess. Her head began to turn back toward the irresistible allure of the handsome form that overlaid the water-horse.

"Back off." Thomas glared at the kelpie, whose pale, river-wrinkled fingertips halted an inch from Tess's arm. "She's not interested."

"She certainly seems to be," the kelpie asserted. "We're going to take a stroll and have a chat."

"Not tonight."

Tess watched the byplay for a moment, then interrupted. "I was just asking about my friend and his problem, Thomas. That's all. No harm done."

"You shouldn't be here, T—" He stopped himself from speaking her truename just in time, because it had hovered on his lips with such pleasure from the moment he saw her from his window. "It's not safe." He was relieved that his arrival seemed to have broken the kelpie's spell.

"I'm all right." She turned fully toward him at last and the kelpie thrust an ugly gesture at the two of them behind her back before slinking away into the evening drizzle.

"You don't even have a raincoat," Thomas fretted at her, "and you're talking to dangerous strangers. I'm not certain you understand what 'all right' means."

Now Tess seemed offended. "I have adequate judgment and can take care of myself. You're making me sound like an idiot. Surely you can't mean that."

Thomas drew a deep breath to control the turmoil inside him. He reminded himself Tess could not see through the fae glamour and had no idea she'd been dealing with a creature from a hidden world, one with different rules and moral code, not to mention menus. In her mind, she'd been talking to a street boy, a very pretty and forward street boy. She didn't know that pretty boy would have drowned her and dined on her delicious, salty liver without thinking twice about it.

He glanced over his shoulder and saw that the market seemed back to normal on the surface, but the denizens were still furtively eyeing them. He'd drawn a target on Tess as surely as if he'd walked into the center of the milling crowd and shouted, "Look, a foolish human! Free for the taking!"

He'd have to do something about that, but what? He couldn't work magic well enough to throw a glamour over Tess to change her appearance, nor make the fae forget they'd seen him take her from a kelpie. The best he could do later would be to spread a tale about the kelpie and make the water-horse seem at fault somehow. Maybe something about how the city seemed to be concerned about the number of drowned and gnawed girls that washed up lately. Urban fae well knew they had to keep their inhuman behavior within limits in order not to be discovered by the hundreds of thousands of humans living so near their mound.

It might work. The market fae knew him and trusted him, as far as Unseelie trusted anything not Unseelie. They knew he did the Queen's bidding, and for all they knew, he had her ear. After all, he'd been her lover once upon a time, in a fairytale. One of the rare few who survived their trysts with her.

"Thomas? Just let him go." Tess drew his attention back from the darkness where the kelpie had gone to squat near the railing along the riverbank, glaring at them, his eyes shining like coins in the dark. Good thing Tess couldn't see what those eyes belonged to.

"I'm sorry. It's just…like I said, it's not safe here, and he looked like he was feeling a little too comfortable. How've you been?"

To his relief, she smiled. The stilted moment had passed. "Fine, though work's a bit frustrating at the moment. You?"

"The same." A rattling noise behind him alerted him to the hobs, still playing knucklebones. And listening. Thomas reached out and tucked her hand into the bend of his arm. "I'm up for coffee, even though it's way ahead of schedule. You?" Her fingers were warm, and with the touch, he could more effectively convince her with the little fae magic he possessed.

She resisted, but only for a moment, then his charm pulled her along, out of the market. "I was trying to find out more about Aaron and his dealer. That's what I was asking that boy about when you came along."

"So I gathered. I'm serious about how dangerous it is here in Underbridge."

"What an interesting name you've given it, like Goose Hollow or Irving, as if it's a Portland neighborhood." When he quickened his pace, aware he was giving away too much, she matched his stride and kept chatting, her hand snug in his elbow. "It really is sort of a neighborhood, after all. So many of these people live here, more or less."

"That's why I know so much about them. Look, why don't you let me do the asking around for you? They know me, and I'm big enough that no one messes with me."

"Nobody's messed with me, either." They paused at the corner to wait for the walk light. Thomas nonchalantly turned up the cuffs of his oilskin sleeves and popped his collar, then retied his belt knot backward. It was the closest he could come to turning his coat inside out in order to thwart any pursuers.

"That kid tonight…if he'd managed to get you to come along, he'd have tried to rape you. Worse, maybe." Thomas turned his head to the right, where he could see the ornate red gate into Chinatown. He subtly increased his pace and hoped Tess would not suggest cutting through there tonight. But he didn't want to make Tess suspicious by resisting entering Chinatown, either. She picked up on nuance far too quickly.

"How can you know that?" Tall as she was, she still had to look up at him, just a little.

"There's our light." They crossed and continued walking west. Thomas let out a breath when the red gate was out of sight.

"Seriously, Thomas. Do you know him?"

"Yes. And he might look like a nice enough kid, but he's

not."

"I didn't get a bad vibe from him, and I work with addicts and thugs all the time. I've learned to trust my instincts."

Thomas stifled a sigh. "Just this once, please trust mine." He was going to have to do something about Tess. If she kept messing around Underbridge, she'd end up hurt or worse. If the Queen got word that a human was on the track of one of the Queen's lovers, it would definitely be the "worse" option.

Tess pulled her hand from his arm and knelt on the sidewalk to tie her shoe. Thomas heard her say, "Huh. Look at that," as she reached for something tucked into a cavity, a bit of damage at the base of a light post.

Thomas saw the glimmer of fae magic too late; it was in her hand, and Tess was smiling.

"I find the oddest, most interesting things down here in Old Town. Look." She held up her hand, palm flat. A glass thimble sat there, glinting with the electric purple that was the Queen's magical signature. He knew Tess would only see the clear, greenish glass of the thimble.

Thomas's gut clenched sickly, and it was all he could do not to strike the thing from her hand. Instead he reached out slowly, taking the thimble as if he only wanted to examine it.

Those are my possessions, and I will not have them taken from me.

With a shiver, he knew what the Queen had been talking about at last. But he was no closer to understanding why they were at or near the goblin market.

The golden band on his left arm began to warm, and he saw his mistake in touching the thimble. Because he had, the Queen had been alerted to the movement of her trinket.

He had to get Tess out of here, and now. He glanced at the wristwatch on his arm, the one he wore because certain human devices entertained him, and because it helped to dress like a human if he wanted to pass as one. "You know, I was so pleased to see you again that I forgot about my evening appointment. I can't go with you for coffee. We're still on for our date Friday?"

Tess blinked, slowly rising. "Sure, Thomas. I wouldn't miss it."

He saw her uncertainty at his sudden departure, a little line of concern puckering between her brows. *Give her something else to think about.* He smiled, feeling the armband burning. Any moment, if he didn't head for the fairy mound, he'd smell the stench of his own flesh cooking. The Queen would not be ignored for long.

"Thanks. Where's your car?"

She pointed up the street. "In the parking garage, for a change. That ticket cost me an arm and a leg."

"Promise me you'll go straight there? I don't like the thought of you blundering around Underbridge without me, especially tonight."

"Don't be silly, I—"

Thomas leaned down, not really knowing he was going to kiss her until suddenly that peony mouth was beneath his, and her words had stopped, and her eyes flared wide and then fluttered closed.

Her lips burned in a way the Queen's shackle never would. A sweet fire, electric, without the thistly prickle of the bone and gold on his arm. The skin hunger surged even more powerfully than it had when Tess first touched him last week. How long had it been since he'd kissed a woman, someone not fae…someone not the Queen? Decades.

It was Tess who closed the gap between them, taking a step toward him. Her face tilted. Her mouth pressed his firmly, and when he reflexively put a hand at her back to steady them both, he felt her lips part under the pressure of his own.

She was sweet and salty together. As he tasted her, tongue sweeping slowly between her lips, his fingers slipped the thimble into a pocket of his oilskin. Her hands came up and clutched at his lapels. He cupped the side of her neck and jaw in his empty palm, his thumb on the pulse beneath her ear, where he could feel the blood throb past in a quickening tidal rhythm. Her breath hitched in a gasp and he caught her even closer.

His fae nature flared for a moment at the taste of her, but it was his human side that swamped his iron control. Her hair caught between his fingers as he kissed her ever more deeply. He had to lock his knees when her arms went up around his neck.

She was lithe and lissome, swaying with him as he swayed, both of them blind to their surroundings. Portland and Underbridge and his dread for her sake all swept away. There was only the places where they touched, skin sharing warmth and the wonder of what it meant to be human again, to live and want as humans did.

It was the overpowering urge to whisper Tess's truename as his lips grazed along her jawline that finally pried him loose. He needed all the control he had, bolstered by the increasing sting of the band, to lift his head and step back. She gazed at him, speechless, eyes dazed and dark.

"I won't apologize, because I've wanted to do that since we met, but I've got to go, and I didn't want you to think I was rejecting you, when it's my own forgetfulness that's the problem."

Tess's fingertips came up and touched her mouth, and Thomas swallowed hard. "I'll see you soon. Remember to be careful."

He turned on his heel, almost running.

At the next corner, Thomas looked back over his shoulder. She was still standing under the streetlight, fingers to her lips, watching him hurry away.

He wondered how long it would be before she noticed he hadn't returned the thimble. He melted into the shadows out of sight, let the trow-form with all its strength and speed and magic surface, and raced to Forest Park.

☥

The Queen was in a rage. To a casual observer, she might have appeared coolly aloof. But Thomas knew the signs, the little tell beside her eyes where a flicker came and went in rhythm with the fist that clenched, hidden by the cobweb drape of her sleeve.

"You touched one of my things, Thomas."

"I did, my Lady."

"You moved it."

"I did, my Lady."

"You moved it, when you knew it was mine. You must have known I would discover you, bound as you are to me."

"I did, my Lady." He stood, the trow-form uppermost, legs apart, head bowed, hand out, thimble rocking in his palm with his pounding heartbeat. He had every expectation she would kill him without a single qualm or warning. "I have it here, safe."

"Why did you touch it?"

"A human had hold of it. I took it back."

The Queen hissed, and her pupils slitted to a snake's. "You have caught the thief! Did you kill him?"

"I did not catch the thief, my Lady. Merely someone who stumbled upon its hiding place by accident. I saw it happen."

The Queen stepped down from her bristly throne, her eyes on the slow-quaking thimble. Thomas flicked a glance at her countenance and saw that he would not die tonight. Now if only he could distract her from questioning too closely about Tess.

Thomas could not lie to the Queen, but like any fae he wouldn't necessarily give the whole truth. It was a neat trick he had learned over the centuries, dissembling. It was what passed for courtesy and social lubrication among the fae. The fae of the Unseelie court were masters of it, though every fae Thomas had met seemed to possess the skill to some degree.

I find the oddest, most interesting things down here.

Tess's words kept echoing in his ears.

He told himself that didn't mean she was the thief, but the pit of his stomach lurched each time he visualized Tess kneeling by the lamppost, the thimble in her hand. But what if she was? How could he keep her safe from the Queen's anger? He had to find a way. It was a good thing the Queen couldn't read his thoughts, but he'd have to guard carefully against revealing his suspicions. He didn't want to examine his motives for protecting Tess too closely. He preferred to put it all down to an evening spent drinking lattes with a kind, friendly woman, assuaging his longing for human contact. Not the kisses, or the concern for her well-being that he was rapidly beginning to feel.

"Shall I put it back for you, my Lady?"

The Queen pursed her lips and lifted the thimble from Thomas's palm. "I will give it thought, but no, not at the moment. I'll keep this with me for a time." The glowing thing vanished into the folds of her skirt. She trailed a tender hand down Thomas's cheek. "You have done well." Her hand cupped his jaw, then his throat.

At her touch, his human form surged outward, pushing aside the trow in an instant. She had always preferred to look at his humanity, though she both tempted and punished him with the trow's abilities and appearance. He could feel her long, curved nails lingering where his pulse beat in the hollow of his collarbone. She held his eyes with hers and drew her nails—bird claws, owl talons, cat claws, the ragged nails of a crone—down his shirt, slicing it open from neckband to belt. She put her hand beneath the jersey fabric and used her claws around the nipple closest to his heart.

Thomas's body betrayed him, reacting with the same mix of fear, loathing and impossible desire the Queen always roused in him. She was a horror, a painful ecstasy, a bitterly intoxicating drink. And when she tugged at his belt and led him to her couch of thistledown, he went.

"Pleasure me, Thomas," she whispered, her face shifting between the beautiful, luminous young woman who had led Tess's friend away at the riverbank, and the nightmare of fury that was her normal face. "Please me well enough, and in return…" Her owl's talon lingered on the bone and gold band. "One strand will part."

"Two, my Lady." Thomas followed her down onto the deeply cushioned surface, his knee between her legs, pressing upward in a way he knew she liked. "One for services already rendered in returning your possession, and one for services about to be rendered." It was only at times like this, when she was indolent and distracted, that he could bend her will.

"Ah, my beautiful boy." She stroked his cheek, then reached into his trousers and took hold of him. "Drive your bargain...this *hard* bargain of yours..." She gave him a wicked squeeze, and laughed when he gasped. "And then perhaps we will see."

The world turned red, and though he was choked with pleasure and bleeding from the scrapes on his back, it was ordinary brown human eyes that swam before him. Only fear made him remember to call out his Queen's name.

⤳ Chapter Eight ⤳

"**W**ere you able to find the knick knack Rory Morris pocketed the other morning?" Seated at her office desk, Tess spoke into the phone.

"No, Ms. Gordon." The day-room attendant's voice seemed certain and a bit annoyed that she was still harping on the issue.

"But it must be there. I have no idea what he did with it, but it's got to be there. I don't know what's in it, and I'm concerned it could do him, or another resident, harm."

"Oh, but there's been a tremendous improvement in patient Morris. I'm not at liberty to give you details over the telephone, but he's had a breakthrough."

"A breakthrough? What?"

"Like I said, I'm not at liberty—"

"I know, I know—federal law prohibits you, and I'm not his physician." Tess sighed in irritation.

"Sorry," the attendant said. Then he laughed. "Maybe your knick knack was magic."

"Ha," said Tess. "Well, thank you, I guess, and please let me know if you find the thing." She hung up and stared at the telephone. Rory, a breakthrough? She wondered what that meant. She thought she'd glimpsed a moment or two of clarity, but since she had only observed him through their counseling sessions, and not during his hospitalization, she didn't have a good behavioral benchmark against which to compare.

Maybe the damage the drug had done wasn't permanent. Maybe there was hope, hope for Aaron, hope for the other young men who'd been in her care, and for the unknown others whose families didn't have the money to spend on private rehabilitation. Rory had been at Ridge Manor for nearly six months. A former client, Anthony Sparks, had been hospitalized elsewhere for even longer, but for the last month she had not checked on his progress. He was no longer the responsibility of the rehab center.

It ate at her, gnawing like a rat at a wall that separated it from food, to have failed so utterly. The center had come too late to cases like Rory and Anthony, but Tess couldn't help feeling she still had a chance with Aaron. He was still walking, thinking, experiencing the world. Whereas Rory and Anthony were locked away in their own minds, to say nothing of the hospitals. They were silent, distant, not present in their own lives. No longer taking the drugs, whatever they were, but not able to return from those personal nightmares. What kind of drug could do such damage?

Tess fished in her locked file cabinet for Anthony's folder, then hastened back to her desk to make another telephone call.

Fifteen minutes later, she was no closer to solving the mystery of Rory's breakthrough. Anthony's condition had not changed in months.

She doodled on her notepad, listing the names of the young men with Aaron's symptoms who'd come through the rehabilitation center. There seemed to be no link between them except their rapid declines, the delusion that they were elves or sprites or other magical creatures, and the unresponsive state their addiction ended in. She knew of no common schools, friends, jobs, interests or neighborhoods.

But something had to be at the root of the evil. A point where all of them touched. She couldn't help but wonder if it had something to do with the people under the Burnside Bridge.

She tore off the doodles and wrote Aaron's name at the top of a fresh page. She underscored it twice, as though the bold strokes would summon a solution. Then she listed everything she knew about his condition, including the confusing mentions of the lady and a brief description of the girl he'd met along the river in Waterfront Park. She also listed the young man who'd offered to chat with her—the one Thomas had driven away.

Which brought her to the topic that hadn't been far from her mind since the night before—Thomas's kiss.

It had left Tess bemused and pleasantly shaken, warm with arousal. She hadn't expected the kissing, but it hadn't been unwelcome, even though it was only their second meeting. Her lips parted even now with the memory.

What a long time it had been since she met a man whose

company she enjoyed and whose touch didn't make her wary. Their encounters had been unconventional, but she looked forward to their coffee and dinner Friday night.

Thinking back over those few minutes together, she remembered the green glass thimble and wondered what Thomas had done with it. He had probably forgotten he had it, given their embrace and his sudden departure. She'd have to ask.

Tess shook her head to get herself back on track. Aaron, "the lady," the Burnside Bridge. Rory too had reacted to mentions of the lady and the bridge. The more she thought about it, the more she wondered: had Rory met the same woman, perhaps? Or was "the lady" a slang term for a new street drug? Was Aaron's paramour also Aaron's pusher?

She accessed the center's appointment schedule on her computer. Her appointment with Aaron was not until next week, but what if she spoke to him before that, got him to meet her somewhere they could talk in complete privacy? What would he tell her then? Or did she dare follow him a second time, see if he went back to the bridge and met the woman again? Could she even come up with a remotely plausible reason for being where Aaron was, filled with obsessive questions about whom he was seeing, and whether the woman knew Rory or Anthony or any of the names on Tess's notepad? A reason to insert herself into his personal life? Question his girlfriend, demand to know if the woman had introduced Aaron to something devastating?

Tess rubbed her eyebrows, trying to press away the headache that was building as her questions piled up and up.

She knew what her colleagues would say: don't let it get personal. Don't get sucked into their lives, their delusions, their private nightmares. Before she knew it, she'd be trying to do Aaron's thinking for him, trying to shield him from all harm, trying to *be* his cure instead of helping lead him to it. He had to want to get better for himself. She could not make him do it—he would only backslide.

Like any other addict, her colleagues would remind her.

Aaron had to hit bottom, she could not point to it and say, "There it is. Walk away from it." His family had staged their intervention by bringing him to rehabilitation. And while Aaron claimed to want to get better, he nevertheless insisted he wasn't on drugs, even as he declined week after week.

She couldn't say why it seemed like a personal failure, except that here was a case where nothing had worked, not even for a few days or weeks.

Nothing.

Tess stared at the computer screen, unseeing. She would meet Thomas for their dinner date in just a few days; she held onto that thought like a lifeline. She wasn't Aaron. She still had a life. She simply had to keep it that way. If not for Aaron, she would not have met Thomas. Maybe at their next session she could explain that to Aaron and pull him into reality, get him to confide in her, show him that life mattered more than fantasy, more than drugged dreams. Maybe it wasn't too late.

Her computer beeped for an appointment reminder. With a sigh, Tess cleared away her doodles, turned the leaf on her notepad, and buzzed the front desk to send in her next client, a young woman who'd been very successful losing weight on painkillers. So successful, in fact, that to get more prescriptions, she'd faked being struck by hit-and-run drivers in downtown crosswalks.

Twice.

Everyone's reality was different. If only those realities could also be healthy. Including her own. She bit her lip, then folded her hands and put on a welcoming smile.

The last client departed just after four o'clock. Normally Tess would have spent the remainder of her day with paperwork, but Rory's change in condition was never far from her thoughts. Ridge Manor had visiting hours until dinnertime. If she left now, she'd be able to get in to talk with Rory, see firsthand what had changed in the young man virtually overnight.

Ridge Manor was its usual peaceful self in the late autumn afternoon light. Tess checked in with the nurse at the front desk and was just about to pin on the visitor's badge the nurse handed her, when the woman blinked in surprise at her computer screen.

"Hold on a moment," the nurse said, busily clicking at her keyboard. "Rory Morris, you're sure?"

"Yes."

"It's probably just timing on the paperwork, but I guess nobody let your center know that Mr. Morris's family came to take him home just an hour ago!"

"Home? Today?" Tess repeated, startled.

"Yes."

"So...he's not here."

"No. Did you still want to go back?"

"I..." Tess floundered. Rory, gone home? "I—could I speak to his case manager, please? I'd like to follow up on this personally, not wait for the paperwork to come through. It's quite a surprise."

"A pleasant one. I'll buzz for you. Just a moment." The nurse smiled.

Fifteen minutes later, Tess was back in her Jeep, staring out at the salmon sunset sky. Other than hearing from the case manager that Rory had inexplicably emerged from his catatonia two days before, becoming quite lucid and insistent about contacting his family, she had no further information. She felt like she was trembling inside, burning with excitement. The next step was simply to contact Rory at home—tomorrow would be soon enough, but that task had gone straight to the top of her personal calendar—and speak with him and his family. Follow up for the rehab center's records.

Then she would apply what she learned to Aaron's case as

soon as possible. It was good to feel hope again.

⇒ Chapter Nine ⇐

Thomas had almost forgotten what pizza was like. One of those foods he'd never eaten as a human, living before pizza became so popular. He'd tried it off and on in the past few decades, the way he'd tried many things that changed with the times and kept his human side more or less current, always planning for the time when he would be human again and not trow. But of late his trow body had craved the sorts of things Sharpwit cooked. Fae food. Things that spoke of power in the dark, things that haunted, hunted, or hewed to the night.

But here, in this small Italian place Tess had chosen, he was downing slabs of the stuff, greasy with cheese, volcanic with tomato sauce lava, strewn with meat and vegetables. It sat heavy and warm in his belly, a deeply comforting sensation. Tess had matched him slice for slice until the last two on the platter, when she leaned back, her hand upon her stomach, and her smile wry.

"I thought I could do it when we ordered this pie, I really did." She reached out and turned her glass of beer on the tabletop, studying the bubbles that clung in lines and clusters to the glass. "I was starving, but I can't manage another bite. You?"

Thomas grinned. The ballast of the pizza helped anchor his human form uppermost, which was a relief. He might pay the price later for having consumed the cheese and processed flour, but for the moment he was contented, almost blissful. "I think I'm done for as well." He patted his own stomach and could feel the dinner mounding there as if he were a pup, full of milk and meat. "I could really go for a long walk on the beach to help settle this bulge."

"Or maybe through Forest Park. If only it were summer and sunny. This time of year, the trails are slippery. Leaves and rain and mud, mud, mud."

Forest Park. She said it so casually. She had no idea what lived there, the sorts of things that would find her tasty in any number of ways. He fought down his reaction and shook his head. "No, the beach, for me. A long walk, right where the water meets the land."

She took a sip of her beer. "We could go, you know."

Thomas sat up straighter. With her agreement, a new thought had occurred to him. Tess wasn't willing to believe Underbridge was the dangerous place he had painted it, but what if he could prove differently? He wasn't likely to be able to convince her to smear fae ointment on her eyes so she could see through their glamour, but there was another way.

"We could? Now? It's night."

"Not now, but tomorrow. I don't have to work, it's Saturday. We could go to the seashore, walk all we want, have a little clam chowder somewhere. Spend the day. Take our time coming back."

And I could find a stone with a hole, and use it to show you the reality you think you know. Beach stones were the best for seeing past the glamour. Their holes, worn by the waves, were more rounded, less fractured than stones chipped from cliffs or dug from the earth. He sometimes took a fairy road to the coast and remembered what the area had been like two centuries ago, before so many people came. He'd found a few of the stones over the years—almost as if he had a knack for it. Given a long enough stroll on the rocky beaches of the Pacific, sooner or later one would turn up. They'd all gone to Sharpwit in payment for information or meals. No telling what the hob had done with them and he did not want to ask if she had any left.

He would show Tess his real self and in that way convince her to stay away from Underbridge. It meant she would stay away from him as well, but the urge to keep her safe was becoming more primal the better he got to know her. If she continued with her search for Aaron and the lady, she would run afoul of the Queen, and Thomas feared her life would be forfeit.

"I'd really like that." He couldn't keep the warmth from his voice, and Tess responded to it by coloring faintly.

"Me, too. Did you want to drive, or shall I? Passenger buys the chowder."

"I...uh, don't drive."

Tess's eyebrows went up. "No phone, no car? You live a

pretty streamlined life."

Thomas shrugged, watching her closely for her reaction. "It's not hard, when you live in the city. Everything's right here. I don't need to go far." He wondered if she thought he belonged to the streetfolk.

"I guess that's true. I'm just spoiled by my conveniences. All right, I'll pick you up in the morning."

"I'll meet you at our coffee shop. My place is hard to find and there's not a lot of parking."

Tess sat back and looked at him carefully.

"The coffee's on me," he added. He had to tread softly. He was about to overplay his hand. He could feel her caution simmering to the surface. "And the chowder."

"Is it that you don't want me to see where you live?" Her voice was quiet, but her wide brown eyes were direct and piercing.

"Partly," he admitted. "It's not in a great part of town, and it's…well, you could say I'm a slob."

It was the right tack to take. She relaxed and smiled. "Okay then. So…shall we say the coffee shop, nine a. m.? And I'll have—"

"A hazelnut mocha, two shots. I remember."

"Make it three. I'll need the jolt, especially after all this pizza." She looked ruefully at the two slices remaining. "Those go home with you. Otherwise I'll eat them for breakfast and seriously overdo it."

Thomas smiled at the pizza wedges. He already had plans for them. Given the example, Sharpwit could make something similar, and it would be a change from fungus and bug wraps.

"Walk me back to the Jeep, Thomas?"

"Of course. My pleasure."

Once he'd seen her to her car, Tess insisted he at least accept a lift down the mad spiral of the parking garage. Thomas could have taken the stairs, but after the discussion at dinner, it seemed wiser to accept Tess's courtesy instead of continuing to rouse her caution. He climbed into the passenger seat, doing his best to ignore the seasick feeling caused by so much metal around him. The fae portion of him had difficulty with iron unless it was well insulated by concrete or space. It was one reason he'd chosen his home in the pier of the Burnside Bridge. So much iron kept the true fae at bay and allowed him a certain privacy. Even the Queen had never bothered to visit his sanctuary, though she knew exactly where it was.

Over the years, as the trow nature asserted itself more integrally, his home had become less pleasant, and he could see that in the long run, unless he were able to break the armband, he would have to move. But by then he'd be more fae than human, and he'd want different things.

The thought was not a comfort.

"Too much pizza?" Tess said, as he settled himself irritably.

"Yeah."

"Me, too. But it was delicious."

The Jeep rolled steadily down the twist of concrete that led to the street. Thomas fought the pull of the forces that dragged him toward Tess, and clung to the side of the car, even though the metal made his skin prickle.

Outside, she didn't pause at the exit. She turned left and headed in the general direction of the Burnside Bridge.

"Anywhere's good," Thomas suggested. "I can walk from here."

She slid him a glance while tending to the traffic, minimal so late in the evening. "I'll at least get you closer to the bridge. Even if I can't get you to your door. You're not the only one who wants to make sure someone's safe. All right?"

"All right." He hid a smile and struggled with his trow self. It was late, and he was tired, and the closer to the goblin market they got, the more habit insisted he shift. But all the same, it was nice to think she cared.

Because by tomorrow afternoon, that would all be over.

In a few blocks, she pulled over by the Skidmore Fountain, put her Jeep in park, and turned off the engine. Thomas looked around with a quick assessing glance. The place was, as always, crawling with the fae, something in every shadowy corner. He opened his mouth to turn and ask Tess to drive south a few more blocks, where it would be safer for her, when she gently laid her hand over his. Thomas let go of the wrapped slices of pizza to turn his hand beneath hers and lace their fingers.

Then he sat very, very still and looked down at their hands.

His heart thundered in his chest. They were inches from being seen by the fae, he was half sickened by the iron of the Jeep, and yet the only thing he wanted was to sit hunched in the squeaky bucket seat holding her hand forever.

"I had a nice time tonight," Tess said. "Thank you."

Thomas had to clear his throat before he could speak. "The feeling is mutual. It's been a long time since I enjoyed myself that much."

"Are you sure I can't drop you closer to your home?"

She was almost like the fae themselves, making their offers in triples, waiting for three confirmations or three negations, before they considered a deal done one way or the other. "I'm sure." The chill of the outside air meant that as he spoke, his breath condensed on the inside of the windshield and fogged it. He exhaled a little more, putting up a thin scrim between the two of them and the fae loitering outside the car. Thomas closed his eyes for a moment, concentrating hard on the foggy windows, thinking of the fog as glamour and encouraging it along.

Tess gave a short laugh. "Wow, looks like I need to get the Jeep in for service. The windows are fogging up awfully fast. The defroster must be having trouble now that it's getting colder at night."

"It's all the garlic on the pizza." Thomas tried for a joke, opening his eyes to see the extent of the fogged windows, and relaxed a little. They were better out of view of the fae, but the effort had made him tired and a little twitchy.

Tess gave a soft laugh, and squeezed his hand. Thomas turned to gaze at her in the dim cab of the vehicle. Her eyes had the liquid gleam of ripples on the Willamette long after midnight, and the crescent moon shadows of her eyelashes lay over her cheeks each time she blinked.

When she leaned toward him, he met her halfway, his free hand reaching out to cup her shoulder. Her lips met his in a soft kiss, nothing as startling or overwhelming as the unplanned kiss beneath the lamppost a few nights ago, but far, far sweeter. There was trust in the kiss's softness, in its slow bloom from shy tenderness to heat.

One kiss. That's all he would allow himself tonight. One perfect, trapped-in-amber kiss to take with him into sleep and beyond.

When their lips parted, he touched her mouth with the tips of his fingers. The trow shuddered within him, but he controlled it for a few moments longer. For the length of the kiss, he had forgotten the iron sickness, forgotten the prowling fae in the darkness beyond the bubble of Tess's Jeep, forgotten the Queen's shackle on his arm, and forgotten that Tess almost certainly had the Queen's baubles. Now all those things crashed over him like a fall of earth inside one of the Forest Park tunnels.

He stroked his thumb over Tess's bottom lip and whispered, "Sleep well till morning." Then he opened the door and hurried away, pulling up his collar and hunching his shoulders to hide whatever trow bits might escape his hard-fought glamour before he was out of Tess's sight.

⇒ Chapter Ten ⇐

Long rides in the Jeep were often chilly because of its soft-top and aging heater, but the trek over the Coast Range to the beach south of Lincoln City was doubly so, with Thomas insisting on having his window down all the way. Tess was glad she had dressed warmly. As was so often the case, the weather at the coast would be windier and wetter than inland. Thomas didn't seem to mind the damp blowing in, or the raindrops that shone like dew in his close-cropped hair.

The fresh air smelled of rain and wet earth. Though Tess liked the smell, she preferred the sugary fragrance of balsam in the summer heat. As they crested the Coast Range, Tess looked for elk but saw none. The towering Douglas firs and Sitka spruces lined the roadway, giving over to stands of yellowing birches where the roadcuts and loggers had denuded the slopes of evergreens.

As if the sight of the birches had summoned Stephen's ghost, she heard her brother's singsong in her head. *She's like a birch girl, a birch girl, a birch girl, all white and golden and green and beautiful and I am her dark elf.* Tess gripped the wheel harder, trying not to scowl. She didn't want to ruin the first good day in weeks with unhappy thoughts.

The road took them through part of Lincoln City before it joined the highway edging the coast like a doily frilled with sea foam. Thomas seemed to relax once he saw the ocean, and turned to her with a smile.

She parked in one of the viewpoint pullouts along the highway, and they went down the steep cliff-hugging staircase to the beach of mingled sand and pebbles. They had the quiet cove to themselves, which pleased Tess, and seemed to please Thomas, as well. In simple accord they turned north, with the Pacific curling eagerly to shore to their left. They trudged through the soft dry sand until they reached firmer footing at the tideline, dodging the more ambitious waves.

Thomas wandered slowly, his eyes on the ground like any good beachcomber. Tess lifted her face to the spotty sunlight, watching gulls soaring overhead and ravens hopping from wind-bent tree to battered rock on the cliff to their right. At one point Thomas paused and dug at the sand with the toe of his boot, then bent and pocketed whatever he'd found. Tess, waiting for him a few feet farther on, met his smile with one of her own. As he rejoined her, their meandering strides brought them bumping together, arm and hip. When the backs of their hands bumped and bumped again, it seemed natural that their hands should link. She studiously ignored her racing pulse and hid her sudden joy by looking at the cliff face again.

Conversation was unnecessary. Tess felt there had never

been a more perfect moment between the two of them, never such an exquisite unity of communication, despite the long evenings of conversation and the kissing. A half-mile along the crescent curve of shoreline, Thomas drew her to a beached silver log whose stumps of branches were draped with sea-wrack and delicate, dried algae strands. They sat leg-to-leg and shoulder-to-shoulder, staring out to sea, hands still linked.

Tess wondered if he would try to kiss her again, or if she could try to kiss him instead. Either solution suited her.

"I want to show you something," Thomas said, after they'd been sitting in silence a while.

"Oh, really." Tess allowed herself a little humor in her tone, and was rewarded with a sidewise quirk of his mouth.

"This stone I found." He let go of her hand to fish in the pocket of his oilskin. He shifted to his left to make room between them. He brushed the damp sand from the stone until it was clean, and Tess saw there was a hole in the rock. "It's a stone with a hole, one not drilled by the hand of man." He held it up to his eye and looked at the waves through it.

Tess blinked a little at his odd phrasing. "Those are kind of rare, but I've seen them before."

He half-turned and held it out to her. "The old tales say that if you look through one of these, you can see what the fairies don't mean for you to see. You can see through their glamour to what lies beneath. Why don't you try it?"

Tess took the stone from his hand, feeling the brush of their fingers. She lifted the perforated stone to her eye, smiling. She did it to please Thomas, because his story was so preposterous and charming. An ocean-drilled stone, proof against fairy glamour? What kind of nonsense was that? But she'd learned in her years as a counselor that sometimes the oddest statements held a nugget of wisdom or truth concealed in outrageous metaphor. She watched the waves for a moment, then turned and looked at him through the hole. She blinked once and dropped the stone.

Her heart rate rocketed into the stratosphere. What she had seen looking back at her through the hole was…*not Thomas.*

It was something…*other.*

I am her dark elf, birch girl, birch girl…I am a Green Man, a Man of the Forest.

Her hands began to shake, so she clenched them and jammed them into her lap. A stab of pain in her mouth made her realize she had bitten the inside of her cheek, and she jumped up from the log. She took two steps backward before getting control of herself.

Thomas bent and picked up the stone, brushing away the sand afresh. He set it on the log between them. "Look again. See me as I am. *Really* see me."

Her voice was as shaky as her hands. "It's a trick."

"It's no trick. Sometimes the legends are true." He sat very still, his eyes anxious.

Tess bent, keeping her eyes on him. She reached for the stone and turned it over in her hands. It was simple wave-tumbled agate, flattish and smooth, shaped like a fat raindrop with its narrow end curved to one side. The matte, whale gray of the stone was starred with a spiderweb of white quartz. Near the center of the spiderweb, the stone had been soft enough to be worn away. The hole was large enough for her fingertips, and she put her index finger into it, as if to satisfy her brain that there was no optical trick, no distorting glass.

"Please." He shifted a few inches farther away, as if to reassure her of his good intentions. "I know you trusted me until now. Nothing's changed except you can see the truth of me now. You can trust me still. Just...*look*."

Until this moment, Tess had thought she knew Thomas as well as anyone could know someone with whom they'd spent a few hours and a few kisses. But now he wasn't making sense, and the trick with the stone was disturbing. Tess wondered if his reality was warping, somehow, the way her clients' did. How many times had she heard addicts begging for someone to believe them, trust them, only to prove time and again they were unworthy of that trust, however sincerely they wished for it, and however pure their intentions? But whenever the source of their addiction was present, pure intentions fell by the wayside. Tess stared at him. Her eyes opened wide as they flickered over his earnest expression.

The trouble was, she *did* trust him. But she also trusted her own eyes, which had just deceived her. Slowly, she lifted the stone to her right eye once more, and peered at him through the hole.

His face was blocky and rough like something carved from teakwood or brownish stone, flanked by large, tufted ears. A peculiar shock of thin, spiky hair, blondish in color, slid along the center of his scalp like a goth kid's Mohawk 'do. A large nose, blunt and somehow sore-looking, as if it frequently ran into fists.

She took the stone away and there was Thomas. She heard herself panting, quick breaths of near-panic.

"How is this possible?" she demanded. "How are you doing this?"

He shrugged while she watched again through the hole in the stone and saw shoulders built like boulders rise and fall. "It's what I said. The glamour vanishes."

Tess couldn't look away. It was like examining a laboratory specimen through a microscope. Something so strange, and yet of this world? Her gaze kept returning to his eyes. As unfamiliar and un-Thomaslike as the rest of him seemed, with the stripe of hair and the muscles in his neck as rough and strong as tree roots, and the ears...dear God, the ears, with bobcat tufts at their pointed tips...his eyes grounded her. Throughout the quivering, shuddering shift of form, Thomas's eyes remained warm and human, that same undecided, entrancing smoke-blue hazel they had always been. It was as though he were simply putting on a costume, a Hollywood monster suit, and if she were to search beneath the black oilskin duster, she would find the zipper.

Thomas fidgeted.

Tess stared out at the ocean through the stone, but it looked just the same as always. She looked at the log, and apart from a faint glitter like fine diamond dust on the silvery wood, it looked as it had.

Before.

Before I learned there really is something weird in the world. Something different and strange and...wrong. But why did he show this to me? What does he hope to accomplish? Birch girl, Green Man, dark elf. Oh, Stephen, is this how it began for you? Will I fall too?

"Are...are you...*what* are you?" she whispered.

"I was human once...I still am, some of the time. A lot of the time. But it's a hard form to hold."

"But you're also...something..."

"It's called a trow."

"A troll?"

"Not a troll. Those are bigger, uglier. Like rocks."

She took the stone away from her eye. It was easier to talk with him when she wasn't looking at a creature from God knew where. The laugh that broke from her was confused and shrill. "Uglier!"

He looked away, and Tess saw she had hurt him with her startled exclamation. The idea that something so strange and disconcerting in its appearance had vanity... "I mean...I don't know what I mean. I can't think. This is insane. *I'm* insane, or you are, or maybe both of us—" Her babbling ceased as Thomas gripped her by the wrist. She flinched in terror, but he would not let her go.

"Neither of us is insane. Just...listen, can't you? Put the rock in your pocket. You'll want it later."

Tess shoved it on the log. "I won't want it."

"You will. Now listen. It's not a long story, but you need to hear it for your own safety."

Now he was using keywords that triggered alarm bells in someone trained to deal with addicts and other dysfunctional personalities. *This is what stalkers say to their girlfriends. This is what abusive spouses say: it was for your own good, the safety of the family, you need to learn...*

"Let me go, Thomas. You're scaring me."

Instantly he released her, scooting backward, hands up, palms open. "Please hear me out."

"You've got two minutes, and then I'm leaving. Sooner if you do something stupid."

"Two minutes is all I need." He took a deep breath. "Back when Portland first became a stop on the river routes to the sea, the Unseelie Court moved from somewhere in England to here."

"Unseelie what?"

"They're not Seelie." Thomas dragged his fingers over his scalp. "It's hard to explain. The Unseelie belong to the court of the dark fae—the dark faeries. English people and farms crowded out the fae and ruined the forests. So the fae fled, and they came here."

"Fairies. In Oregon." Tess snorted.

"You promised me two minutes." His gaze pinned her where she stood, and at last she nodded. "Right. So the Unseelie Court has a Queen. She likes to take human lovers, and she picked me. For some reason, she decided not to kill me when she was through with me, but she bound me to her and gave me the trow-form. It's been almost two hundred years since she did that, and every year it's harder to stay human. But I'll do it. I won't be like this forever. I'll get my own life back."

Tess stood very still. If she hadn't just seen something completely outside her reality through that stone, she would have thought Thomas's story was by far the most unique delusion she'd ever heard.

Thomas continued. "Some of the fae think you're involved in something at the goblin market, and I was afraid for you. That's why we came here today, so I could find you one of these stones that will let you see the fae as they are." He spread his hands wide. "As *I* am."

"Me, involved with fairies. And what goblin market are you

talking about?"

"Under the Burnside Bridge."

"That's the weekend artists' market—"

"Sure it is, at the weekend. But other times, it's the goblin market. Humans shouldn't go there. The fae aren't above taking advantage of the ones who do."

"This is nonsense."

"You've met some of the fae yourself. The fortuneteller, for one."

"You've been spying on me! Are you stalking me?"

Thomas's smile was grim as he looked up at her. "No. The Unseelie Queen has told me to watch the market. There are thieves, and she wants them caught. You just happened to be there last week, more than once. In fact, I've seen you there for months. But this time you caught my eye."

"And you think I'm in danger now."

"Yes, I do. Because other fae have noticed you, not just me."

"What other fae? The fortuneteller?"

"Her, yes…she's a banshee, not exactly a fortuneteller—she can only tell you when you'll die—that's if you give her your truename. And the three men at the barrel…they are redcaps. If you hadn't let on you knew the Queen's latest lover, they would probably have dyed their caps in your blood just for speaking to them. And the young man you spoke to—he's a murderous kelpie. You need to stay away from the goblin market."

The Queen's latest lover...the lady, she ride him...not drugs, but enchantment? What are redcaps, what's a kelpie? Stephen's singsong rang in her ears. *Birch girl, birch girl...*

Tess backed away, shaking her head at her own inflamed imagination. If Thomas could be believed, Aaron was the Unseelie Queen's paramour, and she had cast a spell on him. "No. This is crazy. I have to go now, Thomas, and I'm really, really sorry, but I don't think I can take you back to Portland with me. This is...I have to go."

She hurried back up the beach the way they had come. Thomas followed, but at a distance that respected her boundaries. She had to give him that.

She waited at the top of the stairs to the parking lot, arms crossed over her body, car keys in her hand.

"I'm sorry," she said again. "I hope you'll be all right. Do you need some money to get home?"

"Don't worry about me." Thomas reached out slowly and she saw he had the perforated stone in his hand once more. "Please. You need it to keep you safe."

Maybe if she took it, he would leave her alone. She took it from his hand, stretching to reach it, and very careful not to touch his skin. She shoved the stone into the pouch of her hoodie and repressed the urge to wipe her palm on her jeans.

"If anything at all seems odd, look through it. Know when you're dealing with the fae. I won't ask another thing of you.

Please."

She stood, shifting uncertainly from foot to foot. "I need to think about this, Thomas. If that's your name."

"It is. My truename. Like I said, I was human once. I give it into your keeping. If you were fae, it would give you power over me. Likewise, you should guard your own name where the fae are concerned." He nodded toward the road. "I'll find my own way home. I've done it before. It'll be a nice change from the city."

"I could...I don't know, maybe call a ride for you?" Guilt began to nag at her.

"Who? How? You want to go to the market, maybe, tell them you left a trow at the coast? For them to send a kelpie down the Columbia for me?" He shrugged, and all Tess could think of were those burly, bestial shoulders under the oilskin. It was better if they simply ended this now.

Tess drove away, leaving him standing in the little parking lot. She watched him in the rearview until the curve of the road hid him from sight.

The stone weighed heavy and cold in the pouch pocket. She pulled it out and tossed it into the passenger seat. Never in her life had she left someone standing by the side of the road, but her sanity wouldn't let her turn the Jeep around.

It might mean she believed him, and she couldn't have that.

⋟ Chapter Eleven ⋞

Thomas watched Tess's Jeep until it was out of sight. He sighed, shuddered into his trow-form, pulled up his hood and jammed his hands into his coat pockets. He strode due east, disregarding roadways and hopping over fences. Somewhere nearby there would be a fae-door underground, or a ley line to follow, and he'd use it to shorten his return to Forest Park and Underbridge.

He had frightened Tess with the view through the hole in the stone. His stomach was heavy with regret. No doubt he'd seen the last of her. Ordinary humans didn't take well to being shown the raw flesh beneath the glamoured skin of the fae. Trows were hardly beautiful creatures. They weren't thugs like trolls, but their bulk lacked in grace what it gained in strength and speed.

The forest smelled richly of moss and fern, the spice of balsam and the musk of lichen. The odors made him hungry, and he wished for some of Sharpwit's winter stew. No chance now for the chowder he and Tess had planned on as part of their day at the coast. Thomas closed his eyes to concentrate on testing the air for a fae link of some sort and drifted northeast, following the urging of his senses. A mile or so further on, he found it, a ley line that started at a hillside spring and aimed straight for Portland.

When he stepped onto the ley, a chill tingle rose up his legs, as if he had stepped in cold water or a flood of winter air tight against the earth. Each stride moved him many yards along the pathway. Firs, spruce and hemlocks slid past; rocks bulged beneath him and were behind him just as quickly. He had gone several miles in only a few minutes when the line gave a tremendous snap like a whip, flinging him from the track. He landed upside-down against a big hemlock half a dozen feet from the ley.

Thomas staggered to his feet, dizzy and shaken. He clutched his iron-edged knife in his palm, where it bit and stung, but not so much that he couldn't hold it. Not many fae had the power to clear a ley like that; most would have met a fae traveling in the opposite direction and negotiated who would step off and have to wait for the other to be a mile beyond before returning to the ley and continuing on their way. But Thomas had been ejected. He readied himself.

"Hail fellow, well met!" Hunter and his fae hounds—gaunt redcaps, bogles, a kelpie or two, others of the lesser, more bloodthirsty fae—paused in front of him. The hounds milled restlessly, eager to be gone.

Cold dread sank into Thomas's gut. He'd never met Hunter outside of Forest Park, where the Queen's wishes and will held

Hunter in check. He was deep in the Coast Range now, far from the Queen's senses and spies. Hunter never made a secret of his dislike of Thomas. The Queen had soiled the Unseelie Court with her human pet, instead of discarding Thomas when her interest waned, the way she did with her other lovers.

Hunter's expression was as unreadable as always. Nothing showed behind that antlered mask.

"Hail," Thomas replied, sidling to the east along the track. "I yield the ley to you, Hunter."

"Naturally." Hunter angled his long wooden staff in front of Thomas to block his path.

"As I said, I yield the ley."

"Tell me, Half-made…what brings you so far from home? I thought you never left the market except to do our Queen's bidding."

"I don't have to explain myself to you."

Hunter's hounds shifted and gibbered at Thomas's audacity, dancing close to Hunter's mount and risking a skull-shattering kick when the horse's eyes rolled, lit with a feral green light. A hound showed its fangs to Thomas.

"Ah, but there's where you're wrong. Any foolish human cluttering my Queen's court will answer to me."

"I answer to *my* Queen and no one else."

Hunter shook his head. "You need a friend at court, Thomas. You are being replaced, you know. Two human centuries is long enough for the Queen to tire of your novelty. She seeks fresher flesh than yours." The staff moved, prodding at Thomas's shoulder in the oiled duster. "Change is coming. I could be that friend—save you from the worse that's to come."

"What change?" Thomas took hold of the end of the staff, keeping his knife hand low at his side. Hunter was no fool. He'd be ready for any weapon Thomas could wield, but his hounds might not.

"The Queen is ready to make her move. You'll only be in the way, and you know what happens to toys that have outlived their usefulness."

Thomas did know. He'd been astonished to last this long, frankly, and had wondered what appeal he still held for the Queen. He pushed the staff away from himself and retreated even farther from the ley. "Speak plain, Hunter. What is it you want from me, and perhaps—I said perhaps—we can strike a bargain."

"You have had her ear long years and long. Bed talk reveals much. You hear things at the market. Simply come to me with your knowledge, and I will speak for you when the time comes to shed your blood for her own purposes."

Thomas laughed.

Then he laughed some more.

The red eyes behind the deer skull flared.

"If you are indeed her trusted counselor, Hunter, why would

you need a spy? And a human one at that?"

"I but seek to serve my Queen."

"As do I." Thomas began to walk east again. "The ley track is yours, as I said. But we will make no bargain here today."

Hunter growled out a command, and one of the bogles showed its teeth, walking backward on the ley to flank Thomas like a panther stalking dinner. The bogle's skeletal hands twitched and clenched in anticipation.

"Oh no you don't." Thomas put his hand into the front of his duster, where the breast pocket concealed the half-dozen iron nails he'd carried for decades. "I'm not the prey you hunt today. I know the rules—the Hunt cannot take that which is not its quarry."

"The Queen's rules." If a deer skull could sneer, Thomas would have sworn it was doing so.

Thomas's head tilted. Was Hunter making a bid to rule the Unseelie? Why did he think Thomas was an important player in the Queen's court and seek him as an ally, however hostile? This required more thought, but right now it was time to rid himself of the immediate problem.

"*Our* Queen's rules." Thomas grasped one of the nails, stifling a gasp at its raw, rasping burn in his palm. The cloth pocket was enough to insulate him from the metal's effect, but naked skin was another matter, especially when the rust bloomed. He blessed the little part of him that remained human and made touching iron possible, if painful.

"Take him." Hunter tried to turn his mount, but the directional force of the ley was too much even for that brutal beast. The bogle hurried backward even faster, leaping, trying to overcome the forward pull of the ley and overtake Thomas, who was running next to the ley.

A half-dozen more strides saw Thomas safely beyond the bogle's reach. He leapt onto the ley track itself, knelt, and stabbed the thick iron nail into the earth between himself and the bogle, then let go and flung himself backward away from the spike.

Too late he realized he should have jumped from the ley, instead of falling upon it.

There was a flash—not of light, but of energy that burned and flared—and then the ley reacted like a snake that had been cut in half, or a rope under tension. The energy frayed at the point where the cold iron intersected it, then snapped apart, jerking Hunter and his pack to the west, and Thomas to the east. The interrupted ley reeled them away from each other at tremendous speed, the broken ends retracting to their respective anchor points east and west.

Thomas heard Hunter cursing over the frightened, frustrated howls of his hounds. He shot backward through the firs on the flailing sizzle of magic. The eventual crash at the ley's next anchor point was going to hurt like a son of a bitch.

Like an eel thrashing in a net, he struggled to turn and face his direction of travel. Thomas had just made himself a target. He'd bested the Queen's Hunter, however briefly. The thought was bitter, especially when he saw the next anchor point zooming closer and closer: a massive, round rock, balanced on a creekside crag. He wrapped his head in his arms and waited for the world to explode.

☙ Chapter Twelve ☚

Monday was more of a Monday than it had ever been. Preoccupied with the strange events of Saturday, Tess worked doubly hard to restore her life to normal by focusing on paperwork and administrative tasks. Her files had never been so organized, her desk so clean, her calendar and email so up to date. She tried for the fifth time to reach the Morris family at home, but like all the other times, no one answered. She left the same voicemail as always, asking them to return her call as soon as possible. With each call, it was more difficult to keep the pleading urgency from her voice and remain professional. Perhaps the family simply wanted to put what had happened to Rory far behind them, but Tess needed to know.

As she completed each task and the end of the day drew closer, the more certain she became that she had to try and find Thomas. She had to see if he'd made it safely home after she'd abandoned him.

He had revealed himself a monster, and yet she was concerned about him.

All she needed to do was make sure he had returned, and then she could get back to her life without the cloud of dread and guilt hanging over her. It wouldn't necessarily mean she cared, or that she believed his wild tales of wicked fairies alive and well in Portland, or shared his drugged-out delusions.

Except...

Except...

It all fit so neatly, Thomas's tale of the Unseelie Queen and her destructive, dangerous taste for young men. When added to the fact that Aaron's blood tests had never showed any unexpected or illegal substances, enchantment began to sound like a plausible explanation.

And of course there was what she'd seen when she looked through the hole in the stone. The beast with Thomas's eyes.

It was dark when Tess left her office for the night. During the walk to her Jeep, she tried to convince herself she didn't mean to go to Old Town to look for Thomas, but by the time she fitted the key in the car door, she was already thinking about the route she would take. She'd stay in her car as much as possible; look for a glimpse of him on the streets surrounding Underbridge. Damn it, now she was using his word for the market neighborhood. She shook her head hard, and locked the car door as she climbed into the driver's seat.

Naturally, it began to rain, which would only make her task more difficult. She turned the windshield wipers on low as she pulled out of her parking spot. Nervous twitches cramped her stomach, half-belief fighting with rational thought and guilty conscience. It was the most awful emotional stew she'd ever experienced.

Street after street revealed no Thomas. In the steady drizzle, people walked quickly, hoods up, or heads down. No one bothered with umbrellas—those were for tourists. Twice she drove past the Skidmore Fountain and parked for a few minutes, watching people come and go in the area of Saturday Market. No Thomas, though she saw the languid young man who Thomas had all but called a rapist.

There was nothing for it but to get out and check the market on foot. She found on-street parking only a block away and slung her bag across her body, putting her car keys in the pocket of her trousers.

The shops were already shut or closing. In this part of town, even the eateries rarely stayed open much after seven in the evening. There simply wasn't a dinner rush once the commuters left work for the night. The solitude seemed even more pronounced, especially now that she was watching every step. She tried to tell herself she was foolish to be so frightened, but the hairs lifting on the back of her neck told her something atavistic and instinctual instead. The languid young man leaned against a pillar supporting the market's archway and lifted his chin in greeting. His arms were folded over his chest. The sight of him sent a jolt of adrenaline through her. Thomas's warnings had done that much for her awareness, but her imagination was doing the rest.

Tess paused at the fountain, listening to the splash of water and waiting for her heartbeat to slow. No need to frighten herself further. All the same, she kept her eyes on him. She fished in the outer flap pocket of her bag for a stick of gum, feigning nonchalance.

Her fingers found Thomas's beach stone instead and flinched back as if she'd been burned.

"I don't believe in magic," she whispered, but she was trembling.

Maybe you should. You can't explain how Thomas looked the way he did, not with any science, not with any college degree, not with anything you know except hallucinogens, and you weren't taking anything, not even caffeine.

"A rock is just a rock." Even so, she pulled the little stone from her purse and tucked it into her jacket pocket, keeping her hand closed around it loosely.

The young man straightened from the pillar as she walked away from the fountain. Tess pretended not to know him, not even to see him, but remained aware of him all the same. It was Thomas she sought, not a charmer who would tell her what he thought she wanted to hear.

The blackness under the bridge seemed to bulge from beneath the structure, beckoning, mocking. She could see people milling—more than she remembered from previous visits—as she approached. The burn barrel glowed, and the men stood around it, their faces lit from beneath. The fortuneteller sat at her tiny table, hands leafing through her deck, though no one came to have their fortune told. Tess put her back to a bridge support pillar, clutching her bag close, feeling more uneasy than she'd ever felt around street people. Thomas's claims had stuck in her mind, and the past two sleep-deprived, guilt-ridden nights had taken their toll.

Her gaze traveled over the market area, scanning for Thomas's broad shoulders and long coat. She didn't see him right away, but that didn't necessarily mean he hadn't made it safely home. She decided if she didn't find him in five minutes, she'd start asking questions. Nearby, two men haggled over the cost of a soft hat, just one among many strewn over a plaid wool blanket the seller sat behind.

To her left, the fortuneteller had half turned away, shoulder lifted, shutting out Tess. The hanging edge of the dark cloth on her small table rippled in a slow breeze that Tess could not feel. That disparity triggered something in her subconscious, and she scooted back into the shadows, out of easy view.

The rock was heavy in her pocket, slowly warming to her skin. She turned it in her fingers, feeling the hole in its center.

This is ridiculous. I'll just...I'll prove I'm right. Thomas worked a trick of some sort.

Tess brought the stone to her right eye and looked at the fortuneteller through the hole. But she wasn't the fifty-something woman with gray hair. She was a squat, hook-nosed crone with hair like forest lichen, and a cluster of moths clinging to her clothing, creeping slowly over her, wings vibrating, antennae sweeping back and forth like exotic fans. The deck of cards was no longer a familiar tarot. It was a collection of brown leaves, dried petals, torn butterfly wings, and what looked like sheets of translucent skin.

Tess turned away, stifling a gasp. Her heart jolted into her throat. She heard ragged breathing and tried to calm herself.

Laughter and a shower of sparks at the burn barrel caught her attention, and she lifted the stone once more, looking at the men who, to her naked eye, seemed to be pulling apart paperbacks and phone books for fuel in the rainy night. The creatures surrounding the barrel—what had Thomas called them, during his two minutes of recitation at the seaside—redcaps?— were squat manlings, not as tall as her shoulder, with teeth like tigers' and eyes the same red as their fire. Suspended above their burning barrel was a battered cauldron, bubbling away with something darkly viscous. *They would probably have dyed their caps in your blood just for speaking to them.* They were dunking what looked like wool beanie caps in the cauldron, and watching the fabric drip.

Tess's gorge rose.

"Thomas," she squeaked. "Oh, God, Thomas."

It was easier with the stone away from her eye, and yet ever so much worse at the same time. Better to know, or better to remain ignorant of what the market truly was, here in Underbridge when the humans had departed? She turned away from the redcaps and looked across to where someone was shaking out a blanket. Through the stone, she saw an incredible, prismatic net like a bedewed spiderweb lofting through the air, shaking free glinting dust like Sunday-school Christmas glitter art and leaving behind petals and butterflies. The creature doing the shaking was spindly as a birch sapling, and as pale, with hair like silver twigs and eyes as blank and luminous as drops of dew.

A fat toad at the creature's feet sneezed and hopped out of reach of the slow-falling sparkle. A man squatted just a few feet away, staring upward in adoration. Traveling sparks of slow, bluish light worked their way along the seams of his clothing, but otherwise he appeared human.

Without the stone, she saw a street woman and her waddling little dog, and a man wrapped in a rough coat made from a blanket.

Such horror, and such delight.

"Now, where'd you get a clever toy like that one, sweetling?"

The drawling voice startled her, and the guilty need for secrecy made her thrust her hand behind her back. Her head flicked to the voice, and she found the slouching, handsome young man again.

"I don't know what you're talking about." Tess took a firm

grip on her purse and shouldered her way past him, intending to return to her Jeep. She needed a safe place behind locked doors to process what she had seen, and the prickles that rose on her skin at the sight of the young man urged her to hurry.

He pointed with his chin as he wrapped his long fingers around her upper arm. "That toy, there. Your little spyglass. Why don't you let me take a look through it, too, see what you were seeing. Must have been something special."

"Let go of me." Tess fought the pull of his hand as he began to drag her arm from behind her back. She broke away and put distance between them, glancing behind her but not taking her eyes off him longer than a second. Swiftly she transferred the stone to her other hand, and brought it to her eye. *I have to know, I have to...*

Like a double exposure of nightmare sandwiched over sweet dream, Tess saw something lanky and animalistic—legs like a horse's, even to the hoofed hand that somehow could bend to grip her upper arm. The thing was a dark, wet gray, with streaks of black through its hide, and a white shock of hair like a forelock falling across a shifting face. Her eyes fought for dominance— young man, horseface, long nose, white teeth, drowsy sexy smile—all streaming with water that shone like slime in the glow of the streetlight.

Protruding from the bluejeaned pelvis and horse hip was a nightmare phallus. It bobbed erect, knobbed and immensely long, a collar of dank waterweed dangling from its midpoint.

Screaming Thomas's name, Tess ran, heedless of the direction. She knew without looking that the thing was following her, and it was fast. She dodged like a rabbit, dashing across the blanket full of hats, wondering with a terrified thrill what the hats actually were.

"Catch her! Catch the human girl! She can see us!" The horse creature called to the rest of the market. Heads turned as Tess raced, gasping and sobbing, through Underbridge.

The whispers sounded like the dry rasp of autumn leaves scudding over pavement. *She can see us. Sees us. She can see! Catch her, stop her, damn her eyes, damn her very bones!* People closed in on every side, directing her terrified flight into a spiral that curved back through Underbridge and toward the redcaps and their barrel.

"I will have her teeth for my dice," said a wet, hungry voice to her left.

"And I her toes for my necklace," said a different voice.

"And I her hair, to make nets to catch the fat pigeons!" gloated a third.

Tess felt panic, beyond bone-deep, settling into her, as the spiral of people—creatures—tightened and became a circle with only one exit…the glowing barrel. She halted, facing that ominous gap, her breathing harsh and rapid, teeth bared. She plunged her hand into her shoulder bag and fished for the pepper spray, holding it out like a talisman.

Still the circle tightened. Some of the people were smiling, but some twisted their mouths in rage. Even worse were the faces that were eager and hungry. She felt tears on her face, but now was not the time to focus on that. Tears only revealed weakness, the last thing she wanted to show.

But it was only herself and a single can of pepper spray against so many. The ring shrank further, driving her toward that exit, where the three men waited, teeth bared in awful smiles. Someone darted forward and made a snatch at the stone in her hand, but she thrust the rock down her shirt and felt its cold weight settle against the skin of her stomach where her shirt tucked into her jeans.

Now she couldn't see them as they truly were, but perhaps that was for the best. Why ask for her mind to shatter at the horrors they represented? Wasn't it enough to be hunted like a hare? Her gaze settled on the languid young man, flanking one side of the exit. He was smiling, beckoning with his long fingers, but all Tess could think about was the double horror she'd seen, horse and human, denim and hide, crowned by that eager phallus.

"Please let me go," she said. "I didn't see anything. I won't tell. I promise."

"Hark at her!" said a tiny little woman dressed in a muddy bathrobe and rubber boots. "You'd best hand over that stone. And we'll think about letting you go."

"Speak for yourself, Nelly Long-Arms," grunted a fat man,

wheezing up behind the woman in the bathrobe. "Give her to Sharpwit. We've lacked for meat these past weeks."

There must be thirty of them around her now, all staring, all angry. A tall man in a flannel shirt stepped too close, and Tess, shrieking, sprayed him in the face. He made an unholy squawk and growled, covering his streaming eyes. She sprayed again wildly in all directions, and the circle loosened just the slightest.

"Her little can won't last for long," said the languid young man. "And then we'll have her. She's mine, though. I touched her first."

"I can see your slime on her coat," said Nelly Long-Arms. "You'll share?"

"When I've done with her. I'm *hungry*. It's been long and long since I tasted such a one."

"A week." The fat man snorted. "We know you. We saw what's left of your last meal. You left it out where the humans could've found it. Sharpwit had to clean up after you. We ought to take you to the Queen. She'd have something to say about your mating and eating habits."

"We ought to take the girl to the Queen," suggested someone behind Tess. "Let her decide what to do with the human who can see us."

There was a rumbling murmur, half dissent, and half agreement. Tess wondered who the queen was, and if it was the same one Thomas had mentioned on the beach. She decided to try negotiation.

"I'm just looking for a friend. I came here to find him; I think he might be hurt or lost."

"And who would that be?" asked Nelly Long-Arms, rocking forward in her wet slippers. The hem of her bathrobe had trailed in mud and something brown-green.

"His name is Thomas—"

There was a collective intake of breath around the circle, and a few uneasy foot-to-foot shiftings.

"Knew I'd seen her before," said someone.

"Thomas? He'll be angry if we eat her."

"We can deal with Thomas."

"He has the Queen's ear."

At that last comment, there was a brief silence. Then the fat man said, "I ain't afeared of Thomas. I say we kill her now and let Sharpwit make a stew—"

The man's voice broke off when two big hands wrapped around his throat from behind and squeezed. To Tess, it looked like someone from the bizarre world of professional wrestling had joined the crowd. He was tall, with low-set, pointed ears, and a standing stripe of hair down the center of his large, otherwise hairless head. His nose was fat and bulbous, like someone had smashed it one time too many. There were cuts and bruises on his forehead and cheeks. He bent to the fat man's ear and whispered, as if to a lover, "Not afeared of Thomas? And why not, Will Cunning?"

Tess was riveted by the voice and the long black oilcloth coat. Could it be? Was it Thomas? Though she'd tried to block the image from her mind ever since, it looked very much like the creature she'd seen when she first looked through the stone at the seaside.

"Thomas?" she gasped, and knew for certain when his eyes, the beautiful Thomas eyes, flicked over her once. "Oh, *Thomas*, I—"

"Shut it, you," he said to her. "You've made more than enough trouble tonight." He tightened his grip on the fat man. "You owe me an apology, Will, and maybe even a little restitution. I've got an iron nail in my pocket that's for your neck if you don't."

Will Cunning lifted his fat, pawlike hands. "I was kiddin'. You know what a joker I am. I wouldn't have give her to Sharpwit, honest. We're just trying to make sure she don't go tellin' what she's seen. 'Twouldn't be good for anyone."

"You know our Queen has made me the law here. You should have brought the girl to me in the first place." Thomas gave one last squeeze and leaned hard on Will Cunning, who fell to his knees when Thomas let go.

Nelly Long-Arms coughed a short, sharp laugh. "How were we to know she belongs to you? You've not set your mark on her. The only mark is the kelpie's."

Thomas gave a growl, and Tess felt tears starting anew. "That wet slug knows full well what he's doing. Trying to charm what's not his to charm."

Thomas muscled his way through the circle of people and set a clawed finger at the base of Tess's throat, where she could feel her pulse beating frantically. His eyes met hers, and she felt a strange calmness, almost like cool water, pour over her. The claw moved slightly against her skin. He licked the claw-tip, and she knew he had drawn blood. She clapped a hand over the spot, watching as Thomas's eyelids drooped as if he were savoring her salt-copper taste. The crowd gave a collective moan that made Tess shudder in renewed fear. Was this how the turkey felt, just before its trip to the oven?

"We could all have a lick, just a taste…" whispered Nelly Long-Arms. "It wouldn't take much, she's got salt to spare!"

"You see my mark," muttered Thomas. "I will take her to the Queen myself. Because you're correct, the Queen needs to know what's been going on *in her own market*." He gave them all a slow, significant look, and with a mutter the crowd trickled away, abashed and slinking.

"We didn't mean nothing," said Will Cunning, from his position at Thomas's feet. "We was just hungry."

"Speak for yourself," said the kelpie. He moved into Thomas's path. "Nelly spoke the truth. My mark is on her."

"And I have tasted her blood." Thomas loomed over the

young man, who stood unflinching. "I have the greater claim."

"But mine is the oldest." The kelpie spat at Thomas's feet. "You humans…you never forget where you came from, do you? Not even when it would be in your best interest."

Thomas's broad smile, a shark-like note in his damaged face, gave Tess chills. "Never," he agreed, and towed Tess out of what was left of the circle, shouldering past the kelpie and glowering at the redcaps, who had been thwarted in their search for new dye.

"Be sure you do tell our Queen this news," the kelpie said. "For she will surely hear."

Thomas growled in answer, dragged Tess closer, and swung her body over his shoulder despite her flailing and shrieks.

Oh God, out of the frying pan…

➤ Chapter Thirteen ➤

There was only one place secure and private enough to be while Thomas controlled Tess's reactions to the new horrors she had experienced. His own home, the trow-hold inside the Burnside Bridge.

He didn't want her there.

He longed to have her there.

They were ruined. After the disaster at the market, there was no way he could keep her from the Queen. Too many little telltales had too much to gain by exposing Thomas and his pet human to the Queen. He guessed they had perhaps as much as two hours before the Queen came calling. He hoped it would be enough to get Tess calmed down and somewhere safe.

There was no way he'd simply hand her over to the Unseelie Queen. He needed time to think up a plan, find a way to hide her. Or maybe hide them both.

There was just the little problem of the Queen's band around his arm.

Thomas sprinted through the market at top speed, still in trow-form. He dodged through the chain link fence at the pumping station, hearing Tess yelp as some of her hair snagged on the fence. Thomas leapt high to the girders of the bridge and swung up onto it with Tess hanging over his shoulder, struggling and squawking in mingled fright and fury. Even the thick paint over the steel didn't stop the iron burn. His muscles still ached from the snap-back crash landing of the broken ley, making this awkward task even harder.

"Be still," he growled. "Or I'll drop you in the river. You don't want that." He adjusted her so that she was more centered on his front. Her legs were getting in the way, and he maneuvered them around his waist, his hand beneath her ass. At any other time, this would have seemed ideal.

"Oh God," she wailed. "Please, just let me go. I swear I'll never come back here. I won't go to the cops, I—"

"Be. Quiet." He needed concentration to negotiate the web of girders.

Tess craned her neck at the Willamette running dark and ominous beneath them, and screamed again. Thomas ignored her noise, stretching far. "Hold on to me, or you'll fall."

"Oh God." Her voice was a frightened squeak, but she locked her legs around his waist and clutched at his neck with her arms, burying her face in the collar of his coat. Several more acrobatic swings ended with them teetering on his perilously narrow doorstep, and with a push of his big hand, raw from the iron, they were through the door.

Thomas released Tess immediately, putting his back to the door so she couldn't run out and fall into the river. Still panicking, she flung herself against the far wall and groped with both hands along the concrete.

"We're safe for now."

"You call this safe? *Safe?* There are homicidal…I don't know *what* they are, out there, things that—they wanted to eat me, and now you've dragged me off to your lair and for all I know *you're* going to eat me, you gashed my neck and—and—"

Thomas let her sputter while he turned to the door and spun its big latch mechanism. He used his sleeve cuffs to shield his palms from the metal. With his limited magic, no spells he could cast would keep the fae out, but the door's iron bindings and lock would, at least until the Queen got serious about rooting him out of his hole.

"I did it for your own good. Most of them will leave you alone from now on. They know they'll have me to face if they don't." Satisfied the door was as secure as he could make it, he started down the concrete steps to the rooms below, leaving Tess to do as she wished.

What she wished, apparently, was to fling herself at the door and struggle with the latch. Thomas shook his head and continued down the stairs.

It was several minutes before he heard her footsteps coming quietly into the room behind him. He had taken off his coat and hung it away, after checking its pockets for all his tools and weapons. He dunked a cloth in some cold water and stood at the mirror, holding the cloth to his nose. It was still bruised and sore from the ley line accident, and not improved by Tess's flailing. Tess met his eyes in the mirror. She stayed close to the wall and the stairs, but her eyes were unflinching, and in one hand she held the beach stone.

"You're hurt," she said at last, and Thomas felt his shoulders slump as tension drained from him. That kindness at the very heart of Tess was already winning out over the terrified woman he had dragged away from Underbridge. "Your hands are raw."

"It's not bad." He looked at himself in the mirror once more, seeing the creature Tess saw, the trow, and not the human man he longed to be once and for all.

"Why is it I can see you—like this—without the stone?"

"I'm not glamoured." He turned to face her. "The folk in the market, they wear glamours so the humans in the city don't discover the truth of them."

"Then you've worn glamours with me."

"Yes. I had to."

"The…things…in the market, they want to hurt me because I know the truth about them?"

"Pretty much. If the humans knew what—who—whatever—lives alongside them in their city, there would be war."

"Humans would win." She spoke with certainty until Thomas laughed.

"You have no idea what you're up against, Tess. Think about

the nightmares you've just seen. Now multiply that by ten thousand. You and I have to leave here soon and find someplace safe for you to be until this blows over. I think you should get out of town for a while. Maybe a few months. Longer, even."

Tess snorted. "You're crazy if you think a bunch of Halloween trick-or-treaters are going to make me leave. I've got a job, and a house, and...no. And what do you mean? What has to blow over?"

"The fae need to forget you know about them. Some of them will betray us to the Queen."

Tess shook her head and blinked hard several times. "You've lost me, Thomas. What Queen? The one you told me about at the beach?"

After the exertion of carrying Tess away from the market, the muscles on his chest were paining him. He turned back to the mirror, opening his shirt. The bruises on his chest were fading quickly, but they revealed a deeper injury to the ribs beneath.

Behind him, Tess gasped. "You said it was nothing!"

"I said it wasn't bad. I'll live, believe me."

"When did you get those? Was it...was it after I left you at the coast?" She pushed away from the wall and took a step or two into the room. Thomas saw her fingers moving anxiously, as if she wanted to touch him, and she bit her lips. She felt guilty. Part of him was glad, because it meant she cared.

He bowed his head. How to explain everything to her, in the

little time they had before something unpleasant came calling? How to convince her she wasn't safe in her own city? It had taken a nightmare before she believed him about the beach stone, but now she was clutching it like a lifeline. He turned to face her.

"When you left me at the beach, I started walking home. I was able to find one of the fairy roads pretty quickly. They run in straight lines between magical points. Do you remember the old tales of seven-league boots? If you wore the boots, a single step took you a long distance?" He waited for her to nod, though her brows were knitting above her eyes. "Well, the fae roads are like that. One step on them moves you many steps. But I ran into an old…acquaintance, someone who's not fond of half-humans like me, and there was a little problem sharing the road. Somewhere in there I got slammed against a big rock, and that's where I got the bruises."

"It's my fault you were hurt. Because I stranded you." She took another step toward him, her dark eyes wide and brimming with tears. "I came looking for you tonight, to see if you'd made it home safely. I haven't slept well since Saturday."

"After Saturday, I was sure I'd never see you again. It would have been better if you'd just…stayed away."

Tess shook her head. "It's all tangled together, somehow. You, Underbridge, my brother Ste-Stephen, Aaron, this Queen everybody talks about. It's all linked, and if I get to the bottom of it, I can help Aaron. And maybe…maybe my other clients, too."

She was in reach of his hands, and at her statement he could not be still. He took hold of her shoulders, pleased that she conquered the urge to flinch away so quickly. "You are the bravest woman I have ever met. But believe me when I say this is too big for you."

Crystal tears spilled over her lower lashes and left dark blotches on her jacket. "I have to help," she whispered miserably. "I can't just watch Aaron go down into the same nothingness as my brother... If I can do something, I must."

Her head bent forward, and the softness of her hair brushed his chest. Thomas closed his eyes with a groan. "Please don't cry. I can't stand that." His arms tightened and drew her close, and to his astonishment she didn't struggle, letting him bring her to the warmth of his big body. She leaned against him and Thomas felt the last of the tension leave him.

She swiped at her eyes, hiding her face from his gaze. "I'm sorry. I'm sorry—for everything, I guess—I didn't mean to cause trouble, I just want to help, and I liked you so much. And now you say I've made things worse. But I got frightened, can't you see? This is all so unbelievable."

She gave a large sniffle. He got a finger under her chin and tilted her face up. Her lashes were matted together in wet points, and it only made him want to comfort her more. The very human impulse to kiss her rose, and he obeyed, dreading how she would react to his ugly trow face descending to hers.

He touched his lips to her cheek, where the trace of tears wet his skin, and the delicious sting of human salt tingled on his lips. In his mind he could hear the market fae clamoring for her blood and lifted his head. He was no different, lapping at the salt taste of her like a dog, craving more. He swallowed hard and moved away, crossing the room to a chest where he kept certain useful items.

I liked you so much. Liked. Not like.

"Thomas?" she asked, suddenly uncertain.

"We're leaving in a few minutes. I've got to gather some things, but then we're out of here. Got any good ideas where we can hide you for a while, till I've had a chance to talk to the Queen and make sure she doesn't think you'd look nice as a statue on a shelf in her chamber?"

He rummaged in the chest, stuffing things in a sack. When he found a slender piece of cord, he tossed it to Tess. "Thread this on the stone so you can wear it around your neck. Less chance of losing it that way. Now that the fae know you have it, any of them who see you will try to take it away again. But you're better off with a tool, even though it's a dangerous one. Always best to know what you're dealing with."

Tess, wide-eyed, looped the cord through the hole in the stone, then tied the two ends behind her neck. The grayish agate lay on her shirt just above her breasts, rising and falling with her breathing. Thomas swallowed, realizing his gaze was lingering too long on those soft curves and turned away to rummage through cupboards for things he might need. Bits of chain and more cord, another fat nail to replace the one he'd severed the ley line with. Everything stung his already tender fingers, but he persevered.

While he was winding up a loose roll of spider thread, debating whether it would be of use or not, the pier gave a shudder and groan, and a little fine concrete dust sifted out of the walls as if the room had exhaled or sneezed. Vibrations shook the little items in the cupboards.

Tess shrieked. "What is it? Is it an earthquake? Thomas, we have to get out of here—"

"The bridge is lifting, that's all. The mechanism's only a few feet above my rooms. You get used to it. It's comforting."

She looked up as if she expected the ceiling to crash down any moment, and flattened herself against the wall. "Are you sure? It's so loud! The whole place is shaking!"

Thomas chuckled. "Of course I'm sure. And now that I think about it, now's a good time for us to leave while there's commotion to cover us. Are you ready?"

Tess stared at him. "I guess. I mean, I didn't want to be here in the first place, but I don't want to be out there with *them*, either…"

Above them, the mechanism made a grinding, metal on metal sound. Tess moaned.

Thomas stretched out a hand. "Come on. We'll go together."

She looked from his hand to his face, then back at his hand, but at the next bone-shaking thud, put her hand in his. "Together, then." Her voice was shaky, but her grip was firm. "I'm scared."

Thomas closed her soft fingers in his rough, raw hand, brought the tips to his lips and kissed them swiftly, ignoring the nagging internal voice that told him she wouldn't be happy about being kissed by bloodlusting trow lips. "Together," he promised, and led her up the stairs.

➤ Chapter Fourteen ➤

I t was the most terrifying thing Tess had ever done.

Thomas kept urging, with a strangely comforting monotony, "Don't look down, don't look at your feet. Just walk. Hold on to me. Don't look down."

As if she were a star gymnast and didn't have to look at her feet. The steel girders of the underspan were wide—quite wide, if she thought about it—but beneath them, many feet down, was the river, hypnotic and irresistible. The worst part was the steady vibration of the girders as the bridge's center leaves lifted, followed by the massive shudder as the mechanism stopped with the leaves in their highest position. That jolt nearly joggled Tess off the girder, but Thomas turned in a flash and brought her body tight up against his until her gasping squeaks quieted and her balance returned.

At the next big jolt, when the span leaves began their downward trip, Tess and Thomas reached a joint where the horizontal girders met the vertical. Now Tess could clutch at something besides Thomas.

True to his word, he had not let go of her hand. She knew it cost him the better part of his balance and made the crossing awkward for him. In a weak moment she considered asking him to carry her again, but she was too frightened they would both topple into the Willamette. His pace was far, far quicker than she would have managed on her own. She struggled to keep up, so as not to be a hindrance to his balance, but by the time they were over solid ground, still high up, Tess was panting, sweating, and shaking with exertion, adrenaline overload, and fright.

They halted at last. Thomas guided her sweaty, clenching hand to a vertical and held it there while looking into her eyes. "I'm going to drop down first, then I'll catch you."

Tess, speechless with fright, shook her head. There had to be a better place to climb down from the bridge, some place without a dozen-foot drop.

Except she couldn't see one.

"Quick and quiet, here where it's dark," Thomas said. "I'll catch you."

Again she shook her head, trying hard to swallow the lump in her throat.

Thomas gestured toward Underbridge. "If you wait much longer, *they'll* be the ones to catch you, not me."

And with that horrific little reminder, he leapt.

"Thomas!" In the puddled blackness beneath, she could not see where he had landed, and clung desperately to the vertical girder.

"Shhh. I'm here. Just jump, it's not far, and I'll catch you."

"I can't see you." Despite his repeated assurance, she

couldn't quite leap into the darkness.

"But I can see *you*, and that's what matters. Trust me. Jump."

She swung her head back the way they had come, wondering if she'd be able to cross the span again in the gathering dark, knowing she wouldn't be able to open the door if she could reach it.

A half-asleep pigeon shuffled and fluttered in a hole in the girder above her. With a startled shriek she flinched away, lost her footing and tumbled.

Below her, the blackness said, "Oh, fuck!"

There was a scrambling noise and then she landed—not hard, but not easily, either—in the cage of Thomas's arms, on her belly. The air left her lungs in a brutal whoosh and she first curled in on herself, then starfished her arms and legs, flailing in search of air.

"It's all right, I've got you. Your breath will come back in a moment. I think."

Bright blackness starred her vision, purple and electric blue in storm-cloud black. She panicked without the air, clutching at Thomas. Her shocked diaphragm at last kicked in and a gasp of beautiful air, scented with the aroma of the pumping station and Thomas's own peculiar smell whistled into her lungs.

"You smell weird," was the first thing she said. "Like...soy sauce."

Thomas drew in a long breath, as if he'd been holding his in concert with her, and let out a relieved chuckle. Tess realized she was sitting on the pavement between his knees with him squatting behind her like a portable shelter.

"I smell like a trow."

"And you live under a bridge. Like the Billy Goats Gruff." A sort of manic laughter began to bubble out of her, born of panic and pain and the need to screw the reality of her world down tight so it couldn't fray like this.

"That's trow, not troll."

"Is there a difference?"

"Why not catch your breath before you insult me? But be quiet. We don't want the market to hear."

She remembered anew their danger. That killed the laughter. Thomas waited for the space of a few breaths, until her gasping squeaks had quieted.

"Stand up." He rose, taking her hands. "Can you walk?"

Tess nodded. He inched the two of them a few feet toward the chain link fence that surrounded the pumping station, and passed into a small pool of gray security light. Tess stared at him. It seemed he was shrinking, growing his normal close-cropped hair, his face shifting to look like the Thomas that had first attracted her so. He was putting on his glamour, she realized, his human face. He saw her open-mouthed stare and met it with a smile of dark humor twisting his lips.

"This should make you feel better, yes?"

She nodded, held up the stone and peered through it. There was the trow, looking at her in the gloom with Thomas's eyes. "This is insane," she whispered to him.

"Tell me about it." He reached out to the fence and stood with both palms toward it for a brief moment. The chain link sagged out of the way, and Thomas ushered her through. She paused, torn by the impulse to run screaming for the Jeep, and the need to wait for Thomas to tell her what to do next in this strange new world.

"Now what?" She fought the urge to bite her lip and cry. All her therapist training was screaming this couldn't be real. She'd been drugged or had a psychotic break of some sort.

She'd nearly been eaten by a pack of preternatural streetfolk. She'd been *inside* the Burnside Bridge pier, for God's sake, with a trow. And now she was standing in the shadows of the bridge with what looked like a man, though she knew differently. Just now he was tightening the belt of his oilskin coat, looking around as if he expected to meet Deep Throat and pass along state secrets.

Thomas held out his hand again. "Now we run."

"But where?"

"To the nearest ley point."

"What?"

"Fairy road."

Tess, about to take his hand, pulled back. "No. No way.

You're not getting me deeper into this."

"Do you have a better idea?" He wrapped his hand around her upper arm and hustled her along the outside fence of the pumping station, keeping as much out of the light as possible, heading north.

"My car's back there. I'm not leaving it behind."

Thomas sighed, but softly. His eyes flicked everywhere, checking for pursuers as he hauled her with him. "Maybe we can get it later, but for now I've got to get you far away from here."

"We'll go faster if we take the Jeep."

"Fairy roads are faster than that."

"If you think for one moment—"

Thomas's hand pressed over her mouth, silencing her. He froze next to one of the vertical beams stretching up to form the structure of the bridge. Not far away, pigeons disturbed at their rest in the upper girders of the bridge flapped into the night, their wings squeaking. It sounded like the noise of panic to Tess, and she struggled with Thomas, seized by a terror she could not explain, because it felt more basic than any she'd ever felt before. He wrapped her tight in his arms and pushed them both against the beam, in the darkest shadow. When Tess could no longer struggle, he pointed upward, where something darker than shadow was moving stealthily along the skeleton of the bridge. A pair of red eyes gleamed like cats' as dim light winked into them.

"Fuck," whispered Thomas, for the second time that night.

Tess thought crazily how out of character the cursing seemed, but the strange figure above them held every scrap of her attention.

"What *is* that?" Her mouth was close to Thomas's ear as he pressed her against the iron pillar.

"Not what. Who. Hunter."

Something in the way he murmured the word sent an atavistic shudder through her. She heard his dread and fear, and could feel his tension in the way he gripped her. He stiffened for a moment, glanced around, then pulled her back the way they had come. "I wasn't expecting him. Not alone like that, or so soon. Change of plans. Your car?"

She pointed southwest, still staring up into the superstructure.

"Don't keep looking at him. He'll notice."

Tess averted her eyes, but she could feel the pull of the amorphous figure, making her want to glance back and yet dreading to. She was like a rabbit chased by a wolf, needing to look behind to reassure herself she had enough distance between herself and Hunter, yet knowing that to look behind would be fatal. Another burst of pigeons fluttered out of the bridge, and under cover of their noise and activity Thomas broke into a run, towing Tess with him.

They sprinted south along Naito Parkway, staying close to the buildings. Thomas looked behind them every few seconds.

He did not pause, even when crossing intersections. There were no cars on the street, which Tess found extremely odd for that neighborhood at that time of the evening. There should have been traffic. As far as Tess could see, no one from the market had followed them, and she began to wonder exactly how much of this nightmare was real.

A few moments later they turned west and slowed, well south of the market and the Jeep. There was still no traffic, and Tess whispered to Thomas, even though there seemed to be no one around.

"Where are all the cars? Where is everyone?"

Thomas's expression, there in the dusky shadow next to an older building with lime-stained brick, was ominous. "Hunter has that effect," was all he said, before continuing west.

"Who is he?"

"Better ask 'what is he,' but better still not to talk about him. He has a way of knowing when he's the subject and turning up. Believe me, we don't want to meet him tonight."

"You're scaring me."

"Good. Maybe now you'll take this seriously. How far to your car?"

Tess took a long, shaky inhale. "It's a couple of streets south of the Skidmore Fountain."

"Too close to the market."

"Well, how was I to know? I parked where I found a space.

Believe me, if I'd known how crazy tonight was going to get, I'd never have come looking for you, no matter how guilty I felt."

"It would have been better." Thomas's tone was grim.

She yanked her hand out of his and stopped. "Why are you bothering at all? Why not just let your bloodthirsty friends do what they want to me?" She didn't understand why she felt so bitter, and there was hardly time to examine her feelings. It couldn't be that she cared what he thought, what he did, could it? Why should it matter so much that she had the good opinion of a monster?

He glared hard at her, his mouth tightening. She felt herself cringing away from him, wondering if the trow were about to burst from his skin and whether she could escape if it did. At last he spoke.

"Because I'm not like them. *I'm not like them, and you made me care.*"

She stared at him in amazement, her fear of him forgotten. She opened her mouth to speak, and found she had nothing to say except a soft, shaken "Oh, Thomas."

"Yeah," he replied, not looking away, but his expression gradually relaxed. When her groping hand came out and touched the lapel of his oilskin, he caught it to his chest and pressed it there. She could feel his heart thumping under her palm and took a step closer to him, but then a nagging urge to look behind her prickled in the depths of her awareness. Thomas, too, looked uncomfortable. His chin lifted as if he were listening to something she couldn't hear.

"It's Hunter. He's discovered I'm not at home, and now he's looking elsewhere."

The words recalled to instant, shadowy life the dark figure moving along the bridge girders. She grabbed for his hand again and pulled him with her. The Jeep waited not far away.

You made me care.

All they had to do was reach it.

⤳ Chapter Fifteen ⤳

Thomas was glad Tess had the stone around her neck instead of held up to her eye. She would have seen the glimmering tendrils of hunt magic Hunter had strung all over Old Town and the market, snares of enchantment meant to locate Thomas.

Someone at the market had betrayed him. Or, more likely, had never been a friend to begin with. He had hope that Tess's identity was still a cipher. The tendrils were designed for Thomas alone, with no whiff of the human traveling with him. Why the Queen herself wasn't already involved was a mystery. He remembered Hunter's words a few days ago on the ley line and wished he had a safe place to work through this puzzle. Had the Queen not been told of the disturbance in the market? Why was Hunter's interest in Thomas so personal and immediate?

He followed Tess as she raced west. He knew they were close to her Jeep when she started fumbling in her pocket as they ran. He tugged her back against a building where a decorative column provided an extra puddle of concealing shadow.

Hunter's tendrils still followed, questing forward like flickering snake tongues, but they were a block away. No time for a rest, but time for a breath, and room for a little caution. Only two streets over, the market would be in full swing and cry this time of night, with the fillip of Thomas's drama and Hunter's presence adding unusual spice to the dark.

"The Jeep's just around the corner. If we hurry—"

"Let me take a look first. See what's lurking."

But Tess would not let go of his hand, so they edged together to the corner of the building. Thomas put up his hood and peered around the corner. Tess's mostly-yellow Jeep sat under a streetlight. Cautious girl, parking in well-lit areas. But that didn't matter, not with three bogles slouching nearby in their angular fashion, pestering a stray cat. He pulled back, thinking hard. How to cross that block and get into the vehicle without being seen? And before Hunter's enchantment located him. And—

"Damn it, no!" The exclamation was startled out of him when she pulled free of his hand, ducked a quick look around the corner too, saw nothing but the cat, and went swiftly for the Jeep, keys already in her hand.

The bogles noticed. Thomas knew them by sight, if not by truename. They frequently cheated the hobs at knucklebones and snitched scraps from Sharpwit. Their services—lies and truths and everything in between—were for sale to any bidder. He'd chucked them from the market plenty of evenings, but they always crept back like determined flies. One of the bogles turned and ran for the market.

How had they known to watch at the Jeep?

Oh yes. The kelpie, the one who liked to loiter near the Skidmore Fountain.

Thomas, growling, shuddered into his trow-form and exploded out around the corner after the running bogle. He passed Tess, who let out a yelp and cried, "The Jeep's right here!" He ignored her, focused only on the chase.

His strides took him right between the two remaining bogles, who were staring and pointing at Tess. Thomas stamped on them hard, making them shriek in pain and fall to the sidewalk clutching their damaged feet. Then he turned his attention to the fleeing bogle, racing at trow-speed along the street behind it.

As it ran, it was calling to Hunter.

"Aw, shit," groaned Thomas. He was too late; the alarm had been sounded. Hunter's magic, given a focused target at last, splashed against buildings and lampposts like a banner of bruise-colored light escaped from an aurora borealis, gleaming on the wet pavement and glittering through the rainy air. Thomas skidded to a stop and tried to backpedal before it washed over him. A snare of hunt magic tangled the running bogle and brought it to its knees, sobbing, in the middle of the street.

"Master!" wailed the bogle, but Hunter's magic was not merciful or discriminating, and the strangling pain intended for Thomas silenced the creature.

Behind Thomas an engine roared and a horn blared long and

loud, startling him from his horrified study of the hunt magic. Tess yelled out her window, "Get in! For God's sake, Thomas, get in!"

The Jeep braked not six feet from him, one tire up on the curb, and the passenger door flapped open and then slammed closed again as Tess lost her grip on it. She pushed it open once more, and Thomas, praying there were enough iron in the convertible vehicle to do some good against the fully fae bogles, dived for the opening. She had the beach stone in one hand, and from the frightened look on her face, had been watching events through it. Hunter's magic was awe-inspiring, beautiful in its way, but discomforting.

His trow-form did not fit in the seat, and even as he struggled to get the door closed, Tess revved the engine and pulled the Jeep into a tight circle in the narrow street. They bumped onto the far curb and barely missed a parking meter. The two of them jostled like popcorn in the cab and then they were hurtling away from the market. Hunt magic flowed over the car, seeking a way inside. The crack left by his partly open door gave it an entry. He scrambled to close the gap on it, like shutting a slug in a doorway, and a remnant of the bluish stuff ripped free and shot around the interior of the Jeep like a will-o'-the-wisp.

The remaining two bogles, still nursing tender feet from Thomas's stamping, rushed into the roadway.

Tess, seeing nothing, ran the Jeep right over them. The

impact shook the vehicle but didn't stop its forward momentum. "What was that?" she gasped. She looked in the rearview, startled. Thomas swallowed his gorge. He didn't like or trust the bogles, but he didn't wish them dead, either.

The ball of blue light ricocheted around the cabin, lifting Tess's hair. She swatted one hand at it as if she'd been buzzed by a bee. Thomas unzipped the side window panel and knocked the hunt magic out of the Jeep. It bounced on the pavement before blowing back toward where Hunter must be waiting. "Just drive! And a hell of a lot faster."

"It would help if you didn't crowd me so much, you big oaf!" But Tess punched the accelerator and shot away from the market.

It took Thomas a few minutes to settle down enough to restore his human glamour, reducing himself to a more suitable size. The metal of the car made it both easier and more difficult. By then Tess was much calmer, driving with purpose and intent, as though she knew where they were going. As far as Thomas could tell, it wasn't out of the city, since she was still traversing surface streets and passing primary roads that would have led to highways.

"We need to leave town," he said.

"Funny, ha ha," she said, nodding.

"I'm not kidding."

"I know."

"So why aren't we halfway to Washington by now?" He

furtively touched various pockets through the oilskin, taking inventory of his supplies. Nails. Knife. Cord. A lumpy pouch or two. Everything seemed to be present.

"Because I think we'll be plenty safe at my house. It's not like your…friends…know where I live, right? And nothing's following us, right? Not even that freaky red-eyed thing that was up in the bridge girders?"

Thomas turned to look behind them out of reflex, though he knew they'd escaped from Hunter.

For the moment.

The back windshield was clear of Hunter's snares, but he wondered if there was any other torn hunt magic clinging to the car like the stuff he'd shut in the door. It could, if Hunter ever got in range of it, tattle on them as effectively as the bogles. "Pull over so I can check under the Jeep. Just to be sure."

"I'm not stopping until we're safe in my driveway."

"Please."

She glanced at him as she drove down a neighborhood street where wet leaves hissed and slapped under the tires. Something in his look must have convinced her, for she gave a great sigh and nipped the Jeep to the curb in the next block.

Thomas gave the vehicle a thorough going-over, examining every crevice and underhanging bit of metal. Tess got out with him, one arm folded tight around her middle as if to suppress nausea. In her other hand, she held the stone to her eye and peered at her car through it. He shook his head in resignation, squirming on his back on the wet street to check under the Jeep. It would do no good to ask her not to look, and a second pair of eyes might even help.

Soon enough he heard her gasp as she got to the Jeep's front bumper, with its dent and bits of bogle left there. "Thomas, there's...what is that? It looks like...blood?"

"Probably." He spoke from under the back of the Jeep, where he tugged free a small tangle of hunt magic strands from around the axle. The stuff was black and mostly dead looking, probably from the vehicle's iron, but he was taking no chances. It was the only residue he found, and he rolled it into a tight, sluggishly squirming ball and threw it down the nearest storm drain. Let Hunter make of that what he would, if he ever found it. He joined Tess, who was still staring at the front bumper through the stone.

She turned haunted eyes to him. "I ran over someone by Skidmore, didn't I? Did I kill someone? I didn't see anything in the road, but I felt it...when we hit..."

Thomas put an arm around her. "A bogle. It would have called Hunter down on us." No point in telling her it was two bogles. That would only magnify her already epic sense of guilt and responsibility. "There's no way to know for certain it's dead. They're tough little bastards. It might have just been hurt."

"A...bogle."

"Something like a redcap, only not so bloodthirsty. A nasty little tattletale."

She shuddered. Thomas gently moved the stone away from her eye. "Don't keep staring at it, Tess. It wasn't your fault."

She blinked rapidly and Thomas saw a tear slip from the corner of her eye before she wiped it away and set her mouth in a firm line. "Well. I guess if you're done, we should get home."

"We should leave town."

"You keep saying that, and I'm going to keep telling you no. So just…get in the car. And this time put on your seatbelt."

Thomas did as he was told, hiding a smile. For as long as it lasted, he'd relish having her cluck over him, even if she was angry and scared and heartsick.

Thomas's sense of unease reawakened as the Jeep turned northwest. The roads gradually climbed in altitude. His unease increased as they left the square blocks of city streets, businesses and apartment buildings behind for twisty lanes and more trees. Tess at last pulled into the blacktop driveway of a duplex and killed the engine. Thomas's heart sank. He knew the long, dark lump of earth rising like an elephant's spine behind her home.

Forest Park.

The fairy mound.

The Queen's own demesne.

"Fuck," he sighed, defeated.

"What's the matter now?"

"Nothing. Let's just…get you under cover."

They hurried to the front door, where an unlit, smiling pumpkin greeted them toothlessly from an overturned bushel basket on the tiny porch. A shock of dry cornstalks rustled as his shoulder brushed it. Tess unlocked the door and pushed it open. Thomas peered up and down the dark street behind them and saw nothing. He followed her into the house, where Tess was turning on every light in the place. He came behind her, turning them all off again. He could see to the back of the house, where the windows looked out over the black, ivy-choked bulk of Forest Park. Too much light, where any passing fae might peer in, would raise the alarm yet again.

"What are you doing? I need light, damn it! Tonight's been the scariest, darkest night I've ever—"

"Light inside means what's outside can see in." He flicked off the light in the kitchen and strode to the window over the sink, yanking down the blind.

"Oh." Tess's voice was small and frightened. "We left them behind, didn't we?"

"They're everywhere, including that lump of land behind your house. I didn't want to mention it while we were outside where anything could hear. Come on, help me close up. Then you can turn on lights. I promise."

Tess's house smelled like her. Thomas wanted to close his

eyes and wallow in the bliss of womanly fragrances like clean laundry, perfumed soap, and the good smells of bread and milk and coffee. It smelled like what he remembered from centuries ago when his mother loved and cared for him, and later when the sweet, bold ladies of frontier Portland craved his strong body in bed. He moved from window to window while Tess turned in a circle in the darkened kitchen, watching him, wringing her hands.

Finished, he put his hands on her shoulders. "Don't. Come on now. You've been so strong. Don't quit. Is there an upstairs?"

She nodded, gulping.

"Show me."

"This is all so hard. So crazy."

"I know. Do we go down the hall?" He herded her gently back to where he'd seen stairs as they came in the front door. Once she was moving, she seemed better able to continue and led him up the stairs to a small landing where three doors revealed bedrooms and a bath. She reached out of habit for the light switch, but Thomas stayed her hand.

The bathroom's window was already screened by a hazy plastic film to diffuse outside light yet not permit peeping. There was no other window covering, so Thomas reached over the tub and drew the shower curtain across to block what it could. On the other side of the landing was a room filled with bookshelves and a big desk and armchair. Thomas tugged its beige brocaded drapery closed.

That left only her bedroom, and Tess went inside herself to close the curtains, pushing some clothing lying on the floor under her bed. Then her strength seemed to leave her, and she sagged onto the edge of the bed, her hands loose in her lap. Thomas fidgeted in the doorway. In the dimness, her face gleamed like the underside of a mushroom, pale and tender. She looked up at him, her dark eyes enormous and sad. She clutched the stone where it lay between her breasts.

"Go on, look at me through it, if you want." Irritation, born of his fury at having involved her in this mess, roughened his voice. "I'm no different than I've been since you met me. I'm a big, ugly, smelly trow who can sometimes squeeze himself into a human skin for a little while."

She looked down, abashed. "It's not you. I just...do you know how it feels to realize you're going crazy? My whole life just turned into one of my clients' hallucinations."

"It was like that for me, as well, many years ago. All I can tell you is you're not hallucinating. I'm real. The fae are real. The danger is real."

Tess's laugh was bitter. "I use a magic rock to see reality, Thomas. There's no way I'm not crazy. And I may have killed someone tonight." Her voice broke on the last word.

Thomas, galvanized once more by her sadness, hesitated on the threshold of her bedroom and at last plunged across it. He stood awkwardly by the bed, not sure what to do with his hands but wanting nothing more than to comfort her. Tess solved the dilemma by leaning hard against him, burrowing beneath his grubby, damp oilskin. As her arms linked behind his waist, Thomas shrugged out of the coat and let it slump like a cast-off selkie skin to the floor. He could tell she wanted to be held much closer. With a stifled groan he sank onto the bed next to her and let her push her wet face into the angle of his neck and shoulder. A few minutes later her sobbing increased, and somehow in the effort to comfort her, he stretched out on the bed—ignoring the mess his boots must be making of the bedding—and curled her close in the bend of his body, because it seemed to help.

Heaven, for a little while, with her in his arms. As long as he could manage it, to make them both safe. It was only a matter of time before the Queen called for him. But in the meantime, heaven, in a darkened room in a human house on the edge of the fairy mound.

➣ Chapter Sixteen ➣

The morning light seemed gloomier than usual, even for the rainy days before Halloween. The front of Tess's body was chilled, but her back was furnace-warm, as was a stripe across her belly. She blinked and groped with her feet to find the blankets and pull them up, but the hard sole of her boot knocked against her shin. She must have fallen asleep with her clothes on. She smelled something meaty and warm, and very masculine, giving a vague impression of stew and childhood comfort foods.

Tess opened her eyes slowly. The warmth across her belly came from a bulky arm and a rawboned hand with large, scraped knuckles. It held her prisoner on the bed.

A trow hand. She remembered everything in a rush of renewed terror. She shuddered, turning to look over her shoulder, and found trow-Thomas huddled against her back, the long line of his big body warming hers from behind. His eyes were closed, and after the first few seconds her heart rate settled. Taken all together, his features formed an unappealing whole. A nose like a turnip. Eyebrows that would have shamed the woolliest of caterpillars. A forehead that was flat and broad, above high, blunt cheekbones. A mouth slack with sleep, fleshy and red, betokening a hunger for foods Tess would rather not think about. A chin like a bulldog's, but startlingly hairless, with roughened, pebbly skin. And that sparse stripe of hair down the middle of his head.

In the midst of that, Thomas's all-too-human eyes, too small for the scale of his trow face, dark-lashed and closed in sleep. They gave him a piggish look, set as they were near the snout-like nose. He was the source of the comforting scent, too. What a collection of incongruities, as though he had been constructed of spare parts.

She grabbed his hand to move his arm and escape him, and suddenly Thomas was fully awake and aware. There was the barest instant when Tess *knew* he would not let her go. She could sense a vast hunger and need within him—and then he was rolling away from her, the trow-form fading as he moved. Tess got to her feet, feeling safer with the bed between them.

"I guess we fell asleep." His voice was somewhere between trow and human, rough and deep, and strangely attractive. He looked up at the window, where a wedge of gray light seeped past the edge of the blind. "Is that the sun?"

"It's nearly seven thirty," Tess replied, pretending everything was normal; just a human girl accustomed to waking up with supernatural creatures in her bed.

Thomas pulled his hand over his face. "Morning."

"Ye-e-s..." She watched, fascinated, as the stripe of hair down his head and his neck—*does it go all the way down his spine? I wonder how muscular his back is*—seemed to vanish beneath the skin while Thomas's close-cropped haircut reappeared. In moments he was just a man in ill-fitting clothes sitting on the other side of the bed, flexing his hands and looking at their raw palms.

He turned to look at her. The last of the turnip nose had vanished, and there was only Thomas's bruised face. Even the bruises were fading, but his skin still showed enough mottling to remind her of an exhausted prize-fighter. With his shift in form, the odor diminished as well. "Dawn means I can't go home. I'm trapped."

Tess blinked. "What?"

"Trow-holds seal shut when sunlight strikes them. I can't go home until dusk."

"What are you now, a vampire or something?"

"Vampires aren't real." He groped at his upper left arm, frowning.

Tess snorted. "But trolls—excuse me, *trows*—and bogles and redcaps are?"

"Mock away. Deny the evidence of your own eyes." He kept prodding at his arm, and finally Tess gestured at it.

"Are you all right?"

Thomas shrugged. "Just wondering why she hasn't summoned me, is all. I would have thought..."

"She?"

"The Queen of the Unseelie court."

"Queen of the Unseelie—" Tess stopped herself, shaking her

head. "I need coffee." She stumped away down the stairs, half surprised Thomas didn't follow, though he did call after her.

"Leave the blinds closed."

In the shuttered kitchen, she put bread in the toaster and ground beans for coffee. Upstairs she heard water running, and then the shower. In spite of herself, she smiled. She could use a shower herself. She was grungy after the frightening evening and sleeping in her clothes. The perverse and capricious imp that lived in her brain suggested Thomas might not be averse to her joining him in the shower, but the part of Tess that was still struggling with her new reality pointed out that what was in the shower was not exactly human.

By the time the toast popped up, the shower had stopped. And only a few seconds after she had smeared the toast with butter and strawberry jam, Thomas appeared in the doorway, with his oilskin over his arm. The coffee maker gurgled its last, and she filled a mug, adding a little milk. She looked a question at Thomas, who was staring at the quart of milk.

"Oh, yes, please," he said, reaching, but not for the coffee. He took the milk jug from her hand and tipped it up, drinking straight from the spout. Swallow after swallow went down, and in a few seconds the quart was empty. When he noticed her open-mouthed stare, he looked sheepish, and coughed a little. "The…uh, the fae like milk. A lot. Warmed, if possible."

"No wonder you like your lattes with only one shot of

espresso in twenty ounces of milk. I thought caffeine bothered you." She opened the fridge, brought out another carton of milk, and filled a large mug, which she put into the microwave to heat. She gestured him toward the table shared by both dining room and kitchen, and put the toast in front of him. He laid the oilskin over the back of a chair, sat down, and set to with gusto. Tess realized she'd better make more toast, as well. While the microwave and toaster worked, she leaned against the counter and said meditatively, "So I'm making breakfast for a trow."

"Wasn't that on your list for someday?" Thomas asked, with a tentative smile. "Now you can mark it complete."

Tess buttered the next round of toast and put in two more slices. She brought her breakfast to the table and sat down. "I think we have a lot to talk about, don't we, Thomas?" She fingered the stone, still on its thong around her neck.

"You still need to be convinced the fae exist?"

"Nnnnooo, but…why do you keep insisting they're after us? We've just…um, spent the whole night together, and nothing came to break down the door."

"I don't think they were able to track us last night, and now that the sun's up, they'll be slowed even more. They can do a lot more in Portland after dark."

"But you were expecting someone—the Queen? to call you. Or something. What was it you said?"

"Summon." He wolfed down the last bite of toast and

looked longingly toward her own plate.

"I'm making more, if you can just be patient. Summon you how?"

"She has a way of calling me. I don't know why she hasn't, that's what I don't understand."

"You know her."

"We all do."

"You say 'we' like you're one of the fae, yet you told me you're not like them. Which is it?"

Thomas pushed away from the table, scowling. He prowled to the window above the sink and lifted the corner of the blind to peer out. "It's hard to explain."

"Try. If you want me to believe you, you have to *try*." The toast popped up, and as she was buttering it, the microwave beeped. She gestured for Thomas to get the milk. He opened the microwave tentatively, as if it might bite him, and reached inside. He sat down again and bent over the mug to luxuriate in the scent of the hot milk. Now that she was seeing his behavior through new eyes—the eyes that knew he was something other than human—she found it odd, instead of curious or charming. All the little mismatches of conversation and action were starting to fall into place. No phone, no car. He didn't want her seeing his home. His insistence on walking around Underbridge, rather than through it. Wanting the windows in the Jeep rolled down. Sudden appearances and disappearances.

She put the toast in front of him and passed him the jam. "Tell me about your Queen, then. Start there."

His cheekbones flared bright red as he spooned large dollops of jam on the toast and spread it thickly. "She's…she's beautiful. Terrible. Fascinating. Horrible. Wonderful. Murderous. She was long ago one of the Tylwyth Teg, a bright spirit, but something changed and she became a solitary fae, and then Queen of the Unseelie court. She took it away from him who was king before her and moved her court from Britain to Portland."

"They crossed the ocean? Those creatures?"

"She enslaved the kelpies. They brought the court over the seas upon their backs with the mer-folk and selkies. She's unimaginably powerful."

"Kelpies."

"Like that young man—you remember, the one who said his claim upon you was prior to mine. Selkies are sea-creatures— gentler than kelpies."

Tess froze in mid-sip, remembering the fearsome angular grace and foulness of the young man who had sought to take her seeing stone from her the night before. Her finger went to the spot on her throat, hardly more than a scratch this morning, where Thomas had drawn her blood.

His eyes met hers and held them. "You believe me when I say you must never be alone with him or any of his kind again, don't you? They are seducers, but what they kiss, they devour.

Some of the young women found drowned in the Willamette are their victims. Your police don't mention how the girls are missing their livers when the bodies come ashore, or how sometimes—"

Tess let out a cry and shot up from the table. "But fairies are beautiful, tiny, magical things…*imaginary* things…"

"Not these." When Thomas took a toothy bite of the toast, spread with the fleshy, blood-red bits of strawberries, Tess felt her gorge rising and hurried to lean over the sink, afraid her breakfast would make a reappearance.

After a moment her stomach calmed and she turned, clutching the edge of the sink. "How will I know them? They look like people! I can't go around staring at everybody through a rock and screaming when one of them turns out to be a waterlogged pony! I'll be locked up as a danger to myself and others!"

"They always give themselves away. For one thing, they're always male. Look for water—tears in the eyes, a damp spot on his shirt, sweat standing on his skin even on a cool day. The smell of waterweed. The way they won't let you look away from their eyes. The way they always want you to walk away with them to someplace less crowded."

She couldn't control the quiver in her voice. "You do the same things. Sometimes when you talk, I can hardly look away. You're always wanting me to go with you, and I do…"

Thomas raked his hands through his hair. "And I haven't

even sniffed at your liver, have I? Come on. I'm a trow, not a kelpie."

"What does that mean? What, really? You'll eat me *next* week instead of right now? God, listen to me. I hardly know what I'm saying."

He sighed heavily and put his palms flat on the table, long fingers spread apart. "I won't eat you at all. Look. I'm half human. The Queen met me years ago, and I became her lover, and she…changed me. Began to make me one of the fae. I've fought it ever since, but it's hard and getting harder, and there may come a time when I can't be human any longer. I want out, but I don't know how to *get* out. All I know is when I'm with you, I'm more human than I've been for years, and I'm holding onto that as hard as I can."

His hands turned palm-up of their own accord, and on the raw pink skin she saw the clear impressions of the rows of rusty bolts and rivets of the Burnside Bridge girders, scalded there like cattle brands. "Will you help me? I shouldn't ask you, but I—"

"Oh, your poor hands." The words came out in a rush as she crossed the kitchen and reached for his right hand, then pulled back, afraid she would hurt him. Half-remembered stories from childhood began to surface. The fairies didn't like iron, or horseshoes, or inside-out clothing. Couldn't cross running water. Had to be gone by cockcrow. Kept pots of gold at the feet of rainbows. Made shoes at night for true and worthy shoemakers.

Thomas let her touch the welts gently, his fingers twitching when she brushed over tender spots. "They'll heal, you know. They always do."

"Why do you live in the bridge, if you have to hurt yourself to live there?"

"Because it hurts the rest of the fae even more. When I'm my human self, the iron doesn't burn me as much. But last night I had to cross the girders as a trow, and so you see." He shrugged. "I like my privacy."

"Let me get something for that." She went up the stairs to her bathroom, where she had some first-aid spray. She needed a moment to and reconcile her conflicting emotions. Thoughts roiled in her head. Thomas—who she was coming to care for more than she wanted to admit—brought far too strange a world with him. She wanted to go back to the time before the trip to the beach, when he was still an ordinary man who could kiss like the best prince in the best dream ever.

And yet…she could not deny her own excitement at perhaps finding an explanation for her clients, no matter how bizarre…

≈ Chapter Seventeen ≈

While Tess was upstairs, Thomas made a circuit of the downstairs rooms, checking door locks and window blinds, peering outside, and seeing nothing to alarm him beyond the wet green and autumn colors of Forest Park. Was it possible they'd really got away clean, at least until the Queen decided to call him? When he'd crawled under the Jeep looking for tendrils of Hunter's snares, he'd been hopeful, but uncertain, that he'd found it all. The smallest bit would eventually call the powerful Hunter to it. Had none of the market fae gone to the Queen? Was Hunter's binding and masking influence that great? For certainly it had been Hunter seeking Thomas—and perhaps Tess—last night. Hunter, back from the snapped ley line in the Coast Range and prowling Underbridge without most of his rabid entourage.

So many questions. Not even Sharpwit, with her contacts in the market and elsewhere, could have answered them. In the gray morning light filtered by the living room blinds, his eye was drawn to a dim purple gleam in the corner closest to the outside wall. He approached, curious, detecting a glamour-like shimmer with a sinking of his stomach.

That shade of purple, like the dark throats of irises and

violets and shadows cast by moonlight, belonged to only one fae that he knew of: the Queen. He should have noticed it the night before as he secured Tess's home. There were a number of small items on the shelf in the corner, but most of them were ordinary. Bird feathers, curiously shaped stones, seashells, glass insulators from utility poles, skeleton keys. And mixed in with these were other, stranger objects more like the glass thimble Tess had discovered a few nights ago.

I find the oddest, most interesting things down here.

His heart jumped like a fish on a hook. Though he had suspected for days, now he'd confirmed the identity of the Queen's thief, unwitting though Tess was. He groaned, rubbing both raw hands over his face. "Oh, T—" He managed to stop himself before her truename tumbled out of his mouth, there where the Queen's things were waiting. She knew when he'd touched one near Underbridge. For all he knew, she could even hear what was said near them.

All he had to do was sweep them into a sack and return them to the Queen without revealing where he'd found them. Not only would the Queen sever more of the strands on his armband, but Tess could be free.

Except he didn't really believe that this time the Queen would let him get away with a vague explanation. She would want blood. She was never so angry as when she had been thwarted in little things. War, the Queen could handle. Simple frustration made her cruel and petty and committed to revenge.

Tess? Or his armband and slavery? What to choose?

While he debated, torn, he looked around for something to put the objects in and something to shield his skin so the Queen wouldn't be alerted the instant he touched them. Maybe he could simply scatter them at the market and let some other fae find them. Then he gritted his teeth. He'd only be consigning other fae to his own fate, or worse. It wouldn't matter to him if some of the nastier fae found the things, for they deserved the fates they earned, but what if it were a harmless, heedless hob or two, or worse, someone he actually cared a bit for, like Sharpwit?

But he still didn't understand why the items were so important to the Queen. That part of the equation had never made sense. He had too many unanswered questions, and his current situation made finding answers exceedingly difficult. Hunter was involved here, in some subversive, underhanded way Thomas didn't yet understand.

He clenched his fists against the temptation to gather up all the things and run. The objects had been safe enough here for a long time, even so close to the fairy mound. Surely another few hours, while he organized his thoughts or even paid a visit to Forest Park, wouldn't matter.

"Thomas?" Tess called, from the kitchen. "Come in here, where there's better light. This spray should take the sting out of your hands."

Thomas did as she bade him, standing next to her at the sink while she first gently washed his hands under warm running water and dried them on a fresh kitchen towel, then spritzed medicine on his palms until the burning stopped.

"There's still rust imbedded in the skin," she fretted. "I don't want to rub it too hard or the blisters might burst."

"It's much better. Thank you." He looked down at her bent head and careful, tender fingers holding his hands. When she looked up, it was as if she had her own form of Hunter's magical snare. Her dark eyes, so wide-set and hopeful. Her peony mouth, inviting a kiss, whether she knew it or not. Their gazes held for a long moment, then she smiled. Thomas couldn't quite return a genuine smile through his worry, but he felt his mouth quirk a little, and that seemed to satisfy her.

After a minute, Tess broke the spell. "More toast?"

"Yes, please." Milk and bread. If the fae knew about the ridiculous amounts of milk and bread humans kept in their houses, there would be more raids for food than raids for changelings. Only the fact that Thomas rarely had human money stopped him from eating nothing else. It took a long time to find enough dropped coins to buy a carton of milk, not to mention bread to go with it. Add to that the summer in a jar that was strawberry jam, and Thomas could have eaten until he was well past stuffed and died happy. He sat at the table again and watched Tess moving from little machine to little machine, warming the bread and covering it with deliciousness.

When the toast was ready, she sat down. "We should talk about the thing that was chasing us last night."

"Which thing?" he asked, though he knew she meant Hunter. He wanted to know a little more about what she had seen. Hunter's glamour had been fraying considerably, up in the darkness beneath the Burnside Bridge, surrounded by so much iron. He didn't think she'd used the stone to see, but he couldn't be sure.

"The one hiding up in the bridge, the one we ran from. It had red eyes, and it looked like Batman. Er, something in a black cloak. You called it Hunter."

"He's the Queen's huntsman. He leads the sluagh—legends call it the wild hunt—and tracks down her enemies or brings her meat."

Tess swallowed hard and put her toast down. "Brings her...meat?"

"The fae don't really live on dewdrops and nectar. You need to stop thinking fairies are sweet and kind and scatter pixie dust to give humans pleasant dreams. They're harsh things who find humans convenient toys or tools."

"But this...Hunter...was looking for you. Us."

"Yes. And I'm not sure why."

Her brows furrowed. "Does the queen want to eat you?"

Thomas shrugged, shaking his head. "I doubt it. I'm not

convinced she sent him last night. I think he was working alone, on his own agenda. He didn't have the rest of his host with him, the solitary fae who serve him in return for scraps or a chance to work their nasty magics."

"He had a few bogles with him, you said—the ones I…" She bit her lip.

"Lookouts. They were watching your car, waiting for you to turn up again. Someone at the market knows what you drive and told a tale."

Her expression grew darker still. "That boy. The horse one."

"That's my guess." He finished off the toast and gulped the last of his milk. "Come with me a moment. I need to show you something." He rose, letting the human glamour shred away like shadow. It would be easier to convince her what had to be done if he didn't look so ordinary and human to her eyes. He held out his big trow hand, pleased and a bit surprised when Tess took it and followed him into the living room.

"Where did you get all these things?" Thomas gestured to the curio cabinet in the corner.

"Oh, here and there. Walks on the beach, hiking in Forest Park—" Thomas knew she saw him cringe, but did not comment upon it. Time enough later to drop the bomb she was living virtually atop the largest fairy mound in the world, if he ever needed to do that. Tess was reckless enough that she might take it into her head to visit the Queen on her own, if she knew that

Forest Park was the Queen's home. "Some of them I found at the Saturday Market. Those are the *really* interesting ones. Like this one—" she reached for the thistle made of wood and bronze, but Thomas caught her hand before she could touch it.

"Yes, those are the ones I mean. I've been looking for those things for weeks. The Queen tasked me with finding them, and here they are."

"What?" She shook her head in confusion. "No, I found them—"

"Yes, you did. Now I want you to look at them through your stone."

Tess leaned backward warily, and her fingers went to the gray rock still on its thong around her neck. He was foolishly relieved she hadn't yet taken it off, even though it would almost certainly mean more trouble. It might yet save her, and it meant she believed him and his preposterous stories.

She lifted it to her right eye. He knew from her indrawn breath that she could see the glimmers of magic chasing over the surfaces of the items. She lowered the stone again, clutching it tightly as if it were a talisman.

"You see they're not just things. They're of the fae."

"What were they doing at Saturday Market? If I'd known, I wouldn't have taken them, but they seemed so interesting, and they…Thomas, it's almost like they called to me; something about them seemed familiar, though I can't imagine why. I'd find one every few weeks or so, and there was never anyone around who knew anything about them. So I'd just bring them home, and put them on the shelf. And now they're...*they're in my house.*" She turned to stare at him in dread and confusion.

"The Queen put them there, and she's angry, very angry, that they've gone missing."

"Then why put them where they could be found in the first place? It doesn't make sense."

Thomas shook his head. "None of us know why our Queen does the things she does, but she's been the Queen for centuries. She must be doing something right."

"She sounds like a bloodthirsty old bitch to me." Tess gestured to his trow-form. "Look what she did to you."

"With the fae, nothing is only as it seems. No bad is unmixed with good. I may be smelly and ugly, but I've been alive and young for almost two hundred years."

"You really don't smell that bad." Tess put a comforting hand on his arm. "Just...a lot like a steakhouse. Sirloin, with mushroom gravy."

At his toothy grin, she took a step back, and he laughed. "But not quite good enough to eat, eh? And still ugly." Then he grew serious. "Listen. Today, since I can't go home until dark, I'm going to see if I can find out what's really going on. Hunter has something in mind, but it's not clear. If I can't get the truth out of him, I'll go to the Queen. This has to stop before you get hurt."

"Thomas, no—" Out came her hand again, that soft, tender hand. Other human women, when confronted by his trow-form, had fainted, or looked away in disbelief, or fled in fear. Tess had managed to absorb his reality and still find him likable.

He would do almost anything to keep her kind regard. He craved her touch, her sweetness, her smile. He wanted more than that, but while she might find him a likable trow, she doubtless no longer thought of him as relationship material.

"I'll be all right."

"You don't know that."

"I *have* to be all right, because I'm coming back here so we can get these things out of your house, since you're too stubborn to leave town."

"Thomas—" This time she did put her hand on his arm, bare inches from the Queen's wretched slave band, then moved so the palm was cupped gently over his heart. "Please be careful. Or—I know, let me come with you! We'll take the Jeep, I want to get out and put fuel in it anyway, and—"

Thomas could not stop himself from pulling her into his arms. He tucked her head under his chin. "Listen to me. This is important." He turned them so they were facing the curio cabinet. "If I don't come back tonight, then tomorrow morning you must take everything in this cabinet and put it in a sack. It would be best if you didn't touch the things with your bare hands. The Queen would know if a fae touched these things. I don't think she can sense when a human does or she'd have come for them by now, but better to be safe."

Tess leaned back in the circle of his arms and stared up at him in horror. "You want me to give them back to her?"

Thomas shook his head. "I want you to take them somewhere near Underbridge and leave them. Do it in daylight, as sunny as possible. She wants them put back. Very well, we'll put them back. It's the only way I know to keep you safe, and maybe keep my head."

"We'll give them back now, then! It's simple. I'll get a bag and some gloves."

Thomas tightened his arms when she would have rushed away. "Not yet. There's still too much I don't know. I can't be certain that returning her things will solve our problems. There's still Hunter to consider. But I'll know, one way or the other, by dawn, and if I can, I'll come back here."

"What if you don't come back? Where can I…where will I find you? I suppose I could try to get to your place in the bridge…"

It was enough to melt his heart, that look of hers. If he hadn't been more than halfway in love with her already, her words would have done the trick. As it was, they were like a knife to his breast, plunging deep, gouging out a place in his soul where the image of her would lodge forever, brown-eyed and so sincere.

"You won't find me," he whispered, knowing that neither

the Queen nor Hunter would allow him to walk away if he put a foot wrong. "Just remember to do what I said. Take these things out of here, and afterward, keep away from Underbridge."

Her lip quivered for a moment, then her chin firmed and lifted. "I'll remember, but you make sure you come back, Thomas!"

Thomas made certain Tess didn't see him climb the fairy mound. When he left her on the porch in the cloudy morning light, he walked down the street, hunched and hooded in his oilskin, until he heard her close the front door. Then, masked by an overgrown laurel hedge, he slipped between two houses, hopped a fence, and scrambled up the steep slope onto the mound. The ubiquitous ivy, the Queen's clever warning system, twined up his legs beneath his trousers, wrapping around his ankles and calves above his boots, catching him, tasting his skin with its hairy feet. After that taste, the ivy knew him for fae and did not obstruct him further as he slogged uphill and headed northwest parallel to the spine of the mound.

Entrances to the mound were few and far between, and well guarded, not only by the ivy, but by trolls. This time of day the trolls would be rigid and stony, immovable as glacial boulders, without the great strength his trow-form gave him. Even with that aid, he'd have to struggle. In the process, the Queen and the countless denizens of the mound would be alerted. Relatively few of the fae chose to live outside the mound the way he, and some of the market regulars, did. Most preferred the company of other fae, and the concentration of iron in the human areas was off-putting, when it didn't cause actual illness among the more sensitive.

He paused to think once he was within the shelter of the firs and big leaf maples. He chose a mossy, fallen log to sit on, apologizing when the roots stirred peevishly. He'd woken the thing, but he didn't move away. After a moment or two it settled again, leaving one wet, clay-streaked root where it could keep track of him. Around him he heard the hollow sounds of last night's rain and dew still dripping on the leaves and stones. Many of the deciduous trees in the park were bare, their bright autumn colors dimmed and muddy, the autumn rains and wind having torn loose their foliage. The few oaks he could see still held tight to their leaves, some brown, some red. The birches showed their gold, the female spirits inside the trees growing drowsier with each passing day. Soon, the lovely birch girls would dance their last dances, then root themselves deep and sleep until spring.

Thomas could feel the Eve approaching, only a day away. With Allantide, the barriers between the human world and the world of the fae would be at their weakest. This year, the moon would be a hunter's moon, full on that fateful night. It happened only a few times each century, and Thomas had learned to dread those nights for their extraordinary, bestial toll on the fae and humans alike.

Hunter would ride with his hounds, in full voice and full strength. Even the humans would be able to hear their strange, bloodthirsty cries. Some would go mad, some might throw off the shackles of convention and morality and join the Hunt, but most would lock their doors and toss in restless, blurred and dreadful dreams, waking sick and weary the next morning, with elf-locks knotting their hair.

Inside the mound, the fae who were not out with the Wild Hunt would hold an orgy of dancing and feasting and coupling. In decades past, when Thomas was still bedazzled by the Queen, joyously doing her twisted bidding, he had joined in the spectacle with relish, knowing the dawn would bring nothing but heartache and sickness, but unable to stop himself. Over the years as he realized what he was really doing for the Queen in between excesses of pleasure—killing and torturing so she wouldn't have to sully her bright, sharp claws—his soul seemed to shrivel. The more fae he became, the more he resented the decay of his human self.

A year came when he sat on the sidelines, glowering and sullen, while the dance went on around him. The Queen looked at him from the corners of her serpent eyes, and it was that night she brought a different young man to her couch of thistledown as dawn came, kissing his mouth and twining about him while Thomas looked on in astonishment, from a spot against the wall near the door. Thomas had killed the boy in a fit of jealous rage, afterward vomiting all the delicate fae viands across the Queen's perfect onyx floor while she smiled. The next year Thomas attended as usual, feigning abandon, but despising every whirling step, every sly and insinuating touch from fae hands. He fell on the Queen at dawn with fury and hatred, for the first time taking her in his trow body, and rejoicing when she struck him and cut his face with her claws. She spat and bit at him, but she climaxed all the same.

It was only later, when two strands of his slave band snapped and curled back on themselves, that he realized he'd done what she wanted, after all. Damn her. She knew him too well, for he was the creature she herself had made. She waited like a spider, patient and sticky-webbed, for the last of his human self to melt away, for him to become completely fae. Completely hers.

The year after that, he sealed the door of his trow-hold and spent the night thinking about how he would have liked to destroy the gear room while the bridge was up, to leave its spans forever apart. But the humans would only use other bridges and eventually repair the damage.

He'd never gone back to the mound at Allantide. The Queen didn't command him, and now Thomas knew she had taken other lovers, though she still occasionally bedded him. He had often wished she would kill him, but she only gave him new tasks, slowly whittling away at the bond of his servitude.

Ugly years.

Desperate years.

Now there was Tess.

The hope he felt was as bitter and sharp as the salt of her tears and the richness of her blood. As surely as she would be his ruin, she might be his salvation. There was always a choice, even if both alternatives were dire.

He rose from the log, belting his oilskin around him. He didn't let his thoughts linger on a third alternative that presented itself with monotonous frequency: handing over the thief to the Queen and washing his hands of the whole mess.

⟫ Chapter Eighteen ⟪

With Thomas gone, the duplex seemed too quiet and frighteningly empty. Tess jumped at the least sound—the refrigerator motor kicking on, the neighbor in the other half of the duplex starting his car in the driveway. She walked the rooms restlessly, worrying and fretting and pondering every strange explanation Thomas had given.

The treasures in the curio cabinet drew her back time and again. She examined them through the seeing stone, not touching them, watching the slow crawl of the purple magic—for what else could she call it, after last night?—over their surfaces. An hour before she was due at work, she called in sick. Likely they'd all roll their eyes and think she was taking Halloween off to party, but in truth she was exhausted from the disrupted night and the weary days preceding it, and she needed time to process. Sometimes it was hell being a psychologist, examining all her own motives in microscopic detail.

In the end, Tess huddled in a fat armchair in the living room with a mug of hot tea, staring at the cabinet, wondering what to do and just how much to believe. The trouble was, she'd been given the proof she demanded, and now it was hard to fit reality into the new paradigm. Everything made sense if she believed

Thomas, the man who became something *other* from time to time, and who had wormed his strange way into her heart with nobility, earnestness and vulnerability.

Tess shook her head. She had to find some professional distance again. Get a grip on her feelings.

She woke two hours later from a dream of something dark and flapping, dimly seen, with red eyes, chasing her down the wet, leaf-strewn jogging trails of Forest Park. The half-drunk tea, long cold, splashed down her leg onto the carpet, and made her curse. As she mopped up the mess, she sat back on her heels and stared at the curio cabinet, struck by a sudden thought.

Rory had taken one of the things—the little silver hazelnut. Had it been one of the fae objects?

What was more, after he'd taken the nut, he'd made a spectacular and unexpected recovery, and been released from Ridge Manor.

A wild series of questions raced through Tess's mind. What if the nut *had* been fae? What if its concealed power had healed Rory? What if another object could heal Aaron? *What if she took the things to Aaron's house and one of them cured him?*

The thought was too exciting to bear. She discounted the unreality of it; reality was fluid these days, and too many coincidences aligned for her not to try. Aaron's continual assertions he wasn't on drugs. The way the creatures in Underbridge indicated he belonged to their Queen. The strange, beautiful girl he had met in Waterfront Park. The way all his tests had turned up negative for drugs. His family unable to say what he might be on. Rory's sudden cure.

And, of course, Thomas.

Everything Thomas was changed her world.

Tess got to her feet, went upstairs to shower and change, and came back downstairs with a pair of winter gloves and an empty cloth grocery tote bag. She marched over to the curio cabinet, pulled on the gloves, yanked open the glass door, and froze, biting her lip. The what-if game began again.

What if Thomas was right, and the things did belong to his Queen? What if the Queen knew Tess had them? What if moving them caused real problems, or they made Aaron sick, or drew the attention of the creatures in Underbridge—or other creatures even worse, since Thomas insisted the fae were everywhere in Portland.

"And what if you don't do this, and Aaron becomes like Rory, or d-dead, like Stephen? Get a grip, Tess." Her own voice startled her, but it also firmed her resolve. "You brought the damned things home, and nothing happened. You can take them out of here and nothing will happen."

She set the tote on the sideboard, lifted the seeing stone to her eye, and one by one transferred the Queen's trinkets to the bag, taking only those things with the oily purple shimmer. With Rory, the hazelnut had worked, and maybe it didn't matter which thing she gave to Aaron, but maybe it would. Best to take them all.

The things rattled and clinked against each other in the bag when she lifted it. She worried a little that they might reach some sort of critical mass, crowded together like that, but reasoned that they'd been sitting in her cabinet for months and nothing untoward had occurred.

There were fifteen. A few more sat on the bookshelf at her office, but she'd already called in sick, and it wouldn't do to show up there looking perfectly healthy only to dash out again. If each trinket represented someone the Queen had paralyzed, Tess had found cures for a dozen and a half people. Yet she only knew a few young men fitting the same profile.

If her wild guess was right, who were all the others? How could she find them? Tess imagined herself talking to the rehab center's director, explaining that all they had to do was give each addict a magical toy made by the local evil Queen of the fairies, and they'd be completely healed.

Then she imagined being fired, and her license to practice taken away, and newspaper articles showcasing the sad state of mental health care at a certain rehab center in Portland. Lawsuits. Ridicule. She shook her head and went for her jacket and car keys. Outside, locking the front door, she stared around her, half expecting to see a kelpie or redcap lurking in the bushes. All she saw was her pumpkin, looking a bit more sinister and smirky than she remembered carving. She shook her head at her own overactive imagination, and fought the creeping sense of unease that urged her to go back inside and stay in bed with the covers over her head and the wall at her back for the day.

Aaron lived across the Willamette. The Burnside Bridge was the logical route for Tess to take, but after the previous night, it was the last place she wanted to be, especially given Thomas's warnings to stay away. The creatures in Underbridge knew her Jeep now. What if they were watching for her? If Thomas was nowhere around...would she be able to take care of herself?

As she drove through downtown, heading for the Hawthorne Street Bridge, well south of Burnside, she occasionally lifted the seeing stone to her eye. Some of the people she passed showed flickers of glamour, and at one stoplight a gargoyle on the side of a historic office building snatched an unwary pigeon off its stony head and stuffed the bird into its mouth, chewing with evident relish and letting several tail feathers fall to the sidewalk below.

Shuddering, Tess tucked the stone away beneath her shirt and tightened her grip on the wheel.

They *were* everywhere. Even in broad daylight.

She shivered and drove on.

Once again she parked down the block from the Eisley house and sat watching it, trying to build up her courage to knock on the door and ask to speak to Aaron. This time it was noon of a beautiful autumn day, sunlight firing the red vine maples and yellow ginkgoes. The neighborhood yards were filled with bright leaves raked into mounds on green lawns. Everywhere was the flicker of motion, the endless, slow downward twirl of leaf after leaf. Millions upon millions, all different, all beautiful, like Aaron. Like Rory. Anthony. Stephen. And how many others?

She took a deep breath, grabbed the grocery tote, and walked to the Eisley family's front door. Crazy idea or not, she had to try.

Aaron's mother answered Tess's knock, harried and tired-looking, her hair mussed, staring at Tess in confusion until she placed the tall counselor. "Ms. Gordon! Did Aaron call you? Is there news?"

"Actually, I was looking for Aaron, if he's home. I wanted to talk to him. I've had an idea that might help him, and—" *Just let me sprinkle a little pixie dust on him, and he'll be fine. I promise.*

Mrs. Eisley's face crumpled and she turned away, hiding her eyes behind her hands. She stumbled into the foyer, and Tess, alarmed, followed her. "You haven't heard."

"Heard what?" A sick dread clenched Tess's stomach.

"We haven't seen Aaron for three days now. He hasn't come home since Tuesday."

"Not come home…have you called the police?" Her fingers twisted in the strap of the tote bag, longing to reach out, to comfort the weeping woman in the sunny hallway with its warm hardwood floors and bright white walls.

"Of course we have. And nothing. Nothing! Are you sure you haven't seen him?"

"Aaron's next appointment isn't until Monday."

Mrs. Eisley stared at Tess, fresh tears welling up. "I don't know what I'll do if something bad has happened to my baby boy. I don't know...I don't know." She clutched at Tess's arm. Even through her jacket sleeve, Tess could feel how cold Mrs. Eisley's hands were. "Has he told you anything that might help us find him? Anything at all?"

Tess stood, wracked with indecision. On the one hand, revealing Underbridge as the probable source of Aaron's problems might give his family and the police a place to start. On the other, the idea of sending unprepared people among the creatures there was tantamount to murder. While she opened and closed her mouth like a goldfish, trying to frame words, any words, that might help, the telephone rang. With a loud cry, Mrs. Eisley ran to answer it. Like a craven, Tess slipped out of the house, closing the door silently behind her.

Outside, the wind had picked up. The sky was still bright blue, and a pile of leaves from the yard next door whirled upward. Tess hurried down the sidewalk, ducking her head against a sudden flurry of flame-colored leaves. The flurry thickened around her, the swirl tightening, leaves brushing her clothing and face, snagging in her hair, tangling her ponytail. Tess halted, her heart pounding. Nowhere else on the block were leaves moving, except in the slow drift of autumn. Nowhere else was there a leafy funnel-cloud attacking a pedestrian.

Tess heard Thomas's words in her mind. *If anything at all seems odd, look through it. Know when you're dealing with the fae.* She fished in the collar of her shirt and hauled out the seeing stone.

The moment she held it to her eye, the leaf storm lost energy and focus. Tess saw the crackle of what she now thought of as fae magic, strange glimmers that looked like nothing else on earth, though the rainbow sheen of oil on wet asphalt came close. This magic was dark as a bruise, spitting and sparking from leaf to leaf as they sank to the ground. Red, orange, yellow, bloody crimson, dried-blood brown.

"Are you looking for me?" Tess demanded of the air. "Well, I have nothing you want. Go away. Bother someone else. Go away!" She clutched the tote bag tight to her chest, wondering if whatever had made the leaves swirl could tell she was lying. Tess ran through the settling leaves, hurrying to the safety of the Jeep. Would it have enough iron to block the fae commanding the whirlwind, the way Thomas's house was protected by iron? She fumbled the key into the lock, jerked open the door and threw herself and the grocery tote into the cab of the Jeep, slamming and locking the door behind her.

Could it see her? The swirl of leaves was mostly still, only a leaf or two here and there still spinning downward. It had left a perfect circle on the sidewalk and grass.

"Fairy ring," Tess gasped. But weren't those made of mushrooms, and not leaves? Still, it was too perfect a circle, which made it dangerous and unnatural. She crow-hopped the Jeep down the street while she fumbled for first gear and then second, looking behind her to be sure the leaves weren't following, heading for the Willamette to put running water between her and the fae outside Aaron's house.

⮫ Chapter Nineteen ⮬

"Where is your master?" The bogle swung from Thomas's big grip, kicking and squealing. Thomas had snatched it as it squeezed out from under the roots of a maple, where it had apparently been dozing. He'd smelled the bogle's telltale odor of stale beer as he walked one of the Forest Park trails and caused enough ruckus that it woke to see what was happening. The maple held its roots away from the bogle, reminding Thomas of nineteenth-century women lifting their skirt hems above the muddy streets of Portland.

"I'll never tell the likes of you! Not fit to lick his boots!"

"I leave that to squirmy little meat like you." Thomas gave the bogle a shake and caught its spidery fingers in his free hand. "Tell me, or I start breaking your fingers, one knuckle at a time. You've got a lot of knuckles, and every one will hurt more than the last."

"I won't tell!"

"Your choice." Thomas shrugged and chose the bogle's least finger, ignoring the creature's flailing and screeching. Any humans who happened to pass by the large boulder where the two of them struggled would think a pair of cats were fighting somewhere nearby. He began to squeeze. "Last chance. Look, there's a raven flapping in to have a snack. Think I can pop this joint off the end of your finger for him?"

"Do your worst!"

Thomas had to give the nasty little creature credit. If it lacked brains, it had bravado. He squeezed harder. Tess wouldn't approve of what he was doing, but he couldn't think of another way to get to Hunter. "Talk, you dribble of slime, or summon him." The bogle's knuckle gave beneath the pressure of Thomas's fingers. The sickening pop nearly made him vomit, but the bogle shrieked like a fire alarm and went rigid in Thomas's grip. Around them a number of trees awakened, stirring anxiously in the wet, clay soil. Knotty eyes blinked. Mossy mouths complained about interrupted naps. Two nearby birch girls turned their faces away, lowering their golden leaves to hide their eyes.

Thomas shifted to the next knuckle, and the bogle flailed so hard he nearly dropped it. As he squeezed, every dead leaf within a twenty-yard radius suddenly took to the air in a furious, rushing vortex. Thomas could not see more than an inch or two in the violent flurry, with wet, half-decayed leaves plastering themselves to his face and body.

"Master!" gibbered the bogle, weeping.

"Go back to sleep, trees! This isn't your concern." Thomas flung an arm over his eyes to keep the tide of leaves at bay.

"No, but it is mine, and the leaves obey my command. Release my hound." Hunter's voice, raw and sharp-edged, seemed to come from everywhere.

"When we're done talking. If these leaves are yours, send them away."

"Why do you seek me, human?"

"I told you. Talk."

"The time for talk is done. It is Allantide. Tonight I ride, and the moon makes all the earth mine. Be sure you are not in my path, Thomas Half-made."

Thomas could hear the blood lust in Hunter's voice, an excitement verging on the sexual that appalled him but nevertheless roused an eagerness he could not entirely quell. His fingers tightened on the bogle, which shrieked again.

I am not like you.

It was the only way he knew to set himself apart, control the fae part of him that wanted to wreak havoc on this night of all nights. *Tess.*

"You once sought information from me." Thomas shouted through the ceaseless wet slither and slap of leaves. Twigs and dirt joined the rain of leaves. Thomas wondered when the pebbles, and then perhaps stones, would add their pummeling to the storm.

"You are too late, as always, no matter how clever you were, severing the ley line like that. For certainly you would have escaped me by no other means that day. Who taught you such a trick, weakling?"

Thomas ignored Hunter's jab. How would he have explained the concept of human libraries, reference books, written by humans, about the fae? Sometimes the humans got it right. Instead, he kept on target with the topic he believed would interest Hunter the most: the Queen's plotting. "You were right, she is planning something."

"As I told you." Hunter's terrible voice carried a note of boredom and Thomas realized he was losing his audience. "Kill the bogle or release it, but either way, make that noise stop before I finish it myself."

"I saw you in Underbridge last night. Why were you following me? Was it at the Queen's bidding?"

"I keep my own counsel. My choices are mine."

Thomas knew his dart had hit home. Was it his imagination, or did the storm of debris lessen? "We all think that. It's what she wants us to think. She wants us to believe we make our own choices that just happen to align with her desires." He laughed, knowing a moment of ball-freezing fear when the leaves suddenly fell like stones, slamming to earth in ways no leaf would ever plummet. The bogle's eyes shot open, and its mouth closed, as Hunter seized it around its scrawny middle and ripped it from Thomas's hand. Hunter flung the creature away among the trees down the slope, where it rolled to a stop and lay unmoving.

"That's four bogles you've ruined in less than a day. Where will you get more, if you keep wasting them like this?"

Hunter circled him like a wolf circling a bear. Hunter's form was leaner and smaller, but Thomas knew he was no match for him. "You bait me, human."

"I want your attention."

"You have it. Be careful what you seek, for it may be granted."

"You once offered me a share in something."

Hunter's red eyes flicked suspiciously from right to left. "The forest has ears."

"Aye, everywhere. I'll be quick and quiet, then. Tell me why you sent snares after me and mine, and I will tell you what the Queen wants."

"You and yours?" Hunter's laughter was like lightning and thunder—quick and violent, intolerably loud. "That human you won from the kelpie?"

"I'm waiting."

In a movement almost too quick for Thomas's eyes to see, Hunter was upon him, mailed hand at his throat, the butt of his staff pressing between Thomas's legs, where his tender sac tried its best to shrink away. "Do not presume, you gobbet of human meat."

"You came to *my* home, Hunter. You chased us through *my* streets. Underbridge is *mine*. The Queen gave it to *me*."

"Yes, and why is that?" Hunter's tone grew thoughtful. "Why give it to a half-made who can hardly keep himself in check, let alone the entire goblin market?"

"Because I *am* half-human. I know how to let the humans and the fae mix and yet be separate, and still allow the market to flourish. I am the law in Underbridge." *This is going well, don't you think?* He almost gave an insane giggle. Hunter disturbed him even more than the Queen, because Hunter's goals were unclear in ways the Queen's never were. "Do you want the market? Is that what this is about?" Thomas knew it wasn't, but pricking Hunter's ego seemed to be the only way to get the information he sought.

Hunter flung Thomas away in disgust. "I do not want your leavings, Half-made." The red eyes burned, and from where he sprawled on the muddy ground, Thomas wondered that the deer skull didn't burst into flame. "Very well. Say your piece."

Thomas took a deep breath, getting to his feet. He knocked away the worst of the mud from his oilskin, buying time to think. "The Queen has been marking the Underbridge and some of the streets around it, placing small trinkets soaked in her magic there. Someone has been stealing them, and it is my task to find the thief."

Hunter's head tilted to the side in apparent thought. Thomas hated not being able to see Hunter's expression. "Go on."

Thomas shrugged. "You wanted to hear what I know. That's what I know."

"You summoned me for rubbish gossip like that?" Hunter

advanced again, the mailed fingers flexing. "A waste of a perfectly good hound."

"You ruined that bogle, not I. Now, why were you setting snares for me?"

"You have told me nothing."

"You made a bargain." Thomas tried not to swallow and reveal his unease. Hunter despised and destroyed anything weak and uncertain. And today of all days, with the moon building to its Allantide fullest, Hunter was strong, ferociously so. "Think about it. If someone has been taking the Queen's trinkets, that someone must be stronger than we realize."

Hunter's red eyes slitted for a moment, as if the idea of an unknown quantity—a strong one—gave him pause. "Why is the Queen putting markers there to begin with? Has she not told you?"

"The Queen rarely shares her plans with me, unless those plans involve me."

"She is cunning."

"Keep your part of the bargain, Hunter."

The deer skull swung slowly back and forth as Hunter stretched his neck to crack the joints there. "I was going to take what you knew of her plans from you. By force if necessary."

Thomas snorted in disgust. "And the human with me?"

"An unfortunate complication. It was you I wanted."

"But you knew enough to set your hounds on her vehicle."

"I remember all too well the pleasures of the flesh, Half-made. How vulnerable they make one. It's why our Queen enchants all her lovers, so she is never in thrall to human needs and desires. Your mistake was nearly fatal for you both. Next time you won't be so fortunate."

"There won't be a next time," Thomas growled.

Hunter's laughter flared again. "Do you threaten me, Thomas? You may have the Queen's preferment from time to time, but she will never prevent me killing you if it pleases me." He leaned forward, and the sunlight shafting through the naked tree limbs cast a dull glow over the offal-grimed armor. "And it would please me to be rid of you."

"The Queen would be displeased."

"But she would feast on your flesh all the same." Hunter straightened, stabbing the butt of his staff directly into the mound beneath their feet. The ground split, yawning into a great crevice, from which Thomas could hear the clamor of the fae preparing their Allantide festivities hundreds of feet below. "Go and tell her your news. See what it wins you to reveal her own plans to her."

Thomas shook his head. "I will go to her when I have the thief in hand and not before." He tilted his head. "Though it does interest me very much to know you're planning to take her place in the court. I wonder what she'd say if I were to mention that."

As a gambit, it was spectacularly successful.

Hunter ripped his staff from the earth, which slammed shut. Around them, the wakened trees tossed and creaked, reacting to the snares of hunt magic that spewed from Hunter's gauntlets and staff. Thomas was caught in it, and tendrils menaced his face like striking snakes. He fought the instinct to close his eyes, and instead struggled to get a hand inside his oilskin, where his iron nails lay wrapped in their pocket. He doubted such a trick would work again, but he had to try. It was not in his nature to go down without a fight, even against such an invincible warrior as Hunter.

The snares dragged him over the mound to where Hunter stood.

"You would have done better, *human*, to become my ally." Hunter stared into Thomas's wide eyes. "Mark me well. Tell her, and I will hear of it. But I will not come for your life that instant. I will come for that of your pet's, and I will give her to the kelpies for their pleasure—and their meat. Choose wisely. And if you value your own life, make certain you are inside the mound before I ride tonight. Because if you are not, I will hunt you until cockcrow, and only when you weep for mercy will I kill you."

Hunter's staff thumped Thomas's chest. "Mark me well."

Thump. *Thump*.

Thomas tried to get his hand beneath the lapel of the coat, but Hunter's red gaze flicked there, and he uttered a single phrase: "Stone be ye." And Thomas was as stone, unmoving, but not deaf, and not blind. The net of the snare magic lay wherever his skin was not covered by clothing, and burned there, hot as the Queen's armband could sometimes be. It was excruciating, like being covered by biting ants or stung by wasps. Thomas felt his heart slowing in his chest as the stoniness penetrated deeper and deeper. His breathing slowed, and then stopped.

This was how it would end, then, with magic, beneath the hard pearl sky of Allantide, atop the Queen's proudest accomplishment. He felt stupid for not realizing Hunter must have magic beyond that of his snares.

Even the fae perished when their hearts were breached or broken, and Thomas was only partially fae. His senses began to swim as he struggled to draw breath. He longed to sleep. A deep ache filled his bones like cold sap, slow and thick.

Thomas fell backward onto the wet, stony earth. The deep pile of Hunter's driven leaves made no cushion beneath him, and the trees pinwheeled above him against the shattering sky. He might have heard when Hunter vanished, with a noise like a clap of thunder, or it might simply have been his heart exploding. He couldn't tell, but he was grateful it was over, no matter what, except for Tess, who would never know what had become of him, and who would take a sack of fae trinkets to Underbridge in the morning, tender and naive as a sacrificial lamb.

Oh, Tess. I'm sorry…

⇒ Chapter Twenty ⇐

How had the world become so strange, in so little time? Tess sat in a fast-food restaurant parking lot just off Sandy Boulevard, waiting for her hands to stop shaking. She held the seeing stone clenched tight in her fist, wondering if a cheeseburger would still look like a cheeseburger, or if it would have the oily rainbow sheen of fairy magic upon it.

Nothing was safe any longer, not a person, not a building, not a lamppost. Not even dead leaves. It was all changed, all frightening, unless Thomas was near to explain it, defeat it, or drive it away. She was unnerved by how much she had come to depend on him. She wondered if he was safe wherever he was now, or if the things that had hunted them the night before hunted him still.

When she started to tell herself the leaf attack was simply an aberrant breeze, she knew she was feeling better. But she still felt shaky, so she locked the Jeep and went inside the restaurant for a sandwich and a caffeinated soda, and some nasty, delicious French fries. She bolted her food too fast, peering through the stone every now and then and finding nothing out of the ordinary. A few customers looked at her curiously, and at last she put the stone inside her shirt, where it lay cool and smooth against her skin.

An hour was too long to linger at a burger joint, even at midday, and finally Tess visited the washroom, then went for the Jeep. A fallen leaf, brown and curled dry with autumn, scudded past her on the asphalt like a toy boat propelled by a gust of wind. She screamed.

Not loudly, but all the same, it proved a point. She locked herself inside the Jeep and sat there with the grocery tote in the passenger seat, her heart pounding anew. The fries, so welcome while they were hot and salty fresh, sat like a rock in her belly. She fumbled the stone out of her neckline and stared through it wild-eyed, turning to examine the entire parking lot, particularly the edges where the curbs trapped the fallen leaves.

Nothing out of the ordinary.

Of course.

There had been nothing different about that leaf.

"I'm fine," she whispered to herself, gripping the steering wheel. "I'm alone in my own car and I'm *just fine*." Speaking aloud made her feel a little steadier.

Determinedly she cranked the engine and pulled out into the noontime traffic, heading for her office. She could just tell them she had slept and felt better. She wanted to be around people, good, ordinary people, who didn't change shape or pull mysterious bits of nothing out from under her car and tell her a monster was chasing them.

Except that she knew the monster *had* been chasing them. Ordinary people, or even streetfolk, didn't climb the skeletons of bridges in the darkness with their eyes glowing red.

When she neared her office, she sat at a long traffic light. She happened to glance at herself in the rearview mirror, and saw there a woman who looked completely out of control. Some of her hair had frizzed out of her ponytail. Her eyes were open too wide, and she could not make herself relax enough to stop looking terrified, no matter how hard she blinked or how deeply she breathed.

She couldn't go into the office looking like this. When the light changed, she kept driving, and passed the entrance to the office parking lot.

A moment later she found herself crossing the Burnside Street Bridge, the most direct route home from her east-side office. She sucked in a sharp breath and her foot stuttered on the accelerator. Stupid. *Stupid.* How could she have been so distracted that she neglected to consider the market and the fae beneath that very bridge, especially after having been so careful earlier?

Nowhere to stop. Nowhere to turn around.

There was no barrier in the center of the bridge. If she just pulled gently to the side, as if she had car trouble, eventually the traffic would clear enough that she could make an illegal U-turn and head back to Sandy Boulevard and the east side of town, and a different bridge. She began to slow down, her right turn signal on. The traffic from the west was already diminishing; the stoplights must be with her. She pulled to the right, checking her rearview and side mirrors. In another few hundred feet she would be directly over Thomas's house, across the leaves of the bridge, and into the frightening territory of Underbridge.

Tess checked her mirrors one last time and blinked.

There were several vehicles halted at the east end of the bridge, blocking traffic there. She could hear the noise of horns honking.

Every single vehicle was black.

She jammed her foot on the brake, stopped on the empty bridge, and turned in her seat to look behind her.

Not just a few of the vehicles.

All of them.

She counted quickly: twelve, with their headlights on. For a disjointed moment she thought it must be a funeral procession, but for that they'd have been in single file, following a pilot car from a mortuary, not gathering at the base of the bridge like a group of racers about to burst from the starting blocks.

Twelve. All black, shining things. In the lead was a monstrous SUV, making its slow way onto the bridge deck. Behind it were arrayed little sedans and coupes, a truck or two, but nothing so ground-pawingly macho as the SUV.

Thomas's voice echoed in her head. *If anything at all seems odd, look through it. Know when you're dealing with the fae.*

Twelve black vehicles with their lights on in the middle of the afternoon seemed odd to Tess.

She fumbled the seeing stone out of her shirt and held it to her eye.

They weren't cars at all. Nor trucks. Not vehicles of any kind. They had to be heavily glamoured to be out and about in the human world in broad daylight like this. Glamoured to look like iron, which seemed crazily appropriate and impossible at the same time, given Thomas's reaction to riding in her Jeep and touching the steel girders of the bridge. In the lead was a skeletal horse, gray as steel in the daylight, champing at the bit in its mouth and dripping gobbets of froth from its bony muzzle.

And its rider…dear God, its rider was the cloaked thing that had skulked the girders above them as she and Thomas fled his house. She could see the red glints of its eyes even from a third of the way across the bridge, but it was not hooded now, and she saw what could only be the immense rack of an elk or a stag adorning its ferocious head.

Behind the rider was a milling of smaller creatures, things with too many legs, too many teeth, and not enough flesh to be anything but famished.

And among them, the wet, horselike monsters Thomas had called kelpies. If she'd had any doubt left that the boy-thing that had tried to woo her in Underbridge was ill-intentioned, it was gone now.

The group roiled at the edge of the bridge as if they were reluctant to take that first step onto the deck. Thomas had chosen his home wisely, well protected by iron and running water. But she didn't think the water would hold back the kelpies in the group. They'd probably rejoice if she suddenly entered the Willamette. It would put her in their element.

The warning blast of an air horn woke her from her frightened trance and she turned in her seat expecting to be obliterated by a massive truck bearing down on her from the west end of the bridge. Instead she saw the lights of the bridge warning system flashing, and the red and white striped arms beginning to descend. Through the body of the Jeep she could feel the thrum and groan of the Burnside Bridge machinery, the same shuddering vibrations she had felt the night before in Thomas's strange little bolt hole.

To the south, a ship was headed for the bridge.

Behind her, the collection of black cars crept onto the bridge and began to gather speed as if they had recognized her as their prey, and with that recognition, had found their courage. Their speed began to increase, narrowing the safe gap by the moment.

Ahead of her, the arms were almost down across her lane.

She slammed her foot on the accelerator, cut the Jeep hard to the left, grabbing for gears as she sped. She looked over her shoulder to see the black posse forming a barrier across all the lanes of the bridge. If they thought she would drive right toward them, Tess had other plans.

Even the terrors of Underbridge were preferable to the things waiting at the east end of the bridge. She rounded the end of the gate and zoomed into the no-man's-land between the red and white striped arms, where the leaves of the bridge would separate.

She pushed the Jeep faster, cutting back into her own travel lane, racing for the dark crack she could see in the middle of the bridge. Sparing a glance in the rearview, she saw the SUV and several of the chase cars coming fast, oh, so frighteningly fast, passing the first arm.

Through the windshield she saw the bridge operator out on the deck of the western tower, waving his arms to stop her. But there was no going back, even if she and the Jeep went into the Willamette. The Jeep neared the center of the leaves, where the crack in the bridge was widening ever so slightly and the deck tilt was becoming noticeable. Tess stuffed the Jeep into third gear and torqued the engine harder than she'd ever pushed it before. Fifty, fifty-five, sixty, sixty-five, and the Jeep crossed the center of the two leaves, bumped sickeningly across the little maw that was opening there in the bridge, sixty-eight and the engine was screaming and the RPMs were into the red but she was across, *across*. She slammed the Jeep into fourth gear and shot past the line of east-bound traffic waiting politely behind the second barrier, slewed down the slope of the bridge and sob-blessed the red light at the bottom when it winked green. She dared a glance behind her.

The SUV alone still followed her. Had the rest of the things been too afraid to cross? Too slow? Halted by the iron and the running water beneath? Or would they come slithering in from elsewhere, like rain-drunk worms from the earth? She recklessly jammed the stone to her eye to scan the area at the foot of the Burnside Bridge, but there was no plague of fairy things swarming up from Underbridge. At last she had to jam her foot on the brake to gain enough control to negotiate the city streets without killing herself or someone else in the process.

The Jeep smelled hot and angry with the stink of scorched clutch as she pulled it sharply to the right into Chinatown, beneath the ornate crimson welcome gate flanked by two guardian *fu* dog statues. She knew she had pushed the old engine too hard, but she hoped with all her might the faithful vehicle would continue on just the way it always had. It was the only thing she had to get herself out of this mess.

The light ahead of her turned red, and a stream of pedestrians flowed into the crosswalk from both directions. A sob built in her throat and she turned to stare behind her through the stone, where, sure enough, the black SUV had just turned the corner into her street. Tess heard the note of eager triumph in its deep-pitched engine growl, but suddenly the SUV slewed to the side and rocked hard, nearly off its wheels. She couldn't see what it had struck to knock it so, but then it occurred to her to use the stone—*I should just build it into a pair of glasses, never take it off, look like a freak the rest of my probably very short life at this rate*—and what she saw next made her jaw drop in utter astonishment.

It was one thing to see a gargoyle coming to life on the side of a building and snacking on pigeons.

It was another to see the *fu* dogs launching from their pedestals on either side of the gate into Chinatown, ripping at the rider and his mount with claws the size of dinosaur teeth. The skeletal horse reared and tossed, a spray of sparks like fireworks spewing from the damage the dogs' claws left wherever they struck and tore. The noises she heard were no longer just the SUV's roar; somewhere mixed in was the outrage of the guardian dogs as they protected their territory, tails lashing, giant heads tossing like dragons in the Chinese New Year celebrations. The rider lifted his bow and shot an arrow into the air. From the fletching trailed a net of brilliant oil-slick light, rippling over the dogs and falling harmlessly on their golden backs.

Chinatown's guardians didn't like the hunting, prowling creature any more than she did. But they had better weapons with which to fight it, and fight it they did, driving the beast backward slowly but steadily. The rider launched arrow after arrow, which passed through the *fu* dogs as if they were only smoke. Yet she could see the *fu* dogs' claws laying open cloth and flesh.

Here in Chinatown, something other than the fae held sway.

No wonder Thomas had always walked around its border, rather than through.

The car behind her honked, long and loud, and she flinched, meeting the irate gaze of the driver in her rearview mirror. The light had changed; the pedestrians were back on their curbs, safe and waiting, and though half of her needed to stay and watch the astonishing scene behind her, to *know* the SUV and its driver had been stopped for good, the wiser half knew this was the moment to flee, while the dogs kept the fae monster busy, before it realized other streets weren't guarded by such ferocious power.

Tess let out the clutch too fast, hopping the Jeep across the intersection, and sped away, the battle growing quieter behind her with each successive city block.

She kept going, barely pausing even at red lights, pushing her luck, expecting a police car on her ass every second. *I'm so sorry, officer, I know it was wrong to cross the bridge like that when it was opening for the biggest boat I've ever seen, but you see there are evil fairies after my boyfriend and me. Here, you can see them if you look through my magic rock...* She dodged left and right and left and right and always trending northwest, always looking in her rearview, missing parked cars by inches and scaring pedestrians back onto the sidewalk, headed for the only safety she knew, however dubious: Home.

⇒ Chapter Twenty-One ⇐

The breath that slammed into his lungs hurt worse than anything he had ever felt. Thomas put an arm across his eyes to shield them from the glaring daytime brilliance above, gasping and thrashing, not ashamed to weep. Apparently Hunter had gone, and with him the spell that turned Thomas to stone. He rolled onto his belly and coughed weakly.

"Not dead," he gasped.

But why not? Hunter wasn't known for his mercy or his self-restraint. Therefore he must still have a use for Thomas, or else he was not certain the Queen would excuse Thomas's death so easily.

That meant Thomas still had an edge somewhere. He just had to find it. The very thought of looking for it overwhelmed him, and he lay still on the chill earth of the mound, simply breathing, feeling his heart calming from its desperate panicked restart.

A noise downslope caught his attention and he turned his head, careful to move slowly and make no noise. It was Hunter's hound, the broken bogle, struggling to its feet and wailing pitifully, screeching like a wheel on an ungreased axle. Thomas could hear it calling for help but felt no compunction to assist it.

At least the thing hadn't been killed outright. He could take some cold comfort in that fact. He lay where he was until the bogle was out of sight and earshot.

Did he dare go to the Queen and try to learn more? Did he even care any longer? What if he simply turned his back on the whole mess and walked away?

He rolled onto his back again and stared up into the bare branches. Leaving wasn't a real possibility. The Queen would use the band to call him back, and he would go. She owned him body and will. Meanwhile, his need to protect Tess was rising again like a will-o'-the-wisp in a marsh, driving him to sit up, and then to get to his feet. Protecting Tess meant he needed information only the Queen could provide. He stared downhill in the direction of Tess's house, not visible through the trees and undergrowth and the choking, ubiquitous ivy.

He could end all this right now if he were to go back, gather up the Queen's things, and drag Tess into the mound to face the Queen's displeasure whether it was deserved or not. The temptation was strong, but his stomach churned with dread. The easy way out was not the right way out. He hated himself for his cowardly but very human thoughts.

I am not like them.

Thomas squared his shoulders, stretched out some of the sore places Hunter had left with his stony magic, and hiked along the ridge to find a troll and an entry into the mound. He might have earth and stone magic himself, but it wasn't sufficient to create an entrance into the hollow hill the way Hunter had. It would behoove him to remember Hunter wasn't simply a bad-tempered killer. He was an ageless thing of guile and power and motivation, likely second only to the Queen in ability and skill.

The troll, when Thomas found it, was unresponsive and immovable. Daylight turned them to massive stones, an admirable deterrent to any curious human who might suspect the large, moss-free boulders hid an opening into the hill. Thomas used what little magic he had to dig his way past the troll, who was wedged among the massive roots of an old-growth oak tree. He charmed a little earth back into the gap he had made, but left the soil loose in case he returned this way before nightfall.

Just beyond the troll, he found himself in a tunnel sloping steeply downward. The walls were lit with the usual meandering clusters of glowworms and the faint fae magic keeping the tunnel open and dry. Stones pressed into the clay soil walls sparkled occasionally. It was an entrance he had not used before, and he took the way slowly, pausing often to listen. The whole place vibrated with the excitement and magic of Allantide. The closer he got to the series of enormous caverns composing the fae's festival halls, the more he felt the eagerness that had always meant ferocious, unrelenting pleasure was in store.

Soon the tunnel was more crowded and more complicated, with side tunnels stretching away into the depths of the hill where the Unseelie kept their dwellings. Pixies flitted past with fierce, joyous cries, colliding with Thomas and the other fae, occasionally snatching glowworms from the walls and devouring them on the wing. This was their season, brightly garbed in the leafy forms of their home trees. The pixies were little more than self-aware pets for many of the fae, who tolerated them for their frolics and utility in carrying gossip in the mound.

At last the tunnel opened into one of the halls, where clusters of the Unseelie swirled and laughed. They waited excitedly for night, for the moon to reach its zenith. At that moment the trees above the mound would pull their earth-clogged roots aside, creating shafts for the cold light to blaze down into the interior. Thomas pressed himself against the wall behind a spindly, cobweb-laced column and waited to hear news of the Queen. The whispers bouncing through the cavern were confusing and scattered, deflected a thousand times by the jagged, glittering crystals that formed the ceiling and walls. At last he heard one that mentioned the Queen—not by name, for even here, speaking the Queen's truename could bring her awareness or wrath down upon the unwary—and her night's attire. A shallow topic that passed for importance in the minds of the mound fae. It was just one more reason Thomas chose to live outside the mound, where he could find more of interest and substance and humanity.

Yet part of Thomas longed to see the Queen garbed in her

fae glory, a gown made of webby silk and desire, flame both burning and quenched, a gown that concealed even as it revealed. He wanted to dance in the drugging spirals the fae would weave through their mound and sate himself without consequence wherever his fancy suited—drink, food, sex. But the rest of him wanted nothing more complicated than to walk into Tess's quiet house and dine on milk and new bread with her seated across from him at her little kitchen table.

I want to be human again. How the urge had grown so strong, he didn't know. Tess was part of it. Perhaps even most of it.

He listened again and heard that the Queen rested in her divan. The full moon on Allantide meant power beyond imagining, but also a great cost when she harnessed that power. If he wanted to learn her secret plan, he would need all the guile at his command. He closed his eyes and forced away the trow-form, making himself appear as the human who had drawn the Queen's eyes so many decades ago. Perhaps there was still human charm in him despite how long he had spent among the Unseelie, taking on their manners and morals. Perhaps she would find him innocently pleasing and relax her guard.

He removed the bulky oilskin and carried it over his arm, walking through the halls until he reached the doors of her chamber. There, two kelpies smirked and dripped, baring their horsey teeth at him in what passed for a leering grin.

"Is she within?" Thomas queried, staying well back.

"Aye." The left-hand kelpie was the one whose finger he had severed on his last visit here; no hope of help from that one.

"Please announce me."

"She's not alone." The kelpie's leer grew broad. "She's with her new one. Younger than you. Younger than you *were*, even."

Thomas felt a shaft of white-hot fury blast through his body, but it was a momentary jealousy, a jealousy of old habit, a pale thing compared to the emotion that had once led him to slaughter a rival. It was quickly followed by a sense of relief that someone else was servicing the Queen, satisfying her appetites. Someone else she was draining of strength to increase her own.

"Announce me or stand aside."

"I will do neither."

Thomas looked at the kelpie on the right, the one laughing at his predicament. "Do you want to lose a finger, as well?" He gestured to the kelpie on the left. "You can see I mean what I say."

The right hand kelpie looked to its companion, then lowered its eyes. "She'll kill me. You know she will."

"Why should I have mercy on such as you, when your kind does damage to mine?"

"Trow? We do no damage to trow kin. You all taste like mud and cross-eyed badgers."

Thomas slipped his little iron-edged knife into his hand and flashed it carelessly. "I am no trow, and well you know it. I am what she made me. But I was—*am*—human, beneath."

The right-hand kelpie flashed him a wicked glint and pushed the latch. The door opened slowly. Through the gap Thomas saw the violet glimmer that was the Queen's magic, blurred and soft as the light at sunset.

The sort of light that shone when she was well-pleased with—or by—her lover.

Thomas gritted his teeth and flashed the blade again. "Announce me."

"No."

"You've already opened the door. If she meant to kill you, she'd have done it by now. Look at that light; she's quiet for the moment."

"She has been well fucked." The left-hand kelpie slid close and looked Thomas up and down, gaze lingering at his crotch. "We never saw that sort of light when you were the one doing the service to the Queen. Did you never please her? Pity. It might have been you in there still, instead of the new one."

"Be it on your own foul heads then," Thomas said. He pushed open the door.

On the thistledown couch, screened by gauzy draperies, the Queen sat up as Thomas entered the room. Beside her lay a young man, apparently sleeping, in a coil of the Queen's snaky form. With a start, Thomas recognized the boy Tess had followed into Underbridge the night Thomas first met her.

He could see the Queen's slow smile even through the draperies and resisted the urge to swallow. He remembered that smile; remembered the violent pleasures it betokened. Unknowable hours spent in sensual excess, driven to take the Queen, and be taken in his turn, until he was nothing but a husk of flesh and bone and exhaustion. By then the Queen would be achingly desirable, plump and beautiful with everything she had drained from him. The strange sleep afterward, broken by even stranger awakenings. Being fed like a babe on hot milk from the breasts of banshees and troll women until he recovered enough to do it all again, age upon age. He had given everything to the Queen simply because she asked it and he could not resist.

"Thomas. How lovely. Come, my knight, join us here." The Queen made a moue of her lips. The draperies blew aside, shredded into mist and fog, and the sweetness of her breath reached him from the distant bed, honey and almonds and bread...

...*and fungus and grubs and rot*, he reminded himself firmly. He remembered how appalled he had been, so many years ago, to discover himself greedily devouring a plate of slow-writhing pupae, their bug fat on his chin like melted butter. And yet he could not have stopped himself, so ravenous was he after his beautiful paramour had ridden him nigh unto oblivion.

Even now he could feel his body responding, the same irresistible scorching mixture of reluctant arousal and loathing he had always felt. He grew hard inside his trousers, and she saw it. She beckoned with a smile.

"Come and meet Aaron," she whispered, rising, the snaky coil vanishing as she became the beauty he preferred to remember. "He sleeps, but when I wake him, oh, Thomas, what pleasures we three will share."

Thomas cleared his throat and looked at his feet. It was easier, better, not to look at the bed, not to remember what it was like to bury himself in her, not to dwell on what unimaginably erotic atrocities she could orchestrate with three instead of two. "I have news, my Lady."

It was the right tack to take. The languor instantly left her limbs. She became the ruler who had brought her people from Britain to the New World, built a haven for them, and protected them from detection by the humans in an ever-growing metropolis. "Have you the thief at last? Have you killed him?"

"Very nearly." It was the truth, after all. Because of him, Tess had nearly died at the hands of the market mob in Underbridge and afterward with Hunter. "If it had not been for the interference of another, the thief would be dead." True, also. Dissimulation: the fae art of lying with the bald truth. He was not as skilled as he should be, to manage the Queen in this manner, but it was the only weapon remaining in his arsenal.

"Give me the name of the Other." She came forward from the bed. On it, Aaron lay like a dead thing, and the Queen's purple glow took on spiky black fringes of ire.

"I do not have his truename," Thomas confessed. "But I know him as Hunter."

Instead of the violent hissing rage he expected, the Queen gave him a heavy-lashed smile, sweet and cloying. "Ah." She walked to a cabinet and took down two goblets, filling each with what smelled like clover wine, sharp and reviving. Thomas's bruised body cried out for it, but he was cautious when she put the goblet into his hand herself.

"My Lady, why did you set another to the task you gave me?"

"Jealous, my Thomas?" She drank deep, the diamond wine glittering in the cleft of her lower lip. "Think. You are no longer wholly mine. You have not been for many years. Lately, I hear new things of you, how you stop the kelpies from hunting for their meat."

His heart thumped painfully. She could only be talking about Tess, but did she know the extent of his feelings for a human woman? He searched her shifting expressions for a trace of cupidity, of deception. "Confused, but not jealous. If I am to protect the market and do your bidding, why shouldn't I stop the kelpies from shitting in our nest? Why do you need another for my task? Have I not served you well enough?"

"Hunter also serves me."

"You did not believe I could do the job." He feigned deep

distress.

"The time is limited. My two best soldiers at the task? I knew it would be accomplished."

"What is the timeframe, then? Why not tell me when you gave me the task? Why set obstacles in my path?" He strode to a spindly table made of stilt-bird legs and a slab of rock-hard bracket fungus studded with crystal. He set down the goblet. The wine called to him, but he needed clarity more than he wanted its sweet oblivion.

The Queen shook her head, smiling at his naiveté. "The time is upon us. The time is now. Can you have lived among us for so long and still have no true understanding of what Hallows Eve means? An Allantide with the moon at her fullest?" She cocked her head, eyes slitting. "No. You know exactly. What do you hope to gain here?"

Thomas gestured to the bed, hoping to throw her off. "Is that why you've taken new lovers of late? Gathering strength for this night?" He put on a hurt pouty look, a trick that had fooled her—or at least swayed her—in the past. "Was I not enough, my Lady? Not enough in your bed, and now not enough in your market, though I wear your band in dedicated service—"

Her laughter was like bells, sweet, chiming, with an undertone of goaty chuckle. "How you men like to believe you and your maleness are all any female should ever need. Thomas, my beautiful Thomas, come to bed now. Take me. Fill me. Give me your strength, for if I am strong enough, it will not *matter* if the thief is taken in time or not. The market will be safe at last, completely ours, at last."

And there it was, laid out for him as bluntly as she would ever reveal. She meant to own Underbridge, not merely allow the fae to squat there as long as no humans interfered. The trinkets must have been some sort of markers, like the anchor points of leys, for what was to come. She was not working through the channels she had used to obtain Forest Park, bewitching the humans. No, she meant to displace them altogether, force them out, and take the place for the fae.

Now Tess had the things, foiling all or part of the Queen's plan.

Thomas shuddered to think what the Queen would do to Tess if he could not protect her. His Queen was dangerously close to finding her.

Thomas gestured to the young man in the bed. "Send that one back to the humans." It was the least he could do for Tess, help her in her cause. "Send him away and I will..." It took an enormous effort to push the image of Tess to the back of his mind. "I will do as you ask. But until then, my Lady...I must decline."

The Queen shook her head in mock sadness. "That one I must have, Thomas, for a little while longer, if not longer than that! Ask something else, and perhaps I will grant it because of the progress you have made, and because you have shown more cleverness and determination than I credited you with."

"Remove this band. Release me from your service."

Now she laughed outright. "One strand. No—two. Little enough."

He heard the thin plinks as two strands on the woven band broke. Crumbs of bone brushed his skin inside his sleeve as they fell. His heart leapt. "I would ask another boon of you." Now was the time to bargain to keep Hunter away.

Her eyes slitted once more. Thomas saw the catlike shift of them. He was pushing his luck.

"And in return? Ask more of me if you wish, but know the payment for the debt." Her eyes turned toward the bed before they returned to rest upon him. "Join me in celebrating Allantide, now in my bed, and later in the mound while we weave the Unseelie magic and grow our land. Return to me, my Thomas. Give up your chilly iron trow-hold in the bridge."

So easy. Bed the Queen, and give up his life once more.

So easy, and so tempting. After all, he'd done it before. He knew what he was getting into.

But he thought about Tess at home, all unknowing, with a clutch of fae eggs on her shelves. He thought about how she treated him, even after she understood his true nature. Tess was the hard choice, but Tess was the right choice. She was the way back to humanity.

He looked away from the Queen. "You set me a task. I'll complete it." *Just not in the way you meant.* "I thank you for the two strands."

She came close, goblet still in hand. "Drink with me before you go." Her nostrils flared delicately. "Where have you been? You smell...delicious and strangely familiar. Not of my Thomas...but of my...of my..." She pursed her lips, pondering.

Though Thomas had bathed at Tess's house, he was still wearing the clothes he'd slept in. He had been so close to Tess for hours as they slept, the Queen would be certain to smell her on him.

The Queen leaned forward and licked the front of his shirt, just above his heart, a long, deliberating stroke. Her tongue pulled back into her mouth, tasting, savoring.

Knowing something. Remembering. Thomas could tell from her expression. Tasting Tess.

"Ah," was all she said, but her smile told him everything he needed to know.

Thomas obeyed her command to drink, lifting his goblet from the table and taking a mouthful. The wine was hot in his mouth, scorching his tongue. He set down the goblet, swung his oilskin around him like a cloak, and walked toward the door without another word, without a kiss goodbye, without looking at the Queen. Behind him he could hear her laughing softly as she moved to draw aside the misty curtains around the bed.

"Wake, my strong one," she said to Aaron. "Your lover hungers for you yet again."

The kelpies sniggered nastily as Thomas shoved the door closed. "Threw you out, did she? She has tastier meat than yours in there."

Thomas spat the mouthful of clover wine at the mocking kelpie and was not surprised to see it burning where it touched. The kelpie cringed and shrieked like the bully it was, whimpering and pawing at the wine running down its river-wet flesh.

Thomas rushed to where an underground stream trickled down the stony walls of the cavern and pooled smooth as a mirror on the floor. He threw himself on the floor next to the pool, pushing his face into the water and sucking it into his mouth like a fish. He spat the water on the floor and rinsed his mouth again, and again, and again.

She meant to poison me. I discovered her plan, and she meant to kill me for it. I know her plan now, but she knows about Tess.

The knowledge both terrified and freed him. He no longer owed the Queen anything, not love, not adoration, not his body or his honor, nor protection.

Nothing, except the debt she commanded with the band on his arm.

Chapter Twenty-Two

A half-mile from her duplex, a wave of paranoia washed over Tess.

What if she hadn't lost them—what if the SUV had fought free of the Chinatown *fu* dogs? What if one of the other black vehicles had made it across the river and was now tracking her through the maze of northwest Portland? They could be behind her even now, glamoured to look like something they weren't. Her heart, which had slowed its panicked thumping, now took on a heavier, slower rhythm of dread. She felt stupidly glad she hadn't gone to her office where she might have endangered everyone inside.

"Thomas lives in that bridge for a reason," she told herself out loud, as if voicing an affirmation would make it true. "I'm safe."

Still, she paused the Jeep at the side of the street in a no-parking zone next to a corner fire hydrant. She got out of the vehicle, leaving the engine running, and took out the seeing stone. First she stared through it up and down the street, then down the cross streets, examining vehicles that passed, cringing inside at the curious glances she earned from passing drivers. Next she scanned the drifts of dead leaves mounded at the curbside and on neighborhood lawns. None of the leaves glimmered with fae magic, nor did they show any tendency to organize into circles or whirling tornadoes. Aside from a gentle breeze lifting a leaf here or there, they didn't move.

Finally, she turned her attention to the Jeep itself, looking at it from every angle, even stepping up on the rear bumper to get a good look at the top of the convertible through the stone, and crouching low to peer beneath the Jeep. She saw no traces of glamour, except when she looked through the passenger window at the grocery tote in the seat.

Nothing. She was safe.

Unless they could follow the queen's trinkets like homing beacons, which seemed all too likely. The tote glowed like a malevolent sample of reactor fuel, gleaming dully but sickly through the cheap cloth. She didn't dare throw the things away. If she was right about them, she'd need every single one, though she couldn't imagine how she'd ever find all the queen's victims. If they were even still alive.

Tess wondered what it would take to convince the fairy queen to restore what she had taken. She visualized herself waltzing into the gorgeous throne room of a Disney castle, demanding to see the queen, who would be coldly beautiful and dressed all in spun silken cobwebs in iridescent hues and holding a star-tipped wand. Given how nervous Thomas seemed about his queen, she was probably very strong, magically speaking.

She'd never listen to a mere mortal who wanted her to undo her dirty work.

Tess realized she was standing in the middle of the street, pondering things that would get her hospitalized, if anyone could see into her brain. Not to mention she was in plain view of any passing fae, and as she'd seen, they were everywhere in Portland. Maybe not right here, not at this instant, but despite the assurances of the seeing stone, she had no doubt that if they wanted to be on this quiet residential street, they could, and she'd never notice them.

She climbed back into the loyal, trusty Jeep, buckled her seatbelt, and started again for home. More dodging and twisting and doubling back, and at last she rolled into her driveway, wishing she had a garage in which to hide the Jeep and its distinctive coloration. The fae knew about her now, knew about the Jeep, too, if last night's chase and this afternoon's were any indication.

It was probably only a matter of time before they knew about her house, but she hoped to stave off that knowledge as long as possible. She scrambled out of the Jeep, gathered her shoulder bag and reluctantly took the grocery tote in hand, glaring at the fallen leaves in the yard as she hurried to the house. Inside, she took the tote into the kitchen and set it in a corner behind the trash can so she wouldn't accidentally see it and remind herself of the day's frights.

Tess decided it would be best to hide the Jeep, so she ran upstairs to the linen closet and found an old quilt. Outside on the driveway, she gave the quilt a shake and lofted it over the top of the Jeep. As it settled, she thought she heard tiny, thin laughter—the sort of laughter an evil fairy leaf might make—all around her, but when she stopped to listen, she heard nothing but a faint breeze blowing.

"Stop making yourself crazy," she fussed, circling the Jeep and tugging the quilt into place. It didn't quite cover the entire car, but it was better than nothing. She looked up into the sky as if fae helicopters would be circling there, marking her home on their fae radar systems. The seeing stone shifted on its cord, rough and chilly against her skin. The reminder jolted her from her dithering panic, and sent her scrambling for the house yet again. Inside, she locked the door, close to sobbing with fright, exhaustion, and the sheer insanity of her own thoughts. She leaned against the door breathing slow and deep until she felt steadier.

But steadiness was an illusion. Only two things seemed real now: the strange certainty she felt about Thomas, and the sick way her stomach twisted whenever she thought about him out there alone, facing down the things that chased them both. She moved backward until she could sit on the stairs and stare out the narrow windows on either side of the front door, and tried not to imagine seeing unearthly things through the dimpled glass.

There was nothing left to do now except wait and hope for Thomas to return. She wondered with uneasy dread what she would do as dusk settled over the city, when the trick-or-treaters came for their ill-gotten swag. Trick-or-treat? Child or kelpie?

⇒ Chapter Twenty-Three ⇐

As Thomas stumbled up the walk to Tess's porch, dim with the early dusk of an autumn evening, the front door flew open wide and a tide of light, yellow as sunshine but infinitely more welcome, spilled out. Tess flew out with it, his name on her lips in glad cries. He hardly had time to set his feet enough to brace against the impact of her body—soft, warm, clinging—before her arms wrapped around his neck and pulled his head down.

"You're safe!" Tess spoke directly into his ear, her whisper hoarse and broken. She pressed feverish kisses to his cheek and jaw, mumbling things he couldn't understand though he got the gist. She'd been frightened for him and had waited and watched. Through his exhaustion and hopelessness, joy crested like a storm surge and he wrapped his arms around her, closing his eyes to savor her nearness and feel the silk of her skin beneath his lips.

Her cheeks were wet, and there was no rain. He licked his lips.

Salt. Tears.

The fae in him threatened to rage forth at the delicious bitter taste of tears shed for him, but then her wandering mouth touched the corner of his and paused there for long seconds, her breath warm and quick and excited and a little fearful, all at the same time. It was her fear that calmed the beast, and though the Unseelie savagery urged him to hurt her more, make her cry, *take her salt and blood and fear*, it was the human in him that won. When she turned her face the bare inch that would bring their lips together, he met her there, and the flood of sensation quickly swamped the fae craving. Lips on lips, the quick rush of breath, the warmth of her as he caught her up against him, one arm lying along her spine to cradle her head, the other much lower to cup her hips and take her weight and balance. His body responded unmistakably.

It was a homecoming, such a welcome as he had not felt for decades, perhaps not since he had been made fae. He couldn't think beyond the way she clung to him, the way her mouth was still whispering his name, the eager yielding of her lips when his tongue slipped out to taste her and then to plunder. He was exhausted, yes, and scraped and bruised and bleeding from the encounter with Hunter, but here was a fresh source of energy— the raw desire that burned in his heart and groin like the coals in Sharpwit's braziers. He tore his mouth from hers to whisper hoarsely in her ear.

"Oh, Tess. Tess." He breathed her truename with all the longing and desperation of his half-human soul, because only her truename could convey the hugeness of what he felt. The swelling of magic within him, around him, was like nothing he had ever known before. Even though Tess had given him her name the first time they met along the riverfront near Underbridge, he had never spoken it aloud. Her truename, coupled with his emotions and her utter trust of him, felt as if it were an expanding star she placed directly in his heart. Thomas cupped her face in his hands to look down at her, falling into the deep pools of her eyes.

"*Tess.*" With that magical third repetition, whatever unspoken bargain they had made with each other was sealed. He felt it inside himself, a thing both closing and opening, fluttering and stilled, starving but sated.

On the porch the cornstalks rustled just as he sought her mouth to plunder it again. Thomas's head came up.

Treachery, his long years with the fae whispered, reminding him that spies could be anywhere, or everywhere and nowhere at the same time. He stared hard into the darkness at the edge of the yellow light from Tess's house, but the stalks were motionless, and it might have been a breeze.

Might.

"We should go inside," he urged her, looking down into her sweetly dazed face with its wide-apart eyes dark with evening, and the slowly burgeoning smile on her well-kissed mouth.

"By all means. Mustn't shock the trick-or-treaters." She took his hand and led him toward the bright hallway, and Thomas hung back only enough to summon his will to make the porch seem toothily fearsome to the children who might otherwise flood the door.

The cornstalks shuddered in his wake, and the candle in the pumpkin snuffed itself with a stink of waxy smoke and scorched vegetable.

Inside, he closed and locked the door and turned off the porch light, and then the hall light, missing its warmth immediately. In the gloom, Tess pointed at the bowl of candies she had standing by. "The neighborhood children will—"

"Not tonight," he said, moving close. He brought her hands beneath his oilskin and pulled them behind his back. "Grant me one thing on this night. Let the knocking go unanswered." Because it might not be a human child at the door. He remembered Hunter's oath to hunt him down if he were outside the mound and wondered if Tess's house, so close to Forest Park, would be shelter enough. Thomas's very presence had brought danger to her house, and to her, but with the Queen's trinkets here, there was no telling what would happen. He would have to remain alert and on guard. Allantide was not the time to move them.

She looked at him for a long moment, gazing steadily into his eyes. She pulled away slowly, her hands warm even through his shirt. As her hands left his torso, they ran over his arms, and at last linked with his own, palm-to-palm, fingers interlacing with his and curving over the backs of his hands. Something about her stillness calmed him.

"Will it…will you…I mean…" Tess cleared her throat. "Yes, let the door go unanswered tonight." She turned, keeping hold of one of his hands, and led him up the stairs to her room. Thomas followed, his heart pounding with joy and anticipation.

It was no trivial matter, undressing in front of Tess, regardless of how eager he felt. The oilskin went first, draped slowly over a chair at the side of the room. Then Tess turned to his wooly sweater, which stretched so usefully when he was shifting between human and trow. When the sweater came off over his head, she gave a gasp. Hunter's new bruises had to be explained in carefully casual language. The cuts and scrapes necessitated a trip to the bathroom where she daubed at them with cotton balls dipped in something that stung at first and then was magically soothing.

But the worst was yet to come, as he had known it would be. Eventually she worked around to his left arm, where she saw the Queen's armband beneath his bicep, with its curled-back strands of gold and splintery gray-white bone.

Her hand hovered above it as if she was afraid to touch it.

"Thomas?"

"It's nothing."

"It's on too tight."

The Queen meant for it never to come off until all his debts were paid. "I know."

"What happens when you...when you change? You're so much bigger, all over..." She seemed to take in the reality of that for a moment, swallowing hard. "Doesn't the armband hurt you then?"

"It hurts all the time. Just more sometimes than others. Really, it's nothing."

"It's not nothing." She probed at it, gently, where the muscles of his arm bulged around it. "Don't you want to take it off?" She got a thoughtful look on her face, and Thomas felt a nervous flutter in his belly. He was beginning to know that look of determined analysis. It would be followed by a stubborn pronouncement or a willful action, like the night before when she raced for the Jeep with Hunter's bogles on the prowl.

"No, I don't."

Her brown eyes searched his. "You're lying. Wait right here. I'm going to see if the guys next door have a bolt cutter. Maybe if I can work one of the blades beneath the band, I could—"

"Stop." He caught her before she could leave the bathroom. "Do you think I didn't try that years ago when it first began to ache? Besides, it's enchanted. Bolt cutters won't work on it."

"If they're steel, maybe the iron would—"

"It's all right," he repeated. He took her face between his hands and distracted her with a slow, tender kiss. Maybe there was a little unintended magic in the kiss, but more likely she could simply sense how much he wanted to be with her, because when he lifted his head, all she said was, "I only want to help you."

Me, and every stray that crosses your path. "I know."

He kissed her again, and when she slid her arms around his neck and leaned in, he lifted her and carried her to where the bed waited. He set her on her feet beside it, seriousness overtaking him. She laid a hand on his chest, over his heart. He felt like it might burst from his chest, but when he saw her pulse leaping in her throat, knew she was as uncertain but eager as he. He undid the top button on her shirt, then stopped, meeting her gaze. Tess smiled softly and simply stood, waiting, and he undid the rest.

Beneath her shirt she was pale and naked. His hand trembled as he brushed his fingertips over the crest of her breast and watched its unmistakable reaction to his touch. She watched his fingers as they trailed downward over her stomach to the waistband of her jeans, where he fumbled for a moment with the button and zipper. She returned the favor.

In only a few seconds more, there was nothing left between them, and when skin came to skin all along their lengths, he shuddered and threw back his head with a hiss to hold in the trow. They tumbled to her mattress in a tangle of warm limbs and searching mouths.

Tess's bed was no thistledown couch, for which he was glad beyond reason. The bedding all smelled of her, soapy and clean and musky. Each moment was filled with skin and lips, tastes and welcoming arms and legs. There came that supreme sensation of joining with Tess, an exquisitely slow push accompanied by her indrawn breath and passionate arch. He looked down at her, meeting her brown eyes. Her soft gasping "Ahh!" was every word he could have wanted to hear.

"Thank you," Thomas said.

She traced trembling fingertips over the bridge of his nose and around the edges of his lips. When she shifted positions beneath him, her legs moving to wrap around his hips and seat his body deeper into hers, he was lost in gladness. She met his thrusts with a lift of her chin, as if savoring each stroke.

She never once looked away or closed her eyes, not even when he felt her body tighten and shudder with pleasure.

And when he found his human form too hard to hold, blurring at the edges, she smiled a small, concerned smile and whispered, "It's all right, I've got you."

Thomas let go, safe in her hands.

A little while later, when she found his tail with her drowsy, wandering fingers, she let out a gasp followed by a squeaky laugh that was half delight, half startled surprise, and all charm.

⇒ Chapter Twenty-Four ⇐

Tess woke in confusion, cuddled deep in her bed and wrapped in Thomas's arms. His odor was all around her, warm and comforting as coming home to the smell of beef stew cooking in the kitchen. But there was another odor as well, enticingly floral. For a moment she thought foolishly, *This must be what sex with the fae smells like. Beef stew and lilacs.* She lay still, listening to Thomas breathe and feeling his chest rise and fall against her back.

A slim bar of moonlight lay across the floor, silvering the carpet. It led her eyes to the window where the nearly closed curtains shut out the view of the Forest Park hillside behind the duplex. She remembered it was a full moon, and on Halloween, no less. If she'd been even a few years younger, she'd have been out in all that glorious wild light, flitting up and down the streets with the trick-or-treaters, watching dry leaves scoot before the wind, delighting in the slight prickle of dangerous excitement. Looking for ghosts and goblins.

Instead, she was snug in her bed, filled with a delicious lassitude that came from making love with Thomas. She thought about how wonderful a cup of hot chocolate would taste at the moment.

Now that she was more or less awake, as always she began to overanalyze the situation. Perhaps she'd been stupid to go to bed with Thomas. Certainly it was the most unique sex she'd ever had, watching as Thomas's form melted back and forth between human and trow. But the pleasure had been unmistakable for both of them, piercingly sweet and completely new.

She turned her head toward the clock on the nightstand and found that it was still quite early, only half past ten in the evening. The post-coital drowse had done her good. She was surprised they hadn't been kept awake by the ringing doorbell, but perhaps the neighborhood children obeyed the guidelines about not trick-or-treating at houses where dark porches did not welcome them.

Still...it seemed odd that not even one obstreperous teen had tried.

Or maybe Thomas had done something, put up some sort of block to keep the beggars at bay. Tess thought about asking him, but he was sleeping so deeply she couldn't bear to waken him. He needed the rest. The bruises on his body spoke of the violence of the past two days, and she frowned. It made her uncomfortable to know he had gotten at least some of those bruises because of her.

Hell! All of this made her uncomfortable. Fairies in Portland. Magical sights only visible through a hole in a rock. A house in the pier of the Burnside Bridge. Goblins selling goblin fast-food under that same bridge. Monsters who wanted to have sex with her and then eat her liver underwater. Actual sex with a trow who smelled like the best steak dinner ever. She suppressed a snort, not wanting to wake Thomas. Uncomfortable or not, she was having feelings with a capital F for him—protective, attracted, and somehow responsible for his well-being and happiness.

It was almost like being in love.

This time, she did snort at herself. It had to be the endorphins making her so maudlin and foolish. Thomas reacted by turning from his side onto his back and flinging his muscular arm, circled by the ragged golden band, over his head. This left her free to creep out of the bed, so she lifted the blanket and slipped from beneath it, watching to see if Thomas awakened.

He slept on peacefully. She gathered a warm robe from the floor at the foot of the bed where it had slithered as the two of them made love. Belting it around her, she padded down the stairs, headed for the kitchen and a glass of water.

The floral fragrance seemed more intense in the stairwell. Tess paused for a moment, wondering where it was coming from. It didn't smell like any of her soaps or lotions, and she didn't use air freshener in the house. She hadn't lit any scented candles, so what was it? Anything seemed possible with a magical creature in the house.

Anything *was* possible, she realized, as her hand brushed over the light switch into the kitchen, and she saw the source of the fragrance.

Her kitchen floor was no longer there. The black and white vinyl tile was gone, and in its place was a garden filled with flowers.

Bluebells, to be exact.

Hundreds of them, perhaps thousands.

Their drooping heads nodded as she turned on the light, almost as if they were hiding sensitive eyes. The perfume of them filled the room. As she watched, more and more blossoms opened, delicate wands of bells emerging from green sheaths, as if photographed in slow motion and then sped up into real time.

The beauty was breathtaking. A smile of delighted surprise parted her lips. She bent and plucked a nodding stem of blossom and held it to her nose. The fragrance of that single stem was faint, but in such concentration, even faint perfume became overwhelming.

If this was what having a fae in her house wrought, she thought she could live with it. Still smiling, Tess picked her way through the bluebells to the sink, where she filled a glass with water. Green ivy seemed to have followed the bluebells in from Forest Park, for hairy-footed tendrils were groping their green, leafy way along the edges of the cabinets and twining attractively through the ladder backs of the kitchen chairs. Spring had come to her kitchen.

She turned as she gulped down half the glass, intending to return to the bedroom and waken Thomas, to thank him for this magical beauty with a kiss. Did he dream the bluebells into existence? Had he worked a spell as she slept?

With a smile, she paused to fill a glass with milk for Thomas. She walked back to the hallway, careful not to step on any of the blooms, but hardly able to avoid the clusters of arching green stems and leaves. The blossom heads seemed to turn to watch her progress through the room.

At her feet, the bluebells were colonizing the carpet of the hallway, heading for the living room and the front of the house. Soon the entire ground floor would be a forest glade! As she stood for a moment, watching, a tendril of ivy crept up the doorjamb and reached out for the curtain rod of the window next to the front door. The doorjamb itself took on a woody look, the silver and white roughness of birch or aspen. A dark spot on— Tess could only think of it as bark—what used to be paint swelled gently, and a bud with delicate baby leaves worked its way out of the wood, for all the world like a questing fingertip testing the air. Tess drew a slow, amazed breath and went up the stairs, looking back at the miracle with each step. The susurrus of spring growth, thousands of leaves and blossoms unfurling, followed her up the stairs.

In her room again, she put a knee on the bed and set her water glass on the nightstand. The clink of glass on wood woke Thomas instantly, and in his blocky trow face, his beautiful murky blue eyes flicked open. Tess spoke softly, reaching for the lamp.

"It's just me. I brought you some milk."

Thomas sat up, the blankets falling to his waist. In the warm bedside light she watched him glamour himself, pulling a fully human appearance out of the ether to mask his trow features. She waited until he seemed to be settled, then offered him the glass.

"I love what you've done downstairs," she told him, sitting on the side of the bed and watching while he drained the milk in just a gulp or two. "It's amazing. I've never seen anything so beautiful in my life."

He blinked, looking at her in confusion. "What are you talking about? What's downstairs?"

"The flowers! Can't you smell them? The fragrance is what woke me, and when I went downstairs to get a glass of water, I found them. They're incredible. Thank you." She leaned forward and kissed his bemused mouth softly, feeling a little shy. "How do you work the magic? Does it happen while you dream? Will they still be there, now that you're awake?"

"You're not making sense, Te—" She heard him stop himself from saying her name, and felt a little bereft. He'd only said it for the first time last night as she met him on the front walk. She hungered to hear it again. He reached past her to put the empty glass on the table, and took up her water glass, draining it as well. "What magic? I have very little."

"Come and look." She stood, holding out her hand. The

robe gaped open a little, and Thomas's gaze went to where the silky lapels revealed the swell of her breast.

"It's warm here," he countered, lifting the blanket invitingly. "You come here instead."

"Can't you smell them? They're incredible, and they've filled the kitchen! You have to explain how you do this. Come on!" She waggled her hand at him, and watched his expression change as he saw she was serious. He took a deep breath of the air, then his gaze flicked to hers, their drowsy expression changing. He flung back the quilt and leapt from the bed, heading for the stairs and taking them in only a few strides. Tess, surprised, followed him more slowly, distracted by the view his naked, muscular body provided.

He stood in the center of the kitchen, turning slowly, bluebells all around him.

"Look how beautiful—" Tess began, but Thomas interrupted.

"I didn't do this. This isn't the sort of magic trows have. They—I—can work with stone and earth, it's why I was able to build my home in the bridge pier, those things speak with me. But this is not my work. This is something deeper, something stronger." His gaze lifted to hers as he paused in his rotation. There was a long moment as he appeared to be lost in thought. An ivy tendril stroked tentatively at his ankle, then more firmly, and began to climb his naked calf. Thomas looked down at it, an expression of horror in his eyes. "Oh, fuck, no." He sprinted from the kitchen into the next room, where he stood in front of the curio cabinet.

Thomas yanked open the glass door, even though Tess knew he must see the cabinet was mostly empty. "Where are they? Where are her things?"

Tess pointed. "In the kitchen, in a bag. I should have told you earlier, I have this idea that your Queen has somehow magicked my clients'...er, essence...maybe their souls...something...into her little things. Drained them, and made her things into...I don't know, batteries? Something like that? She stored them away. Because last week when I went to Ridge Manor, Rory—"

"Who is Rory?" Thomas interrupted. "Be quick. And show me where you put the things."

Tess led him into the kitchen and pointed at the grocery tote, which was slumped in the corner where she had put it when she got home from the failure at Aaron's house. Or, rather, what had been the grocery tote. The black cloth was now a stunning mound of emerald moss, with ghostly mushrooms decorating it like fancy drink umbrellas. Tess groped at her breast, but the seeing stone was on her bedside table along with her wristwatch and the other small things she and Thomas had removed as they undressed. "I think they're in there, under all that moss."

Thomas strode to the bag and opened it slowly, peering

inside.

A flurry of autumn leaves burst out, six or seven of the things flapping around the kitchen like trapped birds. She supposed they had gotten in the tote when the leaves attacked her at the Eisley house, and she'd brought them home with her in the car. She shuddered. There was something very, very wrong about self-directed dead leaves. These smacked against walls, cupboards and appliances with noises that sounded like tiny screams.

Cursing, Thomas went after them, catching two and gripping them tightly. "Catch them! Don't let them escape! If they get out, we're done for."

"What?" she exclaimed, confused. Thomas dashed about the kitchen like a madman, naked as a forest god and equally well-endowed, chasing fluttering leaves. For an insane moment she wondered if Thomas would string them like fig leaves over his manly parts, but his next words jerked her back to what passed for reality in her life at the moment.

"They're pixies, and if they get out of the house, the first thing they'll do is fly back to whoever sent them and tattle like the wretched little gossips they are. Catch them, don't let them get away!"

Tess snatched up a kitchen towel and started after the nearest leaves, but they were quick.

They were vicious, too. She swatted one out of the air with the towel, but when she grabbed the leaf, the thing twisted in her hand and sank tiny, razor-sharp teeth into the fleshy pad of her thumb, drawing blood. Tess shrieked in pain, the pixie shrieked back, its thin, sharp noise splitting her skull, and Thomas leapt across the kitchen to jerk the creature out of her hand and pinch its head between his fingertips.

With a small but sickening pop, the pixie stopped screaming, and Thomas dropped it in the sink, where it lay still.

"You...killed it?"

"Te—just...help me catch them. How many were there?"

"I don't know!" She tried to obey him, but her stomach was turning flips. It didn't seem right, catching the little things only to kill them.

"Then where did they come from, if you don't know how many there are?"

"I..." She lunged for one that had rocketed into the hallway, circled the light like a witless moth, and zoomed back into the kitchen. "I went out today, and there was a—a swarm of them, someplace I was. I thought they were just leaves, maybe under a spell because of the way they behaved. I didn't know they were fairies! I guess a few of them got into the bag. But why did they wait until now to come out?"

Thomas's face was dark. He had seven of the pixies in his hand, and one by one he held them over the sink and twisted their stem-thin necks. Their tiny shrill screaming diminished one dead leaf at a time until the sink was littered with crimson and flame yellow and orange and brown, and streaky fluids that might be blood or stains from old leaves. She turned away, sickened.

Thomas spoke and she peered at him carefully, avoiding the sink. "We'll never know if we got them all. One or more of them might have got out of the bag before now. They might be hiding, or they may already have gone back to the mound."

"But why did you have to kill them?"

Thomas shook his head as he washed the remains of the pixies off his hands. "Because if I didn't, they'd betray us. They may already have done so."

"But—"

"This is Allantide. Halloween. Do you know what that means?"

She folded her arms, feeling her face stiffen. "Obviously not. So why don't you tell me."

"We'll talk while we get ready. Come on, back upstairs."

"Get ready for what?"

"What will surely come. This is just the first stage, and unless I'm wrong, we won't want to be here much longer." He went back to the mossy heap and fished until he found the tote bag handles, which looked like roots, thick and brown and sturdy. He lifted the bag, holding it open and studying the contents. "You took these out of the house today, didn't you?"

"I...yes. I had an idea they might help Aaron. One of them helped Rory."

Thomas knotted the handles together tightly. "You need to explain about this Rory person, but for now, get up the stairs. We've got to get ready."

"Thomas, *what* will surely come?"

Thomas paused, looking at her with his beautiful eyes, and she saw the blurring at his edges that signaled the advent of his trow-form. He took a long, slow inhale and the blurring stopped, leaving him a very naked human male. A sweep of his hand indicated the bluebells, now much trampled. "This is my Queen's work. And at last I know why she was hiding her trinkets in the Underbridge. She's growing the mound. But you've thwarted her. All these months, you've been finding her things and bringing them home with you, keeping her from marking out new space for the fairy mound to grow. No wonder she wanted them found, and you stopped. And tonight of all nights, she's begun the process of turning a part of human Portland into fairy earth. She would have used the trinkets to mark where the mound should grow—she'd have filled the Underbridge, taken control of the goblin market and maybe even the Burnside Bridge, and managed to cross the river that way, perhaps. But instead, they're here. And when she finds out..."

Tess tried very hard to make sense of Thomas's words. "But they're not all here," she objected. "I have two or three at my office, east of the river. What's happening there, do you think?"

"The same thing, I'd guess, only not so much of it.

Underbridge, too, because I'll bet you didn't find them all."

Tess's eyebrows crawled up into her hair. The idea that in the morning her co-workers would unlock the office door and find the place had turned into a bluebell wood...

"Come on. There's not time for this." Thomas caught her unresisting hand and towed her up the stairs. Under ordinary circumstances she'd have been quite taken by the bunch and slide of the muscles under his skin as he climbed the risers, but now she could only fight down a dire sense of dread and nausea.

In her room, Thomas began to dress swiftly. Tess, feeling a little shy, turned her back as she unbelted her robe. Her bitten thumb twinged and she muttered at it.

"You should wash," Thomas told her. "I've had infected pixie bites. They're not pleasant. Go and do it."

"Thomas, I—" She didn't know what she was about to say, only that she felt herself fraying away, one thread of reality at a time, despite the growing urgency to flee as Thomas suggested. "Are they poisonous? Will I die from their bites?"

"Neither." His voice was curt, and he was already dressed and belting himself into his oilskin. "Come on. Bathroom. Sink."

Just as she had done for him the day before, scrubbing and cleaning the rusty iron from his hands, now he cleaned the bite under a stream of hot water. While he scrubbed, he quizzed her. "Why did you go out today? Why didn't you stay in like I told you?"

"It was because of Rory."

"Yes. Rory. Tell me about Rory." He lathered her hands and rubbed them vigorously, water splashing unheeded on the cuffs of his coat. The soapy scent warred with the fragrance of the bluebells wafting up the stairs, and the green scent of the trampled plants. And another strange odor, which Tess decided was the pixies, dead in the kitchen sink.

"He was a client of mine. Just like Aaron. Same symptoms, only he was almost non-responsive, whereas Aaron still has a little of Aaron left in him." She began to shiver, despite the warmth of the water, and wondered if she was going into shock.

"Go on." Thomas pressed on the pad of her thumb, and a thin streamer of bright blood mixed with the water in the sink and spiraled down the drain. She heard him take a deep, shaky breath, and remembered how he had licked his claw clean of her blood only the night before. *Blood. Salt. Milk. Bread. I've got it all in one stupid human package*, she thought dizzily.

"It's like Rory was nowhere in his body. Just…gone. But one day I went to see him, to see if I could reach him and maybe get him to tell me where Aaron might be getting his drugs, and while I was there I had one of your Queen's little things in my shoulder bag. Rory got hold of it."

Thomas, apparently satisfied with the cleanliness of her hands, turned off the water and dried them one finger at a time. "Go on," he urged again. "What happened to Rory?"

"I just thought he'd taken it, hidden it somewhere. A little silver hazelnut, tied up with ribbon. But the aide and I looked and looked, and couldn't find it anywhere. In the end I left—because it was just a thing, after all, nothing important."

"But you were wrong."

"Yes. A few days later I checked on Rory, and he'd been released from the hospital. Because he was better, you see—like magic. All well. They never found the thing he took." She looked up from where the towel wrapped around her hands, and met his gaze.

"Like magic," he repeated.

"This morning, after you'd gone, I put all the pieces together and decided to try taking the...her things...to Aaron's house. Maybe if he touched one, it would fix him. And if it fixed him, I could fix the others. God knows...there are more than a dozen in that bag, and more at my office. And how many others that I didn't find in Underbridge?"

Thomas nodded slowly. "It might have worked. Come on, let's get you dressed."

From downstairs, they heard a creaking noise, like wood under stress. Something popped.

"Hurry," Thomas said, and now there was a new note in his voice, urgency, and maybe even a little fear. Tess went cold. Her teeth began to chatter. Thomas hustled her into the bedroom, where she hurriedly opened and closed drawers. Out came socks and jeans and a sweater, and pieces of practical lingerie, things suitable for running away from home on Halloween night with a trow. She tried not to laugh hysterically.

While she dressed, Thomas ran down the stairs, returning with a grim expression on his face. She was just hooking her bra behind her back. Thomas, like any man mystified by the processes involved with feminine undergarments, seemed amazed she could hook herself into the bra without looking.

"Oh, T—" he stopped himself, then shook his head and went on, as if somehow he could now permit himself to say her name. "Tess. This is not what I wanted for us." He pressed a hard kiss on her mouth, his hands warm on her bare shoulders. "You're almost ready. Good. Come on. We've got to go. Where's your jacket? You need warm things."

"Where *are* we going?" Her voice was muffled as she pulled the sweater over her head and then stepped to the dresser, where a fast pass through her hair with a brush untangled it enough to drag into a ponytail.

"I don't know yet."

"Your house?"

"First place they'll look."

"Why do we have to leave? Why can't we just lock the doors and—"

"When we go downstairs again, you'll understand. Just...come on, Tess, hurry!" As he spoke, there was another creaking noise—more of a groan, this time, and she felt the vibration in her feet. Her eyes flicked to his. She dived for the light switch, staring down the staircase.

The railing looked like birch trees, slender and lithe, and new branches were budding out along its length. As she watched, something poked through the drywall, a spiky greenness that she suddenly realized was a fir bough. At first there was only one, but a second later puffs of gypsum sifted down to dust the moss that crept up the stairs, and a dozen branches protruded from the wallboard. The house gave another groan. The sight was hypnotic, and Tess stood staring as her carpet converted from Berber to forest floor.

Her house—the entire thing—was becoming part of the fairy mound.

She is my birch girl, and I am her dark elf. Tess could almost hear Stephen's voice. What would he have said about this? Would he have rejoiced? Or would he have hurried her away from the danger, the way Thomas was trying to do? Would there have been enough of Stephen left inside him to recognize what was happening?

This, even more than seeing Thomas's edges blurring back and forth between human and trow, kicked Tess into overdrive. She sat on the bed to yank on her boots, then followed Thomas down the rapidly changing staircase.

The downstairs was utterly transformed. Where there had

been carpet, there was soil and bluebells, mosses and mushrooms. Anything vertical—except for the metal—was becoming trees. Wherever a stud was behind the drywall, a fir bough poked through, leaving a mess of gypsum and paint on the ground. And everywhere, along with the bluebells, was a tangle of ivy, the ivy that covered Forest Park. The scent of green, growing things was oppressive, heavy in the air. The perfume of the bluebells and the sharp, spicy tang of the ivy combined to make her feel sick, as if the air were no longer breathable by humans. So many bluebells in one place had even left a drift of strange pollen in the air and on every surface, like an accumulation of dust from long years. Now, too, she saw strange little patches of luminous slime, alive and writhing.

Glow worms? Or more of the fae magic, suddenly visible with her human eyes?

She clutched at her chest, where the seeing stone should have been, and realized she had left it on the nightstand. With a cry she raced back up the stairs, with Thomas shouting after her.

"Dammit, Tess! We have to go before this place crashes around us! It's happening fast."

"I'm coming!" She grabbed the stone and was slinging it around her neck as she got to the bottom of the stairs again, with fir boughs snagging her sweater and her hair. Thomas saw what she had gone back for and nodded.

"Put it out of sight."

She did as he suggested, and grabbed for her jacket and her shoulder bag, its leather greening with algae where it stood on what looked like a stump instead of the hall table.

At the front door, they took one last look around, then Thomas gave himself a shake like a large dog after a bath, and became fully trow.

"I want to be ready," he growled. "Stay behind me."

"Wait. One more thing." She ran for the kitchen and the mossy green grocery tote bag, which was now sporting the rough hide of an oak tree and some bracket fungi. The knotted root handles still held it closed, but Tess wondered if it would soon burst from whatever magical pressure must be inside. She set it down on the floor to dig in her purse for her keys. Where she put it down, bluebells began to grow, opening their blossoms and releasing a fragrance so potent she nearly swooned.

"What do you think you're going to do with that?"

"Take it with us."

"No. No way, Tess. Where those trinkets go, the Queen will follow."

"I know. But…these things, they're people. People I know. People I've never met, too, but people she's damaged. Maybe I can find them, fix them."

"They're just things. Magical things. Not people."

"You know I'm right, and I'm not leaving without them. You go, if you need to. I'll take care of these. I'm going to find Aaron, and I'm going to put him back the way he was before your Queen got hold of him."

"Tess..." Thomas raked his big hands over his nearly bald head in frustration. "No. She has him, and she will not let him go. I've been there. I know how it is. All he knows, and all he wants to know, is that she's his Queen and she needs him, wants him. Nothing else matters to him."

The duplex gave a terrible groan, and over the fearsome and strange noise of things growing at a tremendous rate, Tess could hear her next-door neighbors shouting. Was their half of the duplex converting, as well? She slung her bag over her shoulder and grabbed the grocery tote before Thomas could stop her, then ran out the front door.

Outside, the moon was enormous in the clear sky, and with merciless clarity, it lit the hillside where she lived. Forest Park was on the move, swelling like a monstrous boil just behind her house. She ran across the shared driveway, fishing in her shoulder bag for her car keys, which she tossed at Thomas. He caught them and immediately dropped them, and she remembered the metal content was probably at least partially iron. He bent, pinching them up with the cuff of his coat.

"Go for the Jeep. I've got to warn my neighbors!"

"Tess, come on! We have to go, and we have to go now."

She ignored him, reaching the neighbors' front door and hammering there with her fist. She couldn't very well scream

"The fairies are coming! Run!" so she shouted the first thing that came to mind. "Landslide! The hillside is coming down!"

The front door opened and she nearly fell into the foyer. The two neighbors stood there, fully dressed, and the odor of bluebells rushed out.

"What the hell is going on next door, Tess? Are you having a party? Because it sounds like the house is about to explode," one of them grumbled.

"Landslide," repeated Tess. "Get out. Drive, and drive, and drive. Far away. Do it now."

"Jesus," the other one said. "You're too old for Halloween pranks. Lay off the booze next year, whaddya say?"

Then they closed the door. Tess screamed at the unresponsive wood, and suddenly Thomas was there, grabbing her around the waist, hauling her to the Jeep.

"We're leaving. Forget them. You have to drive, I can't. Tess, if I'm taken, you keep driving. Leave the city."

"Stop talking like that!" She could not keep the shrillness from her voice, even while she was half-dragged by Thomas. "We're going, and we're going together. Nobody's going to…to take you. I'm just…I'm sorry I delayed us. I didn't understand, it all feels so much like a bad dream."

The two of them dragged the quilt off the Jeep and piled into the cab, Thomas trying to wedge his big form inside. Tess put the grocery tote behind the seat, where she couldn't see it, and the idea that it would be back there, festering, maybe doing to the Jeep what it had done to her house, terrified her. Yet she knew she couldn't leave it behind and consign all those people the Queen had damaged to a certain awful fate. There was a chance she could help, and she had to try.

Behind the duplex, Forest Park loomed like a malignant thunderhead in the moonlight. Tess jammed the key in the ignition, fearing for a moment the Jeep wouldn't start.

But it did, and as branches burst out of the wooden uprights of the porch railing and a sea of fungus washed over the driveway, the Jeep skidded out onto the street, crushed mushrooms slicking the way. As she shifted from reverse to first gear, the pumpkin on the porch grew storklike black legs with far too many joints, and scurried across the lawn. Tess felt a scream rising in her throat, swallowed the hard lump of it back again, jammed her foot on the accelerator, and jolted the Jeep down the street.

She couldn't resist staring in the rearview as the duplex vanished, swallowed in the slow roil of Forest Park, a cold tongue of earth and trees and the thin gray shadows made by the full moon. The Jeep nearly rear-ended a parked car while she was distracted.

Her house was part of fairyland now, only the idea wasn't as pleasant as it might have been, once upon a time. The ambulatory pumpkin squatted in the middle of the road, and in the gloom it might have been laughing, toadlike, at the Jeep's erratic passage through the neighborhood.

Tess jerked the wheel, determinedly heading south away from the spur of new land. Frightened tears oozed unheeded over her cheeks as Thomas tried his best to keep his large body out of her way. She wrestled the stick shift and took corners far too fast, dodging away from whatever horrible things might be following them at unknown speeds.

A gasping sob of relief burst from her, and she scrubbed her sleeve hard over her eyes. They had escaped, but what about her neighbors? And what about that sack of gewgaws behind the seat, mysteriously broadcasting their whereabouts to whatever freakish things cared to come looking?

Where to go next? She had no idea. When Burnside loomed, she headed resolutely west, putting the bridge to their backs. Thomas turned, looking east up the street as if he could see the bridge from where they were rapidly climbing into the hills again. She wondered if he thought of his home as longingly as she thought of hers, and accelerated.

➲ Chapter Twenty-Five ⇚

Thomas tried to hold on as the Jeep wound steadily uphill from Portland. The metal in the Jeep's panels, even covered by paint, stung his already iron-raw hands. The moon rode high in the sky, nearing midnight and the time when the Unseelie Court would be at its most frenetic, energized, and powerful. He could feel the surge rising in his body, the pull of the mound so close by, like an itch or an unspeakable craving that could be satisfied by only one thing.

Tess's breathing was rapid and uneven, hitching like a sobbing child's. He looked away from the moonsilver of the road and saw tears on her cheeks.

Of course. The fae had destroyed her house and probably obliterated her two neighbors as well. She was understandably upset, not being steeped in years of fae morality to recalibrate her notions of what was right or just.

"Tess." The surge pulled stronger, which meant they were turning north, not heading away from Forest Park.

"Just...let me drive." She swiped at her cheeks and gave a large sniffle.

"We can't go this way. It's the wrong way."

"It's away from Underbridge, that's all that matters." She

shifted gears as if she were angry, pushing the Jeep harder. "God, listen to me. You've changed how I think about my city. Changed its geography, for Christ's sake."

"No, Tess. We're going closer to the mound. Uphill and north—that will put us closer to them. To her."

"I'd like to meet her. So I can bitch-slap her. Where does she get off, taking over houses and—and—"

She slammed on the brakes with a suddenness that nearly sent Thomas into the windshield. He heard a noise like the whine of a kicked dog coming from her throat and looked to see where she was staring.

Facing them on the road was the Hunt, white as lightning in the glare of the moon, with too-dark shadows pooling around the churning group of bogles and kelpies and redcaps. Red-eyed Hunter, astride his slavering beast, nodded his vast, antlered head at the Jeep as if he knew exactly what—and who—it held.

"It's that fucking SUV again," she whispered, grabbing for gears and executing a hair-raising turn in the middle of the road, racing back downhill into Portland at a speed that made his stomach threaten to return all the milk he had drunk.

"Again? SUV? What are you talking about?"

"Yes. I didn't tell you, but—"

"You've seen them before?" He turned in the seat, his big body unintentionally crowding her. Behind them the Hunt came on like the seventh wave, rushing, frothing, spilling one over the other. He could hear their eager yelping and knew that he was done for at last.

"Today. I got away from them by coming over the bridge, and my God, Thomas! We'll go back to Chinatown! The *fu* dogs stopped them before, they'll stop them again!"

Thomas could hardly sort out her words. "You were in Chinatown? And the demons didn't kill you, with this load of the Queen's things in the car?"

Tess yanked the Jeep into another tight turn and accelerated, checking her mirror obsessively, killing the lights on the Jeep and driving dark. "I dunno, Thomas, the dogs just came off their pedestals and ripped the shit out of that front SUV. They didn't touch me."

"Then you were the first thing to alert them, and Hunter was unlucky enough to be behind you. Tess, we can't go there. It's Allantide, the Chinese demons will be awake and watching for the fae."

"All I know is they stopped the freaks chasing me. Surely they'll do it again."

"Oh, they would. As soon as they killed me first."

She shot him horrified glances, splitting her attention among the road, the rearview mirror, and his face.

"There's a reason I didn't want to eat Chinese food when you suggested it, and it's not because of the taste. It's because the Chinatown dogs and demons have territory of their own to protect. And it's because I'm fae. Never forget that, Tess. Forget it, even for a second, and it could mean your life. Maybe mine as well."

She returned her attention to the dark road, dragging in a long shaky breath. "Then we'll just have to try something else. Involve the cops, maybe. I know where there's a police station. We'll just drive there, and go inside. The fae won't want to be seen, right, and they'll leave us alone!"

"What you should do is pull over and let me out. With the Queen's things. It's me they want, not you. Then you could keep driving. Once dawn comes, you'll be safe. They can't hunt past dawn, even on Allantide. And they stop once they have their quarry."

"No."

It was stated in so flat a tone, that Thomas knew she would brook no argument, would not even discuss it. Part of him rejoiced to hear her say it. He meant something to her. Or maybe the potential she saw in the Queen's trinkets meant more to her than he himself did. The need in her to fix things was perhaps deeper than the affection she felt for him.

But the rest of him knew she would pay for that need.

Everyone who ever loved the fae paid. Some more than others, but they all paid. He was living proof, with the Queen's ownership tight around his arm. He had no idea why she was leaving him alone tonight, but he was grateful for the respite, however short. She must already know her poisoned wine had failed.

"Come on, Tess. Think straight. You can't fight them using human means."

"Human means are all I've got," Tess snarled. "They'll have to be enough." She gritted her teeth and headed east again, toward the river, but now choosing streets south of Burnside. "Right. Iron and water it is, then. It worked on some of them, at least for a little while."

"You can't run forever, Tess. But they can. Especially tonight."

"We're doing just fine so far. Look, they're not behind us."

"Stop, and let me out."

"No. And don't try to escape, either. I'll run you over myself and drag you back into the car."

Her words were bold, but Thomas wasn't entirely sure she didn't mean them. Foolhardy, brave, incredible woman. He wanted nothing more than to close a door behind them, somewhere the fae could not go, and wrap her in his arms forever. Instead, he had to start thinking, and it had to be fast. They could not hope to outrun the Hunt. It was many hours until dawn, here in the thin part of the year, and with the moon not yet at her apex, the fae's power had yet to peak.

"Right. I won't fling myself from a moving vehicle."

Tess checked the rearview again, and he could tell by the

release of tension in her shoulders the Hunt was still invisible behind them. He wanted to turn and look, but it wouldn't make a difference, and there was no point in frightening her further. Hunter could glamour himself into almost anything where humans were concerned, and just because the Hunt didn't look like a mob of street racers at the moment didn't mean they weren't still following. Or flanking them one street over. Or traveling dark, the way Tess was doing. Hunter had his prey—Thomas—in his sights, and that was all he needed. Given Tess's tale of her wild afternoon and the slaughtered pixies in her kitchen, the fae knew all they needed about her and could use the Queen's magic to track them.

Thomas rummaged in the inner pockets of his coat and fished out one of the big iron nails he carried. It stung his hand, but he tucked it into the right-hand pocket of Tess's jacket.

"What's that?"

"Iron. Use it if you have to. Stab with it, just like a knife. Don't hesitate, because they won't."

"But I thought you said they wanted you, not me."

"Well…" Thomas pondered the Laws of the Unseelie Court and the rules that seemed to govern Hunter. "You might be right—I'm the one Hunter wants, he said as much earlier today. But they'll use you to get to me."

"Okay, then." A grim smile curved her mouth. "I'll stick any of 'em that try to take you from me. We've only got to last till dawn, right?"

"Or cockcrow."

"I don't know where we'd find a rooster in Portland. If we can get out to the countryside, maybe, but—"

"Hunter and his hounds would catch us long before that. So—what's your human plan, then?"

"We're going to the Hawthorne Bridge. Just hang on."

"Not through Chinatown!"

"I heard you the first six times." Tess fiddled with the gearshift, and the Jeep made a quiet growl, seeming to understand their need for secrecy. Her head was turning from left to right and back again as they emerged from the residential neighborhood into the more commercial part of town, where the streetfolk roamed at night. Thomas knew they kept moving to stay warm and minimize their chances of being mugged, but tonight they were turning their heads away as Thomas and Tess passed in the Jeep. Block after block, the wanderers, some of them costumed, most of them not, turned to the alleys and walls and doorways.

If he'd had any doubt about being Hunter's prey this night, it was erased now.

Thomas grew cold with sick dread, feeling his glamour stutter as if a hard shiver had taken him. Much like the night before, where Hunter's magic cleared the streets wherever he cast his snares, on this night of all nights the humans turned away, giving the fae their rightful place in the white night of Allantide. He had heard the old tales, how no human could look upon the Wild Hunt and live. What that meant for Tess he was unsure, but each time she had run afoul of Hunter and his hounds, she'd had the Queen's trinkets with her.

Maybe she'd been right to insist upon bringing them along. Hell, what did he know anymore? He had been supplanted in the Queen's favor by a callow youth. She'd tried to poison him, and now he was Hunter's target on the most powerfully magical night in years. Everything had changed, except for him.

Or maybe he was the one who had changed. He could no longer tell.

He felt helpless, as if the decades spent among the fae had gained him nothing, neither knowledge nor power. It galled him to think they might, indeed, be dependent upon human means to defeat the Unseelie and live until dawn.

Keep *Tess* alive, that is. Thomas had no confidence the Queen would let him live, even if he survived until dawn or outran Hunter and his hounds. Tess was what mattered now, which was why he still planned to leave her behind at his first opportunity. He would draw the Hunt away from her, praying that the rest of the Unseelie would leave her alone until morning.

He didn't think past that. Couldn't. Would not. No point worrying where she would go, now that her home was part of Forest Park. Or what she would do with a sack of magical items.

Or what that very sack might do with *her*. No, the critical moments were here and now. Despite Tess's hope that they'd shaken the Hunt, he knew better.

The Jeep was still traveling dark. Tess's grip on the wheel was white-knuckle tense, and she obsessively scanned their surroundings. Thomas wanted to open a window, get some fresh air, let out the breath of iron the Jeep exhaled as a matter of course, but instead he coughed a little and leaned into the turn onto Hawthorne Street.

And there it was, her goal, her human plan: the Hawthorne Bridge, looming monstrous and dark in the Allantide midnight. The Jeep valiantly climbed the first upslope, then gave a cough remarkably like Thomas's own. He heard the engine sputter and felt the vehicle losing speed.

"Oh, no, no, no!" Tess hit the steering wheel with a clenched fist. "Come on, baby, come on, just a little farther! Don't do this now, not now!"

Thomas turned to look behind them. Still nothing. If it weren't for the turned-away people in the streets just behind them, he might have let hope take root in his heart. "What's happening, Tess?"

"Out of gas. I knew it was low, and I should have filled up today but I hoped...oh, I hoped...God *damn* it!" The Jeep hiccoughed and lurched, and Tess pulled it to the right, as snug to the railing as she dared.

Thomas let out his own little curse. She'd blocked his door, locking him in as effectively as if it had been one of the Queen's little oubliettes, those wet pits deep in the dark heart of Forest Park. To escape Tess now, he'd have to climb out over her or rip away the soft top of the Jeep. Tess pulled the keys out.

"Come on." She reached behind her seat for the mossy bag and stood beside the open car door, looking back the way they'd come.

"You have an idea?" Thomas scrambled to exit the vehicle through the driver's side door, struggling to control his glamour. His human form would make it simpler to climb out, but the iron all around them seemed to fill his lungs and his brain. He coughed again. As he squeezed out of the Jeep, he saw the river below them through the grating deck of the bridge. Of all the bridges in Portland, Tess had chosen the one with the least paving, the most exposed iron. It made sense, but it hurt him, almost more than Hunter's beating that morning.

"This is it," Tess said, slinging her purse across her body and taking the mossy bag in one hand, then gripping his left hand in her other. "I was hoping to get the Jeep to the center of the bridge, I guess—as much running water and iron around us as I could manage, but now…I don't know. I guess let's walk."

Thomas coughed again. This much iron would weaken him in the end, leave his mind foggy and slow, if it didn't outright kill him.

They began to hurry east to the center of the bridge. Thomas could feel the Willamette in every straining muscle and breath, a deep, curling pull that changed his heartbeat, turned it into something thumping and slow. Was this strange lethargy the spell the kelpies used to quiet their victims? Or was he truly more fae than ever? Or was it the proximity of the Queen's trinkets? His head was spinning, and he was glad of Tess so close to his side. She looked so small, so human, next to his bulk, yet she was solid and real, and she was in the thick of it with him, determined to see him through.

A vehicle pulled up on the eastern flank of the bridge and paused. Tess halted, bringing Thomas to a stop next to her. He heard her sharp inhalation. The car backed and turned around, returning the way it had come. *No one can look upon the Hunt and live.*

It was only a matter of time before Hunter and his hounds found them, and after that, it was anyone's guess how long the two of them survived. He kept walking east with Tess, his back resolutely to what he knew, in his very bones, was coming.

➤ Chapter Twenty-Six ⬉

When Thomas stumbled, fear clenched Tess's heart. She pushed her shoulder hard against him, propping him as best she could. She looked behind them to the west end of the bridge; still nothing.

"Would it be easier if you changed back to your human form, Thomas?"

"I can't. It might, but I can't. Too much iron, and the river's too close."

He sounded exhausted. In the lights from the bridge she could see how ill he looked. "Maybe this wasn't such a good idea. Maybe we should go back."

He shook his head, lumbering forward. "This is as good a place as any to make our stand. It might work."

"You look terrible. I—" At the west end, headlights swept onto the bridge deck. It was, of course, the black SUV. She fumbled her seeing stone out of her neckline and held it to her eye. No SUV, but the dreadful horse-thing and antlered rider. Its black car escort had changed to the horrible creatures she had seen earlier in the day, kelpies and redcaps and scrawny, twisty bogles. "They're here."

"Keep going," Thomas grunted. "Put that stone away. It

won't make things any better if they know you can see them for what they really are. Better to let them think you're a glamour-blinded human as long as we can." This time it was he who pushed them along. Tess did as he urged, but she kept looking back. Their pursuers waited restlessly at the edge of the bridge, as if the iron was indeed a strong deterrent, but after her glance through the stone, they no longer looked like cars. Maybe she was becoming immune to the glamour, or maybe Thomas was right and the magic of Halloween was building and she was within its fae influence.

The lead rider's mount circled away from the bridge repeatedly, but the rider brought it back each time. The horse put a foot on the bridge and gave a tremendous shudder. The rider raised his hand, and the hounds fell silent. Tess heard her own indrawn breath. The silence was worse than the yelping; while the hounds were noisy, she felt they were stymied and frustrated, and the longer they stayed that way, the better. But now they were silent, and she feared their leader was getting a grip on the situation. She and Thomas struggled on, and at last they were on the span that could lift up into the superstructure of the bridge to allow ships to pass beneath.

"Just a little farther, Thomas." She wanted to be on the other side of that, in case the bridge lifted. The gap could only help them, but more importantly she did not want to be on the deck as it lifted into the trusses above. She envisioned the two of them stranded like flightless birds, high above the river, a gathering of yelping wolves waiting below.

From the eastern slope of the bridge came a yodeling howl. The lead rider at the other side nodded, a slow and stately movement that could have been beautiful if it hadn't conveyed so much menace. Tess looked east and saw a single creature there: a kelpie, with its large, white horseteeth bared in what could only be called a hungry smile.

They were trapped on the bridge.

She wondered how far they could swim, if they had to jump into the river, before something from the dark, poisonous depths of the Willamette ate them for a midnight snack. She didn't want to find out, but it was a chance she would take if she had to.

Finally they crossed the gap onto the eastern half of the bridge, with the lift span behind them. Tess called a halt, and Thomas sank to his knees, and then collapsed onto his backside, his head down. She knelt beside him.

"Is it bad, Thomas?"

"Pretty bad."

"Do you think you can stand it?"

"What's my other choice? Go to them?" His hand flapped weakly toward the Hunt. "Let them take me?"

"I won't let them." She laced her fingers together around his upper arm.

"You won't be able to stop them. Only the iron and water

will stop them, if it can."

"So this is an okay plan?" Tess desperately needed to feel she had done *something* right in all this mess.

Thomas lifted his head wearily and looked into her eyes. "The best ever."

Tess bit her lip. "Not if the iron hurts you first."

"Stop worrying."

"I can't help it. It's what I do." She cupped his face—that ugly, puffy trow face, with Thomas's eyes peering out of it—between her palms, and looked intently at him. "Tell me if you can't do this, and I'll...I'll think of something else."

"Like what?"

"Like...I don't know. I'll go talk to them, or something, and—"

Thomas laughed, a deep, painful rasping sound that made her afraid he would cough up blood any second. "They're not like your clients, Tess. Remember the fae of the Underbridge? Salt and blood is what they want. Mine, foremost, but they wouldn't say no to a tender bite of human woman for an appetizer."

"I'm not going to let them have you." Tess couldn't help repeating her vow, though she had no idea how she would keep it. Thomas's head sagged again, and she pressed a hurried kiss against his temple, where the skin felt rough and clammy, not at all like the warm, suede skin she had felt in the dark as they made love. The iron was making him sick, and she wondered which would run out first: the night, or Thomas's strength.

From Hunter came a long, thrilling call. Tess's body hairs all stood on end, as if an electric charge had run across her skin, or his call had awakened them. Thomas's head came up again, and they stared at where Hunter now sat astride his beast with his back to them, his arms held up to the sky, the antlers silhouetted against the city lights beyond. The juxtaposition of the giant stag in the city tilted her reality right into the crazy zone, but what happened next shattered every notion of reasonableness she'd ever had.

Out of the northwest came a black cloud, thicker than the flocks of migrating starlings that roosted in season on the girders of the Interstate Bridge linking Oregon and Washington. The cloud was dark in the moonlit sky, and swirled and looped just like the birds would, except that birds didn't fly at night unless they were forced to. As the cloud drew closer she could see it wasn't birds at all, but a storm of autumn leaves, borne on no wind she could feel. She clutched tighter at Thomas, who separated his knees and pulled her between them, where he could close her in the cage of his arms.

Hunter turned his horse, slowly, arms still raised, masked face lifted in the moonlight, as if he were calling down the wrath of God upon the bridge.

"Pixies," said Thomas, just as Tess remembered the vortex of leaves that had surrounded her at Aaron Eisley's house, and the fluttering fairies in her kitchen, now lying dead in the sink. If there even was a sink anymore.

"How can there be so many?"

"Hunter must have tolled every pixie out of Forest Park."

"What can they—will they bite us?"

"Maybe we'd better get ready to run."

"Run where?" Tess got to her feet and helped Thomas rise. "Swim for it, maybe?"

"Kelpies." Thomas shook his head. "Sooner the pixies than the water horses."

"Dead is dead, whether by nibbles or mouthfuls."

Thomas gave another of those horrible, sickly laughs, putting an arm around her. "Now you're starting to think like a fae. Keep it up." He never took his eyes off the cloud of darkness drawing closer and closer to the bridge. Tess kept glancing over her shoulder to be sure the kelpie guarding the east end remained on shore, but her gaze returned to the pixies. So many in one place seemed unnatural to her. The pixies swooped and circled through the girders of the bridge, and sick dread overwhelmed her when Hunter turned to face the bridge, arms still upraised. She could see his red eyes, like dire Christmas lights, shining out of his mask, and she could feel them when their glow swept over her.

Thomas felt it too. Tess knew it when he planted his feet more widely for balance and gave his broad shoulders a loosening shake, as if to jostle that stare from his body.

Hunter let out a cry and his arms flew wide, as if he were conducting a savage orchestra. The cloud of pixies separated into two halves and crashed into the girders as if splattered there, thrown by a wicked child's angry hand.

The screaming was horrible, like so many nails on chalkboards, as the pixies tried to avoid the bridge's iron and failed. Tess let go of Thomas's hand and the sack of the Queen's trinkets, hands clapped to her ears to shut out the terrible sound of suffering. The pixies swooped at the bridge and then away, but Hunter overrode their reluctance and fear with his voice and the utter command of his hands. The creatures slammed against the iron and clung there, shrieking their cries of death and fear and pain. Layer after layer gathered on the girders and the roadway grating.

Thomas said something she could not hear through her hands over her ears, so she took them down, gritting her teeth and squinting at the screeching of the pixies. "He's killing them," she said.

Thomas nodded. "Using their bodies as a shield against the iron of the bridge." The two of them looked down at the bag of the Queen's things, where the sides did a slow, peristaltic creep, as if the trinkets inside were crawling over and about one another. Where it touched the iron, there was a faint, dusty brightening. Even here among so much iron, the Queen's magic was working. Tess thought of her bluebell-swallowed home, and her lips tightened.

Tess glanced over her shoulder. The kelpie had not moved, but when it saw her looking at it, shifted into a beautiful young man, nodded and beckoned. Half of her brain seemed to see the motions of a nightmare carousel horse, tossing its head and pawing savagely at the earth. It was as if the influence of the iron stripped some of the glamour, which explained why Hunter no longer looked like an SUV even without her seeing stone. She turned her back, determinedly, and followed Thomas's gaze.

So many human souls and psyches, crammed together in that one little sack. She shuddered, and bent to pick it up again. She hadn't meant to put it down to begin with; she would have to be on guard against such impulses. The fae made her doubt her very eyes and the evidence of her brain. The slow squirm of the things inside the bag made her feel anxious, and her face must have shown it.

"Be careful," Thomas said.

"I'm trying." She looked up at the sky, wondering how long they had until dawn. It must be hours yet, and still the pixies streamed out of the northwest, and still they clung to every inch of the bridge, coating it with trembling oak leaves, maple leaves, sweet gum and sycamore, alder and birch. Every molecule of air filled with the shattering noise of their deaths.

The dark, screaming tide halted a yard from where Thomas and Tess stood. She could not tell if there simply were no more pixies to be slaughtered, or if Hunter had deemed the mass sufficient, or if the Queen's magic held them at bay. The noise diminished, and every now and then a dead pixie fell from the girders above, fluttering down, riding the breath from the river below, falling, falling, a leaf in search of rest, the forest floor, and the quiet peace of rot.

At the west end of the bridge, Hunter's mount stepped onto the carpet of pixies.

"Oh, God," Tess said. Her fingers laced with Thomas's, more for her own comfort than through any faith that he could defend them from the hunter and his shadowy, yelping hounds. "They're coming for us, aren't they?"

"Yes," said Thomas. "You should go. Take that bag and run." But his fingers were tight on hers, and she knew he didn't want her to leave him. Fear warred with the deep burden of responsibility within her.

"The kelpie—"

"The iron nail. Use it. He'll let you pass if you stab deep. In the neck would be best. Leave the nail in the flesh, and keep running."

She stared at him, horror rising. It was a shock to realize afresh Thomas understood these creatures, knew best how to hurt them, skills only obtained through experience. But what else could he do, if this was what his world was like? And how clean and safe had her own world been, despite her job working with addicts and damaged people?

"Come with me, then."

He shook his head, and she could see the weariness and the despairing resignation in his eyes. "They will never stop, and I cannot outrun them while I am weakened by iron like this. But maybe you could get away, if I let them take me."

"I already told you no."

"Tess, it could mean your life."

"And if what you say is true, it *will* mean yours. No. I'm not leaving you." She let go of Thomas long enough to thread the long strap of her purse through the handles of the grocery tote, and sling the whole contraption across her body once more. She had to have at least one hand free, but with the other, she took Thomas's hand and squeezed with all her might.

The Wild Hunt came, slowly, reluctantly, with renewed ear-splitting shrieking from the pixies they crushed under foot.

But come they did, shimmering in and out of their glamour, until the influence of the bridge—despite the pixie coating—and the Willamette's strong current at mid-span stripped it all away at last, and there was only the other-worldly brutality of bone and skin and bare-toothed grimaces remaining.

➢ Chapter Twenty-Seven ➣

Thomas knew he was relying on Tess's strength for much of his support, and Hunter would correctly see that as weakness. He stood a little straighter, locking his knees, and hoped his sick looks could be misinterpreted as menace, at least by Hunter's hounds, if not the Queen's Huntsman himself.

What good was a trow's body if it could be made so vulnerable? He'd lived in his bridge hole for years, fooled into thinking his human body enabled him to stay there, unsickened by the iron, when in reality he was insulated by concrete and layers of his own magic and glamours. He should have known from the rides in Tess's Jeep that iron had become more and more toxic to him.

Even his brain felt weak and sick. Tess would not run, and he could not make her. She was a human who had looked upon—was still looking upon—the Wild Hunt. How did she not turn away? What gave her the strength? He didn't think it was entirely due to the eerie emanations he could feel coming from the things in the grocery tote. Some of it was surely due to Tess's spirit and heart. He'd never met anyone like her among the fae and had only glancing acquaintances with strong women before he became the Queen's lover as a young man.

She caught him looking at her and gave him a smile that didn't quite erase the fear in her eyes.

"You could still run, Tess."

"How many times are you going to say that?" She leaned in for a brief kiss and he obliged, liking the way her hand tightened on his.

"Until you're safe."

"We. Until *we're* safe." She reached in her pocket for the nail he had put there and gripped it in her fist.

Hunter and his pack drew closer. It was slow going over the bridge, despite the thousands of pixies destroyed or enslaved to protect the Hunt from the iron. Hunter continually forced his mount forward, with savage kicks to its skeletal belly and flogging with the butt of his staff. The hounds of his pack cringed and groaned at every step. Thomas could see their breath on the chill air as they panted.

Each step the Wild Hunt took brought him and Tess closer to disaster. There was nowhere to run, and chancing the river was not really an option. His mind circled like a rat in a trap. Their one hope, now, was the very thing he had most wanted to abandon: the bag of the Queen's trinkets. If it came down to it, Thomas thought perhaps he would throw one of the things at the Wild Hunt and see what happened. Maybe it would bring the Queen down upon them, though he doubted even she would interfere with Hunter's choice of prey. The Wild Hunt was governed by laws deeper and older than the Unseelie court's contorted bureaucracy, laws set forth in the time when all magic was wild and only the unstoppable forces of nature held sway. Prey was prey, when it was chosen for the right reasons. The Wild Hunt might be only a vestige of that wild magic, but its rules were immutable.

Thomas was about to die.

There was no changing that, not now.

The Hunt had only another few yards to go, but it was over the Willamette's primary channel, and the current was deep and strong. He saw its pull affecting the pack. The kelpies drifted toward the sides of the roadway, looking longingly into the darkly glimmering water below without touching the bridge railing. The bogles bared their teeth in angry denial of the river's force. Hunter's mount spun in place until he drove it forward once more.

There was really only one thing left to do. He leaned to his left, where Tess's shoulder still pressed firmly against him, providing as much strength and support as she could, and spoke quietly into her ear.

"I'm sorry, Tess. Forgive me."

Her breasts rose and fell on a long, harsh breath. She had heard him, but her gaze did not leave the Hunt, and she brought up the hand holding the iron nail so that it rested near her collarbone, her arm pressed close as if she were cold, or as if something inside her ached.

A moment later, as the Hunt took the last strides on the pixie carpet, she pulled free of Thomas's hand and stepped in front of him, her palm out for all the world as if she were stopping traffic on a neighborhood street.

"No!" he shouted, but she took a step forward, the tips of her boots not quite touching the twitching, leafy bodies of the pixies.

"I command you to stop," Tess said. Thomas heard the tremor in her voice.

Hunter reined in his mount. Its head tossed, and bloody froth dripped at Tess's feet. Maybe Thomas was imagining things, but did it seem as if Hunter's antlered mask was not held as firmly aloft as it had been? The iron had to be affecting him as well. Thomas tried to step forward and instead went to one knee. Without looking Tess stepped back again, staying in front of him. A part of him wanted to laugh; Tess clearly thought her command had stayed Hunter, when it was the edge of the blanket of pixies that had halted him. Hunter was merely gathering his force for the final strike. The greater part of Thomas wondered at Tess's determination and bravery in the face of what was probably the most frightening moment of her life.

"Out of my way, human woman." Hunter urged his mount forward once more. Tess faded back a half step, then squared her shoulders.

"No. You will not take him."

"He is the prey of the Hunt. Mine by right, by law and custom and might."

"You talk like a crazy person. He's not your prey, not yours to take or kill or—whatever you think you're going to do to him. Take your...your *creatures*..." Tess's lip curled in distaste as she scanned the pack. "Take them and leave us in peace."

Thomas swallowed. Tess had no idea what she was saying. He struggled to his feet again, fighting the need to grasp her shoulder to help him upright. The iron felt heavy in his lungs now, leaving no room for air. He heard himself wheeze.

Hunter's laugh was the sound of stone rubbed on stone, the deep rumble of an earthquake. His staff leveled at Tess, a prismatic tangle of the hunt magic blooming at its tip like an unnatural torch. Tess quailed, coming into contact with Thomas's chest. Hunter's red eyes looked around at his pack. "Circle them," he said, gesturing with his staff.

The pack ranged themselves at the hem of pixie bodies, but went no further. The bogles hissed and twisted in terror and fear. Circling their prey meant stepping out onto the iron of the bridge, and Thomas saw the wisdom of Tess's inspired idea. The combination of iron and running water was having an impact.

There were reasons the fae hated the humans, and reasons the humans had crowded out the fae in so many parts of the world. Human means, indeed. She had taken his own concepts a step farther, learning from him, and adding her own ingenuity.

Yet he didn't dare hope, at least not for himself.

Hunter remained facing them as the pack slowly edged onto the iron of the bridge to obey his command. Thomas coughed, then he cleared his throat.

"I'll come with you, Hunter, but let her go free."

"Still trying to bargain, Thomas? You have nothing left that I want."

"He may not, but I do." Tess interjected, and Thomas felt his heart burst in terror.

"T—" he stopped himself before he spoke her truename in their hearing. "Silence!"

Hunter's red eyes were intent on Tess. "Let her speak." His voice had lost that sharp, stony edge, and instead transmitted all the seductive power of any kelpie intent upon its victim.

Thomas tried again. "This is Allantide. If the Hunt returns without its prey, our Queen will be angered."

"There is no law specifying what we must hunt." The antlered head tilted, as if scenting the air around Tess. Thomas put an arm around her middle, and felt the writhing of the mossy bag of trinkets even through his coat. The bag was weighty against his arm, with an electric pulsing that concerned him. He wondered how much longer the bag would contain its contents, and what would happen when the Queen's markers spilled out onto the iron deck.

"But once the prey has been chosen, the Hunt cannot change its mind. You cannot take her, you must take me."

Hunter snarled. It was the law, and they both knew it.

"If you can," Tess said boldly. Thomas groaned to himself. "But I warn you, you must go through me to get to Thomas." She broke free of the circle of his arm and held up the bag with one hand. "This is what you want, not him. And…and…" Thomas could feel her casting about for the right words to make her human bargain. "You will have to wait until dawn to find out what's in here. I promise you, it will mean more to you than killing Thomas ever will."

Hunter laughed again, returning to the honey-sweet tones. "You little know what a thorn in my side he has been, and how much pleasure I will take in carving his flesh to feed my pack and my Queen."

"And yourself, no doubt." Tess sidled closer. "Let me give you a hint of what's in this sack."

"I will have more than a hint," Hunter said, and Thomas would have sworn the mask was smiling. "I will have the bag itself." Hunter's staff tilted down and the hunt magic unfurled over Tess and the bag like a seining net cast by a fisherman in a Willamette slough, but this fish was far more valuable. Thomas stretched out a hand too late to pull her out of its reach, but he needn't have bothered. The snare blazed like dry summer grass alongside the highway. A moment later it drifted harmlessly, brittle and smoking, to the bridge deck.

Hunter's snare hadn't worked amidst the iron of the Hawthorne Bridge.

Tess looked startled, but only momentarily, and then the hand with the iron nail was out, stabbing down, glancing off Hunter's silver-armored thigh and burying deep into the mutable flesh of his mount.

"Shit," Tess hissed. "Missed."

But the beast's flesh sizzled like bacon on a hot pan where the nail entered its flesh.

While Hunter was staring, astonished, at Tess's treachery and the failure of his magic, Thomas caught the back of her coat and dragged her away from Hunter and his jerking, thrashing mount. Hunter sprang away from the beast. Crazed, it bolted forward, coming into contact with the iron deck and spinning a savage dance of pain and destruction. The horse bared its teeth, biting at the smoking nail in its side, missing, rearing, neighing with a noise like a locomotive whistle.

"Now you have angered me." Hunter yanked a stone knife from a sheath at his boot and came toward them, ignoring his horse, which had staggered back onto the carpet of pixie corpses and was sinking to its knees, its neck stretched far in distress. "I will have that bag, and I will have you!"

"I call you to Court, by the will of our Queen and the Law of the ages!" Thomas summoned all the air he could take into his lungs and roared. "You have declared your intention to abandon the Rule of the Hunt."

For a moment there was nothing but silence and the slow, muscular voice of the Willamette, heedless of the deadly drama playing out on the bridge above the current. Everyone stood poised, waiting.

A bogle was the first to flinch, stepping back from the naked iron to the blanketed deck of the bridge, its querulous gaze twitching from Hunter's fury as it moved, signaling its intention. Hunter leveled his staff at the bogle and a bolt of smeary magic, distorted by the iron around it, flew like slow fire toward the bogle. The snare was easily sidestepped.

Hunter's rage at this fresh failure was spectacular, but when Tess's mocking laughter sounded, the red eyes behind the mask became incandescent with fury. Thomas's first impulse was to beg her to be silent, but with rage came opportunity: sooner or later, Hunter would make another mistake, and perhaps it would be the opening they needed to get them safely to dawn, and a chance to live another day.

"Kill him," Hunter said to his pack. His gauntleted hands went to a coil of cording slung at his hip and made a loop in its end.

"He has claimed the protection of the Court," objected a redcap, licking its lips.

"He is our rightful prey, and we are the Wild Hunt. Kill

him!"

The pack began creeping back the way they had come. Only Hunter's red glare and the habit of long obedience halted them.

"The Queen…the Law…" whined a bogle, and the rest of the hounds took up the refrain.

Hunter snarled, "All of you. Dead by cockcrow, by my own hands, unless you do as you're bidden."

"You're losing control of your own pack, cowardly dogs that they are," Thomas taunted, but the effort was too great. Once again he slipped to his knees. Tess went with him, her arms tight around him, keeping him from direct contact with the bridge. The cough that wracked him now brought up blood. Tess stroked his face, tears spilling over her lashes.

"Hold on," she whispered. "Oh, Thomas, hold on!"

At last it was Hunter himself who came to them. Thomas had no strength to fight, but Tess would not let go of him. The stag mask panted clouds of steam as Hunter stood on the bare iron. A second burst of hunt magic fizzled uselessly from the staff. With a growl Hunter spun a loop of cording over the two of them and cinched it tight. Tess grunted with pain as Hunter jerked on the cord and dragged them, Tess uppermost, onto the pixie carpet, but she did not let go of Thomas, nor the sack of trinkets.

"You could have saved yourself, human woman," Hunter said to Tess. "But you had to interfere, and now you will be subject to Unseelie law. You will be judged, and you will die."

"Bring it. I'm not impressed so far. You won't even show your face." Tess's fierce grip hurt Thomas's ribs, but he was rapidly becoming too fogged to respond, and when Hunter towed them onto the crumbling leafy carpet, could only feel relieved that the concentration of iron seemed to lessen.

Hunter looked to where his mount steamed and smoked, falling apart into the bits and pieces that glamour had once knitted whole, then turned his back on its uselessness. He flicked a hand at a kelpie and gestured toward Thomas and Tess. "If you will not kill them, you will bear their burden." He dragged the two of them, still bound, across the broad back of the kelpie, and forced the creature to its feet.

They left the Hawthorne Bridge, picking up speed as they neared the shore, racing into the moonlit night and the blue shadows of the empty Portland streets.

Headed for Forest Park.

⇒ Chapter Twenty-Eight ⇐

Tess clung to Thomas for dear life—both of their lives—as the Hunt clattered off the bridge. Though she tried to jump or fall away from the kelpie, she was unable to pry her body from its wet, broad back, where she sat sideways, with Thomas slumped astride behind her. The cord still bound them tightly, and Hunter held one end of it as he straddled a second kelpie a few feet away.

"I can't get free!"

Thomas coughed, and she was relieved to hear it didn't sound as harsh or deep as before. "That's kelpie magic. It's how they take women to their deaths. Once you're on one, it's over." His arms tightened around her, and she fought a manic impulse to giggle from sheer over-stimulation.

The Hunt rocketed onto Naito Parkway, turning north. As they emerged from the toxic iron-shadow of the bridge, they shivered into glamour. There was a moment of vertiginous perception when Tess saw the fae creatures becoming the prowling posse of black vehicles, but then the illusion stabilized and she only had to cope with the jolting and the terror, which was more than enough. With the loss of Hunter's mount, the dire lead SUV was no longer, but she could see Hunter in a black sedan only feet away, with the cord stretching between like a spider thread, glimmering in the streetlights, invisible in the shadows of buildings. His antlers were gone—*of course, he has to fit into a car*—and in their place was an elaborate tangle of braids and dreadlocks, animal tails and dried reeds and grasses, worn much like a crown.

The speed of the Hunt was breathtaking, as terrifying on horseback as it would have been in a car doing eighty on a city street, taking turns without slowing and heedless of other traffic.

Of which, thankfully, there was none. The power of the Hunt was chilling, and she struggled afresh, still to no avail.

The Burnside Bridge loomed out of the darkness, and soon Tess saw the market, filled with hundreds of milling people, glamours fringed and shattered and flaring bright and then dark. Her heart jolted into her throat at the memory of the fae surrounding her in the market. Was it only the day before? It seemed forever ago, a memory distorted by months and years.

The Hunt plunged into the crowd, driving into a sea of bodies. Every instant Tess's rational brain expected to see someone's broken, bloody body flying up over the hood of the sedan she was riding in. Except that it wasn't a sedan, though sometimes it was. The ever-shifting glamour was making her ill. The wild grasping and clawing of the crowd terrified her. She struggled to draw a deep breath and could only drag in half of one before a gulping gasp burst from her. Her only consolation was that she seemed to be beyond tears.

Thomas's arms tightened around her, helping, but only a little.

The crowd magically parted like a zipper, bare inches in front of them, as they progressed. She could hear the hungry cries, see their strange whirling dances, leaving bright after-images on her vision like fireworks at midnight.

And she smelled bluebells and freshly turned earth. She glanced to the side, where a group of toothy, moth-winged streetfolk danced around one of the Portland water bubblers. Bark had grown up its concrete pedestal so that it looked more like a stump with a birdbath topping it than a city water fountain. Bluebells and ivy radiated out from it, consuming the pavement.

The fae rejoiced in their Queen's triumph. The Hunt bayed along with it, and Tess saw Hunter slide a knowing glance toward the bag she was carrying. She could not hold it any tighter, but she tried.

Then the hunt was through the crowd and the dancers blurred behind them, their noise quickly growing faint with distance. Naito Parkway became Front Avenue as they blazed into the industrial district near the river. Ahead of her, through the glamour, the city shimmered like a mirage. There was a dark fog rising that, for a moment, she feared was another cloud of pixies, but then the kelpie lurched to the left and Tess knew a moment of exquisite terror.

Then she realized they were skirting the edge of the dark fog where the railroad tracks sent spurs everywhere through the district. The fog showed where there was more iron. Suddenly Tess understood what the city must do to the fae, with its iron skeletons and muscles and arteries. Metal everywhere.

The Hunt landed on Nicolai Street with a sickening lurch—but no corresponding crumpling of vehicles—and swept northwest. The black fog diminished, and they chased through a quieter district of smaller warehouses and brick buildings, the occasional blue-collar cafe and pub. The Willamette was still only a block or two away.

"Will we be drowned by the kelpies?" Her eyes opened wide and she only just kept her head from striking Thomas's chin as they bounced like untethered sacks of meal. How they could bounce so hard and not fall off could only *be* magic.

"No," said Thomas. "Not drowned. Worse. They're taking us to Forest Park."

"What—why? What's in the woods?"

"My Queen, and her Court, and her justice." Thomas's voice was flat and brooked no more discussion. "When we get there, let me do the talking. And for God's sake, keep that sack a secret."

"It's going to be hard," Tess said, looking down at the sack for the first time in what seemed like forever. "My…uh, jacket…is growing moss. And bark. And bluebells." She pinched off a budding bloom head and tossed it aside, where it burst like a silent firework against the kelpie's glamour, and vanished.

"Fuck," said Thomas. She couldn't have agreed more.

To their right ahead of them, Tess could see the streetlight-spangled shape of the most beautiful bridge in Portland: the St. Johns, with its gothic buttresses and verdigris paint. It arched over the Willamette so high it needed no drawbridge for even the largest ship to pass beneath it. It too was shrouded in a dark fog, and Tess realized she must be seeing how the fae saw iron, as a dark miasma to avoid. The Hunt turned left once again, leaving the highway for a steep slope upward.

They had entered Forest Park. Tess saw the familiar, ubiquitous ivy on the ground, and the Hunt plowing through it, one moment wheels, and the next, hooves and feet and bodies, as the Hunt abandoned its urban glamour. The trees were black and silver and motionless in the forest's moonlit midnight, except for the birches, which were walking slowly, shedding their brown-gold leaves like droplets shaken from wet fingers.

Walking.

Trees, walking. Looking more like the ghosts of girls Tess had known in high school. Slender and winter-pale, untouched by sun, with lovely, strange faces winking and squinting out of the scored and blotched bark. She fumbled for the seeing stone. She had to see what was truly beneath the surface, or if she was now seeing through the glamour. If, indeed, they were disguised at all. These must be the birch girls Stephen had spoken of. They were beautiful beyond comprehension.

Thomas put up a hand and stopped her. She looked up at him to find his mouth shaping a silent "no" in the gloom. "Guard your secrets," he whispered. "All of them. As long as you can."

"Oh." She couldn't imagine what possible good it would do, keeping the seeing stone hidden, but she trusted him. He knew this world, and she did not. "Are those trees…walking?"

"Ghille dhu," murmured Thomas, as if that meant something. "They are always the last to fall to the wintersleep."

"They're *lovely*." She didn't know what else to say as the trees swayed away from the crashing progress of the Hunt. These were Stephen's birch girls, and at last she knew what he'd been talking about. The faces of the girls turned to look at them, gray-eyed and smiling, pale hair streaming upward, half branch, half silk, defying gravity. The old-gold coins of their dying leaves fluttered in the night wind, seeming to reach toward the moon.

"Yes," said Thomas, "very." She heard the yearning in his voice. It left her bereft. What good was an ordinary human woman in the world of the fae? Even her brother had longed for the birch girls and their delicate beauty. Thomas said he wanted to be human again, but the fae still had claims on his soul and his heart. Fortunately the birch girls were swiftly out of sight and Tess ran out of time to consider them. The Hunt raged uphill, breaking the brittle branches of big leaf maples and crashing through the whippy red alder limbs still dangling the last of their miniature cones.

Tess and Thomas were thrown from side to side on the kelpie's back as it dodged and lurched. Now the pack was yelping, in full cry, hounds of night blasting ever upward, until suddenly they were at the crest of the spine of hills that formed Forest Park. Below her to the south, Tess saw the lights of Portland and the shimmering artery of the Willamette, and then vertigo spun her senses as they plunged downward into a black hole. Hunter looked back over his shoulder at them. The antlers had returned with his red eyes, like the scorched eyeholes of her pumpkin at home.

Home.

It was a thousand years ago and yet only an instant.

Tess saw the hole was really a tunnel. They seemed to be racing as fast as they had through the streets of Portland, but in the blackness it was even more terrifying because she could not see the way ahead of them, and did not know the environment at all. There were spots of glowing things on the walls, and the occasional sense of passing openings to the side, when the pack's yelping echoed differently and the space felt larger. Down and down and down they went, the whole place smelling richly of soil and mold and moisture and rock. It smelled alive, in a way the caves she had toured in the past never had.

The further they went, the stronger the scent became. Much like the swooning intoxication of the bluebells in her house, this was a fragrance that summoned deep summery memories of grass and earth, warmth and daylight, and the heavy sweetness of blackberries so ripe they verged on wine.

Thomas put a hand to the back of her head and pressed her down, still holding her tight. "The ceiling lowers soon." He bent with her, and his trow scent mingled with the blackberries.

Sure enough, within a minute the space around them tightened, giving the impression they were hurtling through an ever-smaller pipe. She pictured them shooting out like storm run-off from a culvert and wondered where this strange ride would end, and what new terrifying things they would find when they got there.

From somewhere up ahead she could hear music and laughter, weird atonal songs that were more chants than music. She turned her head, feeling a pull toward the music, a yearning that made no sense. Somewhere close was a party, and dancing, and she longed to be a part of it.

The Hunt clattered out of the tunnel into an enormous space. The noise of the party burst over them as if a door had been opened, voices calling and singing and shrieking. Everything was confusion and sound and she could not tell left from right, up from down, a sensation as extraordinary and disorienting as floating underwater. The room's ceiling and walls were covered with crystals reflecting and refracting torchlight, candlelight, and darting, flickering glimmers she was inclined to label fairylight.

The Hunt raced along the room's perimeter, their glamour blurring and shredding away like smoke.

It was like being inside a geode the size of a concert hall. Sound came from everywhere, whispers, screams, laughter and joy and terror. On the floor beside them, the fae wound in a spiral that tightened and unwound itself at the same time, whirling both ways. Vertigo took Tess's last vestige of balance, and she closed her eyes against the myriad shapes of the dancers. The singing grew piercingly sweet.

When she opened her eyes again, the Hunt had joined the dance and was spinning and twisting its way to the center of the room, in a spiral like a whirlpool. All around them a tricky wind was blowing. Her hair lifted like that of the birch girls aboveground. She tried to look closely at the creatures around her, but each time her eyes settled on one, it seemed to turn into something she might find blowing down a Portland street in the city's frequent east wind, or trapped in the gutters. A rustle of newspaper here, a scudding leaf there, a sparkle of broken glass, a crushed paper cup, a budding twig, a trodden soda can, a cluster of gravel or sand. And yet, and yet…it was all so beautiful, brilliant with light and sound. As long as she didn't try to stare at any one thing, she could see the shapes of the dancers. They were slender or thick, heavy or floating, all graceful, all beautiful, all horrible, dark and bright and gossamer. Their touch brushed along the neck and sides of the kelpie she and Thomas rode, stroking over her as they passed. What had been a lurching trot became something more dreamlike and swaying, a slow-motion gavotte.

She struggled to be free of Thomas and the kelpie and the binding cord that cinched their waists together. She had to dance, had to wave her arms, leave her heavy clothes and shoes behind, join that irresistible tidal flow, kiss the beautiful mouths that smiled at her…

…and whispered, "Salt. Blood. *Meat!*"

The whisper grew as the Hunt penetrated into the whirling heart of the spiral, until the leafy sibilance became the wild screeching of trees rubbing together in storms, of hellish violins, of the rabbit taken by the owl.

⇒ Chapter Twenty-Nine ⇐

Thomas watched the woman in his arms as her head twisted this way and that, following the movement of the fae in their Allantide spiral. He knew what she needed, for it was the same thing he needed. She needed to dance, to sing and shriek out her madness and grief. To fall into the arms of the male that drifted alongside them, his hand trailing along Tess's arm. Thomas batted it away, but it was back immediately.

Thomas turned her head from the dancers with hurtful fingers pinching either side of her mouth, and stared into her eyes. "Don't look at them, look at me."

She did, for a moment, then her gaze drifted to the stranger's hand on her arm, the one that lifted to touch her collarbones—a sweet, tender place Thomas had kissed and nuzzled only hours ago. He hissed at her harshly. "Look here. *Here*, damn you!"

This time she held his gaze for longer, staring into his eyes, the part that stayed Thomas, no matter what the rest of him looked like. The hand that had begun to coil around her throat slid away.

"Salt. Blood. *Meat!*" the dancers cried. Out of the corners of his eyes he saw their attention following the Hunt's progress the way daisies followed the sun.

"Don't look away!"

This, as Tess's gaze slid sideways. She looked back to him, and then she pulled his head down to hers, closing her eyes.

"You're real," Tess breathed. "I came here for you and the souls in this sack. I won't give in." Her fingers groped for the seeing stone, but Thomas rested a hand atop hers. She settled for wrapping her hand in the folds of Thomas's coat and burying her face in his sweaty neck. He felt her lips touching where his frantic pulse beat strongest. She breathed deep, and he wondered whether she was smelling Thomas the trow, or the whirling, summer-wine decadence of dancing fae. It could not be summer, here at the precipice into winter. It could only be glamour, and glamour was never true. Her senses might fool her, but her heart never would. Of this Thomas was sure.

"Salt. Blood. *Meat!*"

She whispered her doubt to Thomas. "Doesn't it make you need to dance with them?"

His chest swelled on a long inhalation. "Yes. Yes. Every single moment, yes. But I won't, ever again. I don't know if I can get you out of this, but I'm going to try."

The noise of the crowd receded, just a little. "We can do it," she promised him. "We can."

His laugh was brittle and sad, and she held tight to him, breathing him in, her hand cupped above his beating heart. Thomas thought of nothing else. No plans, no thoughts of iron or water or what they could do next. For a little while only Tess existed for him, the warm center of a very small circle scribed by the binding cord.

Then there came a dizzying moment when the center of the spiral was reached, a feeling like the bursting of a bubble inside him, and the coil turned to the other direction. They were coming out of the dance, and the absolute *need* seemed to lessen, the touch of the other dancers along their bodies, and those of the Hunt, less insistent or persuasive. The cries of hunger did not diminish, however. As the Hunt neared the outer arm of the spiral, they grew louder and louder.

Tess being Tess, she would not hide her eyes forever. She peeked out of Thomas's collar to see where they were heading. At the edge of the spiral was the set of arched double doors into the Queen's chamber, guarded by the two grinning, dancing kelpies. The Hunt picked up speed again, fueled by the tingling energy stored up by the spiral, and headed for the doors as if it would crash straight through them.

The kelpies flung open the doors at the last possible microsecond, as Tess was flinching away from the inevitable crash. The pack hit the doorway and stopped as if it had run into a glass wall, yelping and leaping over and over again in thwarted eagerness. But Hunter and their kelpie mount went blasting through, hooves and feet clattering and sliding on a floor as transparently black and glossy as obsidian, shadow given substance.

Hunter's antlers swung round to them as he stopped, his staff aloft in one hand. With his other, he gave a yank on the binding cord. Tess and Thomas toppled from the back of the kelpie, which leaned toward Tess with an unmistakable leer on its face, its penis sliding free of its horse-body sheath.

Tess turned away with a shudder, one hand struggling with the binding cord, the other clinging tight to Thomas where they sprawled on the shining floor.

"I call Hunter to Court, by the will of my Queen and the Law of the ages!" Thomas shouted, over the top of Hunter, who cried, "Salt! Blood! Meat!"

Tess hiss-whispered to Thomas, "Meat? Are *we* the—"

"Shhh."

"Give me another of your iron nails." Her hand groped over his coat and once again he stopped her. He had eyes and ears only for what was going on here in the Queen's chamber until he knew which way the Queen's inclinations lay. Since she had tried to poison him earlier that day, he didn't think he had much chance of winning his life away from the Wild Hunt, but he had to try. Tess might be the variable that changed the game.

Across the room, the curtains of the Queen's bed stirred. They moved like fog, like smoke, draped fantastically over rock crystal stalagmites. Thomas heard Tess's gasp when they drifted aside. He saw his Queen for the first time as if through Tess's eyes: beautiful in her languid awakening. She patted back a yawn in the exaggerated fashion of a stage actress. She sat nude on the edge of her bed, reaching her arms upward, her fingertips beckoning gently. From everywhere in the room came a flurry of pixies in her direction, and the woman was clothed as she rose.

Thomas was very still beside Tess, his attention riveted on the Queen.

Tess whispered to him, "She's the one who met Aaron! Is that the queen?"

Thomas nodded, not looking away from the woman by the bed. Her eyes were taking in everything: Thomas and Tess on the floor, Hunter beside them, the kelpie cringe-prancing in an ecstasy of terror and delight.

Tess moved a little. Thomas allowed himself a glance in her direction and saw that she had settled the tote bag more securely against her body, pressing her elbow down over it tightly. Good for Tess. It was best if she remembered afresh they weren't here for a friendly visit.

The Queen walked toward them. Thomas struggled to his knees, bringing Tess with him. Hunter's every aspect was cloaked in fury, but he had apparently made his official statement and was now awaiting comment from the Queen.

"Which is the meat?" The Queen halted, glancing from Hunter to Thomas to Tess.

"I," said Thomas.

"Pity." The Queen smiled at Tess kindly. "She looks delicious." Thomas knew the moment when Tess felt the compulsion of that gaze, a desire to do anything the Queen might ask of her, if only she would smile or allow Tess to remain in her presence. He saw the worshipful tilt of her face, basking in that smile's warmth. Such beauty could not intend evil. But then Tess's free hand crept into his and squeezed, and her spine stiffened. She looked past the Queen, to where something else was stirring in the bed.

Tess gasped. "Aaron!"

Thomas saw the dawning comprehension on her face as a hundred questions were answered, but he was sure a hundred more rose to take their places. She trembled in Thomas's hold. He tightened his arm protectively. Let the Queen see. She knew, anyway. Of that he had no doubt.

The Queen looked over her shoulder to the bed where Aaron stood naked and slumped in exhaustion, rubbing his eyes. Dismissively, she returned her attention to Thomas and Hunter. "What is it you have brought me, my huntsman? This is unusual."

Thomas and Hunter spoke at the same time, once again. "I throw myself on the Court's judgment!"

"He must trouble me no longer! He is your meat, my Lady!"

The Queen looked from one to the other, and jerked her chin at the kelpie, standing to one side, ribs heaving with the exertion of the long hunt. "Speak."

The kelpie gave Thomas a sidelong glance, and cringed away when Hunter raised a clenched fist. "He was our prey. But there was a moment of doubt, when we should have taken him, and did not, and thus he is entitled to your judgment rather than ours. My Lady."

Thomas saw the Queen's eyes change. A chill went through him as she appeared—only for a moment—to be nothing but blind fury.

The Queen turned to Hunter. "You have brought me my own knight. How came this? Speak the truth. And release them."

"Leave us!" Hunter shouted at the kelpie, which bared its teeth and then slunk toward the exit. Hunter thumped his staff on the floor of the room and the cord binding Thomas and Tess fizzled away like a cigarette falling to ash. Tess hardly paid attention as the kelpie left. She had eyes only for Aaron, who at last seemed to recognize her through his haze. She and Thomas got to their feet, slowly and painfully.

"Aaron!" she cried again, holding out her hand. "Come with us!"

"Come with you where?" interrupted the Queen. "Do you think you are leaving?"

Tess's gaze flicked back to the Queen. "We came to get Aaron and take him home." She beckoned him with an urgent hand motion. Thomas knew what was in Tess's mind. If she could just get him close enough, she could show him the things in the tote bag, and maybe—maybe he would take a marker and be restored, like Rory.

"But he does not wish to leave."

"He doesn't know what he wants—what's best for him—because you have bewitched him."

The Queen laughed, and every pixie in her dress laughed with her, tiny hands waving in mirth, tiny mouths shrilling amusement. "He has made a choice, that is all. We bewitch nothing. If the bargains are not made by free will, they are void." She looked over her shoulder at Aaron again. "Come, my love. Tell her what she needs to hear, so we can get on with this dreadfully boring discussion. Allantide wanes and I am not half done with my work, and my Court has not had its salt and blood and meat."

Aaron moved out of the drifting curtains of the bed, his eyes fixed on the Queen. He wore nothing except a torc around his neck, twisted of the same slender threads of gold as Thomas's armband. Twined amongst the threads were droplets of ruby—blood red, shining dully in the shadowless light of the room. When he was near enough, he took the hand the Queen held out to him, his eyes filled with adoration and need. He could hardly look away from where the pixies fluttered and crept and caressed his lover's breasts, her hips.

"Tell her, Aaron," the Queen urged him, as if he were a foolish child. "Do you wish to leave me?"

"No, my love. Come back to bed."

The Queen gave Tess a sharp-edged smile. "You see?"

"Why don't you let me speak to him alone? He probably doesn't really understand what's going on around him. Addicts sometimes don't, you know. And you've addicted him to something. I don't know what, precisely, but he needs to come. with me."

Thomas felt the blood drain from his face at Tess's words. He would never have imagined speaking to the Queen in such a manner, but Tess had no idea of the fae's power, even though fae magic had chased them out of Tess's house before that same magic swallowed it whole.

The Queen smiled sweetly. "So bold. I see why Thomas is enamored of you. You are much like me."

Tess blinked. "Is that supposed to flatter me? Because—"

The Queen interrupted. "I do not flatter. I have no need of flattery. My people serve me because it is their desire."

Out of the corner of his eye, Thomas saw Hunter's antlered head lift as if he had been stung. Serving the Queen was a duty rather than a desire by now, for both of them. Thomas because he had at last found two things he wanted more than he wanted the Queen—his own humanity, and Tess. And Hunter...Hunter wanted what the Queen had. That much was clear to Thomas. But still she ruled them both, though Thomas did not understand the hold she had over Hunter. Perhaps the huntsman merely stayed close, biding his time. For a moment Thomas wondered what the Unseelie Court would be like with Hunter at its heart and head, and decided it didn't bear consideration. Hunter was a killer.

"I don't think we're alike at all. You've enslaved Thomas. I've seen your *thing* on his arm." Her hand flailed toward Aaron. "You've put one on Aaron's neck. How is that love? How is that desire?"

"So young." The Queen looked at Thomas. "You were once so young. Full of life and ideals, but never so full of spite."

"Aaron!" Tess tried again. "Your family misses you terribly. I saw your mother yesterday. She hasn't heard from you, and she's afraid something bad has happened."

Aaron still had eyes for no one but the Queen. His fingers touched the torc at his neck and lingered there. He stayed where he was, the smoky curtains moving gently behind him as if the bed were breathing.

"You see," the Queen said gently. "Aaron belongs here." Her gaze flicked to Thomas. "As do you, my knight."

"No! Neither of them belong here!" Tess took a step forward, slipping her free hand into the top of the tote. Her fingers closed around something and lifted it out, just as Thomas realized what she was doing and hissed at her to stop.

She held up a snail shell carved of cloudy pale stone and glittering with silver chased through the spiral, between her thumb and forefinger. When he'd seen it in Tess's house, it had seemed a prettily carved stone faintly touched by fae glamour. But now, here in the Unseelie Court, it had a shine all its own, a transient marbling like a curling tress of smoke trapped under glass, and that purple magic dancing along the silver like the sparks from static electricity.

Thomas's hand clenched on hers so tightly she gasped from the pain.

The effect of the trinket on the Queen was like touching a match to gunpowder. The Queen's eyes narrowed and sparkled, sunlight on snow. The pixie gown burst away from her, fluttering uncertainly like a startled flock of starlings with no place to land. Her form changed from a beautiful woman to a circling, weaving snake and back again, as if the Queen could not contain her emotion or her magic.

Suddenly her face was a bare inch from Tess's, the reek of danger absolute and unmistakable in Thomas's nostrils, her head moving and swaying, hypnotic as a cobra's dance.

"That is *mine*. Give it to me!"

Thomas's heart nearly jolted from his body in terror when Tess almost did as the Queen said, but at the last second Tess's fingers closed over the snail shell.

Maybe the Queen couldn't take it away from Tess, Thomas realized in astonishment. What stopped her? He could not imagine, but foolhardy Tess shook her head.

"I found it. I will keep it." Tess's declaration chilled Thomas to the marrow. If only she had kept the things secret a little longer, he might have used them to bargain for their lives, but Aaron's presence had tipped the balance for Tess. She would save the world, given a single strand of hope. It was both the thing he loved best about her, and the thing he feared most. She spoke again, leaning past the Queen. "Aaron! Take it! It will make you well again!"

For a moment the haze of desire cleared from Aaron's face. He looked away from the Queen to the snail shell in Tess's hand, and took a step toward it. "Come on!" Tess cried. "Take it, and take my hand! I'll get you home again." Thomas heard the desperation in her voice, the fear and dread and longing all mixed.

The Queen turned her attention to Thomas, still only inches from Tess. "Is she the thief?"

Thomas looked away from Tess with an effort.

"Thomas," the Queen prompted, the word sickeningly sweet coming from the serpent mouth. "I asked you a question. You must answer with truth."

"Aaron!" Tess urged again.

"Yes," Thomas said at last, wretched.

"Ahh," the Queen whispered, and into the silence that followed came the sharp, twanging sounds of several strands of his armband breaking. Thomas let go of Tess's hand and clutched at his arm. Pain. Relief. Guilt. For betraying Tess, his Queen had rewarded him.

She looked down at the bag of trinkets, still clutched tightly under her arm, and then at Thomas, who would not meet her eyes. "Oh, Thomas."

"And so Thomas betrays you," said the Queen, still sweetly. "Because, like Aaron, he belongs to me. And I have rewarded him for his efforts, you little thief."

Tess stared at the woman, who slowly settled away from her, the pixie gown returning, the sharp smile curving her lips, more human now than serpent, though her eyes were still strange and glinting. Then she looked at Aaron, who put a hand to the torc once more.

"I'm staying here. But it was nice to see you again." Aaron blinked sleepily and walked back to the bed, where the draperies thinned to allow him entry, then thickened and hid him from view.

Tess closed her hand over the snail shell and shut her eyes.

Hunter, a few feet away, laughed softly and drew a stone blade from his belt—stone, not silver, for the ancient wild magic. "Blood, my Lady? Salt? Meat?"

⇒ Chapter Thirty ⇐

When Tess opened her eyes again, hoping against hope that she was waking and the nightmare ended, the Queen was no longer in her face. Tess drew a long breath of relief. The snail shell was still in her hand. The tote bag was still tucked under her arm, though it was growing mossier with each moment and spreading its greenery to her clothing and shoulder bag like a contagion. She had a second or two to observe while the Queen regarded Hunter—and the knife in his hand—thoughtfully and her tongue flicked across her lips.

The Queen's gorgeous gown was made of pixies, Tess saw now, the same leafy fairies that had taunted Tess at Aaron's house and flown out of the tote bag in her kitchen. Tess recalled Thomas's casual slaughter of them as she saw the creatures clinging to the Queen, covering her and revealing her at the same time, a living gown of autumn flame and bronze, in continual motion. These strange, beautiful, biddable and disposable creatures. It was all part and parcel of the otherness Tess could not seem to wrap her mind around. Tree girls, seductive water horses, things that wanted to eat her, things that disguised themselves as rubbish. Ivy and bluebells that consumed entire buildings.

Aaron seemed to have no use for her, no wish to return to his human life. Is this what had happened to Stephen? The idea turned her stomach. Thomas seemed to have survived his encounters with the Queen rather than succumbing to a deathly trance. Tess glanced at him to see his reaction and found he was taking off his oilskin coat. She was transfixed by the droplets of red that dripped from the fingers of his left arm onto the floor. The color was suddenly the only thing Tess could see. Thomas was bleeding.

With a gasp, Tess shoved the snail shell back into the tote bag and hurried to Thomas's left side, where she pushed up the sleeve of his sweater. Blood had soaked through parts of the weave and was dripping from where the curling gold wires pierced his skin in a dozen places. The armband was appreciably thinner than when she'd seen it earlier.

At the sight of the blood, a number of pixies fluttered from the Queen's gown to the floor. The creatures smeared it over their lips in ecstasy, their autumn colors brightening with each lick and swallow. Tess was sickened by the bestial sight. Her trembling fingers worked at the armband, pulling each wire free of Thomas's flesh with great effort. At the same time, her feet scuffled at the pixies on the floor, trying to kick them away from the droplets.

"How could you," she breathed, not looking at the Queen. "You bitch."

There was a rustle as one pixie, wizened and coarsely curled as an old cornhusk, broke from the feeding flock and returned to the Queen, where it offered a palmful of blood. The Queen shook her head with an indulgent smile, and the pixie settled in a spot above the curve of the Queen's breast, licking its hands clean. Thomas's blood did not brighten the weary gold of spent summer cornstalks. Perhaps it was too old. Tess hoped the vile little creature would die. If it came in reach again, she would pinch its evil head just as Thomas had done in her kitchen.

Thomas put a hand up to halt Tess's struggle with the wires. "Never mind. Leave it."

Tess ignored him, her face grim and set, continuing the gory task of bending the wires away at less harmful angles. The pixie, finished with its refreshment, stood at the Queen's shoulder and spoke into her ear while it looked at Thomas and Tess with a mocking smirk on its tiny, pointed face. The Queen smiled again and nodded, and the husk disappeared into the hundreds of pixies that made the Queen's autumn gown. Tess caught a sudden glimmer in the Queen's eyes, and then it was masked, with only her seductive, mutable beauty remaining.

"You really should return my things," the Queen said now, looking at Tess. "Return them, and you may go free."

"I'm not finished here. I certainly won't leave without Thomas and Aaron."

"So noble! Even though Thomas has betrayed you, thief?"

The last wire pulled free. Only a few strands remained intact. She brushed away the splinters of bone and picked a couple out of the sweater before she pulled the sleeve back down over the wounds. There was nothing else she could do for the bleeding right now. "I...know he was just doing his job. He didn't know I was—he didn't know I had your things. I didn't know they belonged to anyone. It's not the same as stealing."

"Stop talking," Thomas said to Tess. She met his gaze and tears welled up.

The Queen took a step forward again. "I can give you what you long for most. Thomas will tell you I can. I gave him his own heart's desire many and many a year ago."

"You made him your slave, just the way you're making Aaron." Tess groped for Thomas's hand and squeezed it tightly.

He returned the pressure but whispered, "Let it be."

"It was what he most wanted." The Queen turned to where Hunter leaned against one of the crystal formations that made the posters of her bed. Hunter flipped the knife in his hand, his feet spread apart in an easy stance. Tess had the distinct impression he was smiling beneath the stag's head mask. She fought down a shudder, that dreaded trio of words ringing in her ears. *Salt, blood, meat.* "Just as I gave my Hunter what *he* most wanted. What I give all my lovers."

Hunter stilled, which was more terrifying to Tess than any of his wicked, casual knifeplay.

Tess curled her lips in distaste, hiding her fear. "To be your slaves."

The Queen came forward slowly, her smile as gentle as summer rain. She ran lingering fingertips over Thomas's shoulder, down to where his muscle bulged over the too-tight armband, into the stain of blood. "You wished to be my knight, didn't you, my love? My strong arm."

It was clear to Tess that Thomas felt the old pull of the Queen's magic and beauty, the sway of her personality. Her grip on Thomas's hand grew fierce as he leaned toward the Queen, his eyes following every bright-eyed glance and every stroke of her fingers. At Tess's painful grip, Thomas swallowed and turned his gaze toward the bed where Aaron was concealed within.

The Queen followed his gaze. "And Aaron, my sweet, sweet Aaron—he does wish to serve me, as you see, but it is with love that he is leashed." The Queen turned to Tess, persuasion evident in every line of her body, every gentle motion of her hand.

"A slave collar," Tess spat. "You've addicted him to you. Let him go."

"Aaron has made his choice. His bargain is sealed."

"You're a lying bitch." Tess's voice broke with anger and disappointment. She could feel she was failing in her quest, but she had nothing else to use except her words, to try and make the Queen understand how wrong her actions were.

The Queen ignored Tess, turning instead to Hunter.

"Remove your mask, my Hunter. Show our visitor we are courteous."

Hunter straightened, stilling the knife and lowering his arms very slowly. "My Lady…"

She gave a slight jerk of her head. It wasn't something to ignore, and apparently even Hunter, powerful Hunter, had no choice but to obey. His hand went to the deer skull and slowly, slowly, lifted it from his head.

Where the deer skull had sat were deep ridges in Hunter's flesh, raw and angry wounds across the man's prominent cheekbones. His eyes still glowed red, but without the dark hollows of the skull mask to accent their light, they seemed less dangerous and frightening. A hundred black braids fell across his shoulders.

Without the mask, he was diminished, which is what the Queen had meant to accomplish. Tess could see hatred in Hunter's eyes. Hatred, yes…and a sick pleasure that the Queen had noticed him, turned her attention to him, at last.

The thing that held Tess's eye was the spiky golden crown circling Hunter's brow, made of glittering razor-edged ribbons and barbs pointing inward, pressing the flesh of his forehead and scalp.

Cutting him, piercing him.

Just like Thomas's armband.

"Hunter wished to rule me," the Queen said, in a voice as

hard and brittle as glass, ringing with a crystalline clarity in the room. "He would be king. I crowned him, as he desired."

Thomas had once told Tess that his armband always pained him, but Hunter's crown was something else again. No wonder Hunter preferred to remain masked instead of displaying the badge of his hubris for all to see. Here in the Queen's chamber, it seemed Hunter was not permitted the glamour that turned the crown into the headdress of reeds, dreadlocks and animal tails. Tess realized there was no defeating the Queen, not here on her home ground where all the rules were hers to make, or change, or break.

"He's like you—" Tess gasped to Thomas.

"Don't listen. She's playing on your sympathy. She's using you."

The Queen cut across Thomas's statement with a hiss. "You could help them both. It's very simple." She put out a graceful hand to receive the mossy bag of trinkets. Her melting, sweet glance was full of understanding and care. "I know what's in that bag. Those things belong to me. Return them. If you do, I will reward both my knight and my huntsman, and give you your heart's desire."

Tess shook her head and clutched the bag tighter. "These...things...need to be returned to the people you took them from."

The Queen's laugh was kind. "Precious girl, so many of

those people are dead. This is the only way they can live on, to become part of my Court the way they would have wanted. Will you refuse to honor their wishes?"

"If they're dead, it's because you stole their lives."

"Not stolen. The Unseelie never steal. Everything is given willingly. They all had their heart's desire, the same as Thomas has had his, even though he seems to want more than his fair share now." When the Queen turned her eyes upon him, her pupils slitted, clever and cunning and judging.

"You would make…what, ivy and bluebells and moss of them?" Tess knew she was treading upon very thin ice.

The Queen drew the back of her hand softly over Tess's cheek, smiling when Tess flinched from her touch. "Is that so awful? Tell me, what would you have them be? Should I return them to the misery from which I rescued them? These were souls the humans had abandoned. Men and women discarded by you and those like you."

"Not Aaron. Not Rory. Not Stephen—"

The Queen gave a sudden inhalation, and a smile. "Stephen. Ah, yes." Her gaze cut to Thomas. "That is what I tasted on you earlier. They were children together, sister and brother, yes? She is very like him." Her gaze turned back to Tess. "Your brother loved me too."

Thomas could almost feel the rupture in Tess's heart as she threw back her head, biting her lips, gazing upward to hide salty tears. In a moment she had controlled the emotion that flooded her face. When she spoke, her voice was brittle and harsh. "He didn't love you. He was an addict. They don't love, they crave. But I loved him. And you took him because he was weak."

"Not everyone is so beloved as you would have me believe. Everyone the Unseelie take has made the choice to come to us."

"Only because you make the poison so sweet! That's no choice at all! I will not give them up. Let me take Thomas and Aaron and leave with these things, and I swear we won't tell a soul about this night, or your home here under Forest Park. You've taken my house—you can have it."

"Not taken. It was given."

Tess's mouth fell open. "Given? Are you crazy?"

The Queen's shrug was eloquent and beautiful. The pixies forming her gown shifted with her, scarlet and gold and bronze with the season, their thin fingers and mouths moving, always moving, caressing their Queen.

"Call it what you will. The fact remains that you abandoned your home to us. You left it tonight and the fae took your place. The same way Aaron was abandoned. And all the others. The fae feast upon human leavings."

"I—" Tess could only sputter, confounded. She was out of logic. "I didn't. I didn't even know what was happening."

"Oh, but you did. I'm sure Thomas told you." The Queen raised a slender finger, as if to beseech a moment's grace from the determined girl before her. With a slow smile, she said, "In free and grateful return for the gift of your home, I give you *your* heart's desire, *Tess*."

What had Thomas said about names? That giving the fae your truename gave them power over you? Who had given the Queen her name? Not Hunter, for Thomas had never spoken her name in his hearing. Nor had she given it herself.

Suddenly she knew. The whispering, traitorous corn-husk pixie. No doubt she and Thomas had missed finding one, somehow. It had overheard them at home and escaped to betray them. She froze, staring first at the Queen's beautiful smile. A warm lassitude, like sinking into a bath of sun-warmed honey, spread through Tess. When Thomas gasped, she turned to look at him. On his face was such horrified sadness that she reached out to cup his cheek, comfort him. The hand that stretched to him was not her own. She flinched back away from this new creature in their midst, and the hand flinched back too.

"No. Oh, no." Thomas moaned and reached for her. His big rough hand caught at the strange new hand. Tess, feeling that trow hand close around the strange hand, knew it was her own. The lassitude ebbed, and in its place was panic. The Queen had done something to her, but what?

She stared at the fingers in Thomas's grasp. Where she had once had pale skin, now there was rough, papery…was it bark she was seeing? She tried to look down at herself and found her movements strangely stiff and restricted. She felt as if she were suddenly taller, yet at the same time more delicate and diffuse, as if her nerves were unfurling and reaching out past her flesh, forming a network of sensation. Her clothing fitted her oddly. Her boots hurt her feet. When she looked down at them, she saw tree roots protruding from between the leather uppers and rubber soles. She shuffled once and the boots flapped loosely, ruined.

Tess leaned forward, intending to push into Thomas's arms, beg him to stop what was happening to her. She was the same height as he now, their gazes on a level with one another. She sought his eyes, desperate to read something there, find an explanation, and saw her own reflection in the darkness of his gaze. Where she had once had hair, now there were twigs and branches stretching upward, and the trembling gold leaves of the birch. Where she had once had lashes, now there were curls of birch bark, black and silver.

She did not recognize herself in the tiny images. Nothing of Tess remained. Horror swept over her. She began to shake. Leaves drifted down from her branches, settling on the sleeves of her jacket and Thomas's shoulders.

Birch girl, birch girl.

➤ Chapter Thirty-One ➤

In that instant Thomas understood it all. The sly whisper of the cornhusk pixie at the Queen's ear. The cornstalks rustling on Tess's porch. His own impassioned murmur of her name as they embraced on the front walk, ignoring the fae truth for his very human desire and hope.

Betrayed.

Thomas clutched Tess's hand tighter and knew it for what it was: the papery bark over the bones, the twiggy fingers of the ghille dhu, the birch girls. Tess had surrendered without even knowing what she was doing, her trusting, kind nature childlike to a player of the Queen's power. It was a brutal wound to learn that Tess's heart's desire was to be something besides what she was, something beautiful and fragile and *other*.

"Thief," hissed the Queen, and made a grab for the sack of trinkets. Thomas supposed she hadn't tried before now because she hadn't had proof that Tess had stolen them. His own admission had strangled their last chance at using the trinkets to buy their freedom.

Yet even now, Tess was still in there, still somehow *Tess*. Thomas wondered again at the strength of mind that held her determination in place like one of the piers of the Burnside

Bridge, bulwark against the ceaseless current of the Willamette. Her new woody body-trunk pivoted, arm-limbs reaching out to push the Queen away even as more twigs passed the tote bag upward into the autumn crown of branches, out of reach. The sack burst at a seam, and a trinket fell, spinning on the floor, a fir cone made of silver and clay. Tess made a noise like creaking house beams, trying to bend after the cone, bare roots flailing and groping uselessly over the slick floor. The Queen's tail deftly slid the cone out of sight among a cluster of pixies.

Thomas roared. "That was *not* her heart's desire, and you know it! Queen or not, you are a liar and a cheat!"

The Queen turned on him, the serpent tail twitching so hard that the pixies upon it were thrashed and broken, and the fir cone slapped to the wall many feet away, whirling like a puck on ice. "She wanted to become something you could love, Thomas. *That* was her heart's desire. I will return her to her human form, in return for that bag. A new bargain for *Tess*, if she will make it."

Tess flinched at the sound of her name, and Thomas swallowed his words of hate, knowing that to speak further would only whip the Queen's anger to retaliatory fury.

She softly touched his cheek, her gentleness cloaking her ire. "My poor knight. Did you never tell her you loved her?" Her eyes searched his, and the birch girl that was Tess twisted, looking at him in confusion. The Queen smiled. "These humans, you must spell everything out for them. They are so literal and unimaginative. How much simpler to be fae." She walked away, leaving him standing clutching Tess's woody hand. "Get me my meat, Hunter, and not this feckless knight of mine. I hunger. I am spent this Allantide, and my work is unfinished because of *her.*"

Tess still held the torn corner of the bag closed by one slender twig hand, but now she was struggling to free the other from Thomas's grasp. He was reluctant to release her. In her new form she was very strong, and rather than upset her further he slackened his grip. Tess reached into the neck of her shirt, her woody fingers clawing over the bark there in search of something.

Her fingers pried under the edge of a blackened tree scar, and gave a mighty pull. A scab of bark broke away, falling to the floor and rocking. Where the bark had been was the seeing stone, imbedded in the softwood of Tess's new body. Her fingers worked at the stone, sap drooling down the front of her trunk.

"Stop, Tess," Thomas begged. There was no reason not to use her truename now. "You're hurting yourself."

"Have to see." Her voice came out muffled, though he could see the knot that was her mouth, moving.

The Queen, having dismissed Tess for the moment, was pouring wine into goblets, enough for all of them. No doubt the same poisoned clover wine, as if it might succeed this time. The pixies that had been cleaning his blood from the floor shifted their attention to the sap—Tess's blood—and giggled drunkenly even when Tess's roots and branches caught and flung them away from her.

"See what? Just stop. It's no good!"

The stone came loose at last, leaving a hole as if the tree had grown around it. A freshet of sap followed, and Tess gave a creaking gasp. Her branches drooped in pain. Across the room, Hunter was following the proceedings with great interest, coming forward a half step at a time, his eyes darting from the Queen to Tess and back again, like a schoolboy intent on wickedness. Thomas moved to put his body between Hunter and Tess, keeping watch on the huntsman over his shoulder. The Queen might have commanded Thomas's loyalty once, but no more. Let her tighten his band until it severed his arm if she wished. He would be free no matter what it took.

Tess held the seeing stone up to one of her large, lustrously brown, ghille dhu eyes. Leaving the tote bag high in her branches, she fished out the snail shell once more and peered at it through the seeing stone. Thomas looked at the shell as intently as she did, but saw nothing other than its smoky pearl and the filigree of silver chased with the Queen's purple glimmers. There was a long, tense pause as she studied the shell, looking for all the world like a fae jeweler with a primitive loupe.

Her lips pursed, then a set of splintery wooden teeth showed in a snarl. The seeing stone fell to the floor.

"This is what she must have done to Stephen," Thomas

heard her whisper, her new voice like a whistling reed, beautiful and thin with music. "Who did you trap in this shell, Queen whatever *your* truename is? You'd just better hope I never learn it! Is this what happens to those whose bodies die? My brother Stephen's body is in the ground, but is his life—his soul—in one of *your things*? Dead but never dying?" She sobbed. "I can never bring him back now, even if this could be the way. Oh, the cruelty of you! Look. Look at what you've done!"

Tess held out her hand. The shell rocked in her spindly palm. Thomas could only see a swirl of smoky pearl inside it, but Tess the birch girl had looked through the stone. Glamour upon glamour upon glamour, covering, canceling, dispelling.

With a mournful wail, Tess closed her birch girl fingers around the shell, tightened them, and crushed it. White smoke poured out of her hand, drifting to the floor like the mists haunted by will-o'-the-wisps, pooling around her roots. She let fall the shards of the shell, which thinned like fast-melting ice.

Another strand of Thomas's armband broke and pierced his skin.

Not far away, he heard a sharp plinking sound, and saw Hunter raise a hand to his head, where one of the thorns had broken away. Its absence left a bleeding wound over Hunter's eyebrow. Hunter's fingertips explored it and his gaze flicked to Tess and fixed there.

The Queen turned from the goblets with a dreadful hiss,

swelling like an adder and then freezing in place.

For Tess had the bag in her grip again, one hand inside. The seeing stone was forgotten upon the floor. Thomas, disturbed by the way the wound in Tess's trunk still wept sap, scooped up the stone and tried to press it back in place—a rocky bandage, but he doubted it would work.

Tess ignored him, drawing a trinket from the bag and crushing it. And then another. Two more strands on Thomas's armband broke.

Hunter let out a roar of pain and triumph. "Yes! Yes, *all of them!*" he shouted. "Release us, all of us!"

Tess squeezed one after another. Where their pearly contents puddled, bluebells and moss, ferns and saplings began to grow in the floor of the Queen's chamber. The Queen herself was strangely immobile after her first reaction, studying Tess with a thoughtful gaze that gave Thomas shivers.

"Every. One. A soul." Tess squeezed, crushed. Chose another. Squeezed, crushed. She wept, walking awkwardly toward the Queen. Hunter moved slowly around the edge of the room, his staff in his hand, a dark smile on his face, blood trickling from a dozen cuts from the ribbons.

"Willingly given," the Queen said, unmoved. As Tess approached, the pixies fled to the chamber door, clustering there with thin cries of fear and loathing. "And now they are become what they longed for, as they would have done had you left them alone in Underbridge."

Squeeze. Crush. Blossom. Jangle. Plink.

"Tess, keep away from her," Thomas entreated. He bent, snatching up his oilskin and jerking it on. Nothing in it mattered now, not the nails, not his iron-edged knife. Whatever he tried here in the Queen's chamber would be of no avail. She knew him too well. She would see it coming and the depth of his bond with her would keep him from more active attempts. But if they could escape...

At another movement from Hunter, Thomas was on his guard once more. "Hunter, stay back!" He moved to keep between them, suddenly certain Tess would become the night's meat in his moment of inattention.

"I'm not afraid of you," Tess said to the Queen. She had not even looked at Hunter.

"Why would you be?" The Queen was poisonously sweet. "I am only making a better place for my people."

"By draining the lives of mine." Burst. Plink, jangle.

"Stop now, and I will let Thomas live."

That made Tess flinch, and she paused. Thomas halted with her, sliding a glance over his shoulder to make sure Hunter wasn't there with his staff, ready to make him stone or worse. But Hunter was edging along the room's side, intent upon the drama in the middle. His crown was ragged and skewed now, its shape held by very few golden razor ribbons and spikes.

"You haven't found them all, you know," the Queen said. "While you are here wreaking havoc and destroying my court, Underbridge is transforming."

Thomas imagined Underbridge consumed by Forest Park, as Tess's house had been. Bluebells along the riverbank, moss and ferns along the bridge, gleaming crystals taking root and growing like crazed plants. And everywhere the ivy, the Queen's spy network.

His house—his trow-hold—what would happen to it? Not that it mattered, if the Queen planned to kill him. The thing now was to make sure the Queen left Tess alive. He had never seen his Queen in such a cold fury, so controlled within her anger.

Tess looked at him, her fingers wrapped around a silvery chess piece. "They're inside, Thomas. Their souls. I could see them when I looked through the stone. She's taken away their lives to make more fairy earth."

So much magic, crammed into such tiny things. No wonder their release was overriding the binding on his arm, around Hunter's brow. No doubt the same thing was happening in the Queen's bed, where Aaron lay in his stupor, drained by his Queen. Thomas looked from Tess's hand to the Queen's face, avid in its focused attention.

The Queen spoke, still softly. "I will kill him. Choose, sister of Stephen. Life for Thomas, in exchange for the rest of my things. It seems an easy bargain, if you truly love him."

"You don't know what love is," Tess spat. "You haven't the first idea. You're mistaking greed and power for love. Just because you can make someone choose doesn't mean you should." She turned to Thomas, tears streaming from her beautiful ghille dhu eyes. "I'm sorry." The wheat-colored leaves fell from her birch-girl branches as she upended the bag. Her roots clutched at the skittering, precious little things, stamping and crushing them all at once. Her boots, pierced by her roots, thumped awkwardly on the floor, but they did the work. "I love you, Thomas, I'm so sorry!"

In the chaos of rising soul smoke and bluebell scent, Hunter laughed. He held in his hand the one trinket that had escaped Tess's destruction, the fir cone. The Queen rushed at him, her hands like claws, and Hunter spoke, blood pouring down his face where now only a single thorn held the crown on his head, cruelly plunged into the flesh above his right ear.

"Get your own meat, Queen of the Unseelie," he said, and crushed the cone in his fist.

The Queen froze.

In the silence, the severed golden thorn sang a thin, brittle note as it broke from the crown. It rang upon the floor bouncing, then settling, its tinkling notes fading only gradually. They all stared at it.

Thomas recovered first. He grabbed Tess's hand and dragged her to the chamber door, where the pixies were squeezing through the crack at the bottom. The Queen's attention and magic must have faltered, because Thomas was able to open the door a foot or so, shoving himself through the slender gap and pulling Tess after him, bending her branches, scraping her roots. Outside, the kelpies were milling, big-eyed at the chaos, leaving the floor wet and slippery with waterweed. Their eyes locked on the crack of the door and what else might burst through it, unconcerned once they recognized Thomas.

"Aaron!" Tess cried, hanging back, but Thomas took hold of her, staring into those dark, drowning eyes, ignoring the wild fury of the dance in the large cavern beyond the Queen's chamber.

"We've all made choices tonight, Aaron included. You and I are leaving while we can. We're going *now*."

"Will she come after us?" Tess wanted to know, her branches flailing.

Thomas didn't answer, because just then Hunter's broken, bloodied crown crashed against the doors and fell in the open gap. Inside the chamber there was an awful silence. Outside the chamber, a stillness fell over the dancing crowd in the crystal hall. All eyes turned toward the Queen's chamber, and light poured down from the ceiling far, far above as the trees opened the mound to the moon.

Allantide was well and truly upon them.

Tess looked at the crown, then to the place beneath his oilskin where Thomas's armband still circled his arm, held by no more than two or three strands of gold.

"All that, and you're still *hers*—" Her voice was loud in the uncanny silence.

"So are you," he said. Bitter, so bitter.

Inside the chamber, Hunter spoke. "Long and long I have waited. Long and long did you deny me, did you bind me. No more. Come to bed, or come to war. It makes no difference, but no longer shall you rule *me*."

"War, then," snarled the Queen.

A fresh stream of gibbering pixies spewed out the gap in the doorway, and inside the Queen's chamber there was a massive crack, as if the room had split. Hunter's staff, Thomas thought.

Thomas bent, picked up Hunter's crown, and flung it into the stilled mob. The eyes of all watched it rise and begin to fall, making way for it as it dropped. It struck the floor with a discordant jangle.

"There is your meat!" Thomas shouted into the hush. "Your Queen keeps not her faith with those she rules. The Wild Hunt bows to another now. Be ye warned!"

Silence reigned for another moment, then with a mighty roar, the fae began to move again. The spiral fell apart like leaves blown in the wind, and in its place clots and clumps of fae began to form.

The denizens of Forest Park were choosing sides.

Thomas caught Tess around the middle, lifting her from the

ground. She would never be able to keep up with him on her new roots, with her ruined shoes flopping. "Hang on, and keep your branches pulled in tight. I'm going to run as fast as I can, and the ceilings will be low." Thomas laughed crazily as he bowled over one of the Queen's kelpie guards and fled into the darkness of the nearest tunnel.

As he ran, Thomas wondered whether Hunter or the Queen would summon him next. Both would kill him, so it made no difference. For now, it was all he would ask of Allantide, to survive until dawn and get his love to daylight outside the mound.

≥ Chapter Thirty-Two ≤

Tess found it less sickening to close her eyes and not watch their perilous passage through the tunnels of Forest Park. Thomas ran so swiftly and changed direction so often that she was immediately confused. Instead of paying attention to the route, she concentrated on clinging to Thomas as best she could, lifting her feet—her roots—from the floor and keeping her branches from scraping the walls and ceiling. It wasn't easy, and it hurt.

Everything hurt, her heart most of all. While they ran, she wept. For Stephen, for Aaron, for Thomas, for herself. For all the souls whose possibility of restoration to life she had destroyed. Somewhere in Portland, the hearts in several people's bodies, soulless and empty, had probably ceased to beat at last. She had killed them as surely as the Queen would have done. But better to be fairy earth, she supposed, than to be imprisoned forever. In her own way, the Queen had the truth of it, even if it was not the truth Tess would have chosen.

After a time, it seemed that their path climbed steadily. A little after that, she thought the air might be more fresh, dew-damp, and chilly. Thomas burst out of the tunnel at last, racing past an ugly lump of something gray-green in the moonlight. The lump turned slowly to stare at them.

"*That's* a troll," Thomas panted. "You can see the difference for yourself." He put distance between them and the lumpen being, then slowed a fraction, his head turning from side to side as he ran. He mumbled to himself.

"Put me down," Tess said.

"It's here—right here somewhere—"

"What is? Put me down."

"The ley."

"The what? Thomas—"

"A fairy road. Like I said, we're leaving. There'd better not be anything coming this way on it, or by God I—there!" He turned sharply, headed once more uphill in the dark, moon-silvered forest. He halted in front of a monstrous Sitka spruce, one of the kind the Native Americans called council trees, using them as landmarks for meeting places or rituals. In its early youth, several of its branches had been trained outward and down before being permitted to grow upward. Others called them octopus trees, with their limbs reaching skyward like an enormous candelabra. Tess had never heard of one so close to Portland before, yet here it was. Thomas set her down, but didn't let go of her.

He pointed at the bowl-like base of the spruce. "The road starts here. This tree anchors this end. The ley will take us over the top of Forest Park and down the other side. We'll end up somewhere near the Columbia River."

Tess saw no road, just the black shape of the tree and the bone-white moon above. Around them amongst the dark trees were other birch girls, pale swaying forms who looked at her curiously, beckoning her to join them. The world was different, and it frightened her. Everything about this world frightened her—her new self most of all. She turned away from the birch girls to the only safety she knew: Thomas.

"No," she said to him, uncertain what she was objecting to, but feeling she must deny *something* this terrible night. Thomas merely took her in his arms, looking up into her branches for a long moment, and then he kissed her woody lips. She felt them soften beneath his, becoming tender, perhaps even human lips, and sobbed against his mouth.

He lifted his head and drew a finger down her cheek. "Trust me just a little longer. You saved my life from the Queen, now let me try and save yours." He took one step to the side, pulling her along.

An uncomfortable sensation, like a flood of ants crawling over her skin and biting, made all her hairs—*leaves, twigs,* she thought crazily—stand on end. Then they were whizzing through the black forest at a speed even greater than that of the Wild Hunt as it tore through Portland.

A massive fir tree came straight at them. Tess fainted.

When Tess opened her eyes, she lay across Thomas's lap, her

head and branches cradled in the bend of his arm and shoulder. The moon still shone on them, though from much farther west and lower on the horizon. The air smelled of fresh water, river weed and wet sand, and, somehow, dawn. Something lumpy was between them, and as she stirred, she realized it was her purse.

"I still have it," she mumbled. "Cross-body bags are the best." She picked a drooping bluebell off its strap and flung it away with distaste.

Thomas opened his eyes and gazed down at her. His back was against a large boulder. He looked unutterably weary in the moonlight, his skin gray and rough. The night was quiet around them.

"Did I wake you? I'm sorry."

"Still have what?" he asked her.

"My purse." She tried to sit up, and he let her. "Where are we?"

"At the far end of the ley, somewhere near the town of Clatskanie, I think." He gestured with his chin, and she glanced where he was looking. Not far from them an expanse of dark water rippled slowly past from right to left—east to west, she thought. "That's the Columbia. The fairy road ends here. It can't cross that much running water."

"Clatskanie!" It was still Halloween night, yet somehow on foot they had traveled more than sixty miles. She got to her feet and stumble-walked to the edge of the river. Her boots fell off as she went, but after one glance, she left them behind. Roots weren't meant to fit inside boots. The soft sand was soothing to her scraped and bruised roots, and as she got to the wetter sand, she realized she could *taste* its moisture through them. The Columbia tasted of tannins, green riverweed, marsh grass and the basalt gorge through which the river flowed. There was also a chemical tang she didn't recognize. She backed up quickly, thinking of fertilizer run-off from farms, storm water from drains, and who knew what else.

Birch girl.

She turned to look at Thomas, who still leaned against the rock, watching her. As tears welled in her eyes, she reached to brush them away, and smelled root beer. Birch sap, she thought crazily. Birch beer. She cried root beer tears now.

"Will she come after us?" Tess asked Thomas. "Will she chase us?"

"I don't know. If we can get to dawn without being caught, a lot of things will be different. Hunter will have to give up, for example. But he owes you a life debt because you set him free. That's one thing in our favor."

"It's not long until dawn. I can smell it."

He smiled a tired smile. "Can you now?"

She stretched out her branches, all of them, to their very tips, where the old-gold leaves trembled, and two or three fluttered loose. The fabric of her shirt and jacket snagged on her rough bark skin, but though the stretching hurt, it also felt good, even where her bark had been scraped away from their flight through the tunnels.

"So beautiful," Thomas said.

She looked at him for a long time, thinking of nothing, but feeling everything.

"I love you, Tess."

She covered her eyes with her hands, and this time, when the tears fell, they tasted of salt and her hands were soft human hands. So she was like Thomas, half fae, half human, and her glamour came and went without her bidding. She wondered if she'd fall into the wintersleep Thomas had mentioned as the Wild Hunt carried them along the mound, or if her half-human state would somehow make her different.

"Why did you do it, Tess? You worked so hard to save those people. Why did you crush the Queen's trinkets?"

Tess felt a rash of rough bark flaring along her jaw line, with anger and a terrible, bitter regret. A tired autumn birch leaf crackled against the lapel of her jacket where her ponytail lay over her shoulder.

How to explain to Thomas what she'd seen through the hole in the stone as she looked at the smoky soul trapped inside the snail shell? The desperate need of the residue of the person to be freed; her certainty that the person's corporeal body was long gone, and for the soul remaining inside, to be slowly drained like a battery when the Queen began to make new homes for her fae creatures, was the purest torture imaginable. Better to destroy them all, hopefully freeing them, and run the risk of crushing a trinket that held something of Aaron or Thomas in it, than leave those trapped souls to wither as Stephen had done.

She shook her head, asking instead, "Why don't you hate me, Thomas?"

"What, because your heart was true? Because you were still yourself, even under all that birch bark? Still the woman I fell in love with?"

She looked at him, the ugly trow, strong and beautiful to her now, all because he was Thomas. "Because I would have let you die if part of your soul had been in one of those trinkets. I chose—" she choked a little. "I didn't choose *you*."

"You did choose me. You just didn't realize it." He touched his arm, where only a few strands of the Queen's binding remained. "You freed me."

"Hunter's the one who's freed, not you."

Thomas shrugged. "It's nearly the same thing, I reckon. I've made my own choice. If she calls me again, I won't go. Freed."

Tess scrubbed at her face, where her tears smelled faintly of root beer again. She had to take a deep breath to call back her human self, and found it could be done. Not completely, but somewhat. She wasn't as sure as Thomas that he could ignore the call of his Queen, but she also wasn't sure the Queen still had her job, now that Hunter no longer did her bidding.

"It'll get easier, the glamour," Thomas said. He got to his feet and came to put his arms around her, careful not to step on her rooty bare toes.

"Promise?"

"Promise. I'll teach you."

She leaned against him. Her hair drifted upward, becoming twiggy, growing leaves. "I'm frightened. I don't want to be fae." Yet somewhere deep inside, she wondered if she wasn't fooling herself. Had the Queen seen through her to her deepest longings? Was this truly her heart's desire? She didn't want to be lonely any longer. Standing beside the strong-tasting Columbia with Thomas's arms around her, she felt a new sort of contentment like an undercurrent in her soul. Thomas was here with her. Loneliness seemed like a bad dream that was already fading.

"It's not so bad, being fae. Just different."

"Then why do you want to be human?"

He was silent for so long that she began to fear she was wrong—he didn't actually want to be human. When he spoke, his tone was thoughtful and quiet. "For a long time I only wanted to get back what she took from me. Beat her at her own game. Revenge." Thomas tipped her face up with a rough-skinned trow finger under her chin. "But lately, I wanted to be human for *you*."

"Oh," was all she could manage, but it made him smile, despite his exhaustion. He kissed her softly.

They stood twined together for a while. The smell of dawn grew stronger and the wind off the river slackened before it changed direction. "Are we safe?" she asked. "What are we going to do? Where will we go?"

"I might know a few places. Not the market, and not my trow-hold. Maybe not even Portland, not right away. We'll wait until we hear some news."

"What if the Queen—"

"We'll make plans. Over breakfast. How does that sound?"

"Let me guess. Milk and fresh bread?"

"Nothing better in the world." He grinned, all his big teeth showing. "Is there still a wallet in that famous cross-body bag of yours?"

Tess lifted the flap and reached inside with fingers that were rough with bark at the knuckles. Her wallet was still inside. "Yep."

"Then let's go see if Clatskanie has a grocery store open this early in the morning. I'm hungry."

"You'll have to do the buying. It might be awkward if a tree-girl walked into the store."

"It will be my pleasure."

Hand in hand, they put the Columbia at their backs and walked south through marsh grass and moss. From the east came the thin, faraway crow of a rooster.

Hunter chose not to be seated when his hounds—a motley mix of bogles, kelpies, redcaps and one ragged boggart—dragged Thomas Half-made and his fair lady, Tess, into Hunter's audience room. Hunter stood with his arms crossed. His wooden staff leaned against the arrangement of massive basalt hexagonal columns that served as his throne. He wore his crown of reeds, animal tails and dreadlocks, but his stag's head mask, with its broad rack of antlers, rested atop his throne like a crown itself.

King in the East, those who had followed him from Forest Park at Allantide had taken to calling him. His band of the solitary fae grew every day, as more and more slipped away from the Unseelie Queen's great mound west of the Willamette River. They came one at a time, or in pairs, arriving in the darkness, or just before dawn, when the humans of Portland slept. Hunter's halls lay beneath Mt. Tabor, an extinct cinder cone inside the city limits. From its top, he could see the long line of hills that bounded Portland to the northwest, and housed the Queen and her court.

At Hunter's left sat a squat basalt column. On its top was a brazier, and behind the brazier was the one fae Hunter knew would command Thomas Half-made's trust: Sharpwit the hob. She had once tended her grill in the goblin market beneath the Burnside Bridge, but at Allantide, the Queen's work was done and Underbridge became an outpost of the mound at Forest Park. Sharpwit, having heard of the war begun that night within the Queen's chambers, and the ill treatment of Thomas Half-made, had crept away from the market. Now she fed the fae in Hunter's halls, making do with raids into human kitchens and shops while she worked to establish her supplies of more traditional fare such as grubs and fungus.

The ragged boggart grinned wildly. Tess—for Hunter had learned her truename two weeks before on that fateful Allantide—marched in front of him, trussed in a coil of Hunter's own snare magic. The boggart's stone knife lurked at her ribs. Her torso and arms were wrapped like a spider's bundle.

Thomas Half-made, the Queen's former trow barrowguard and guardian of the goblin market, accompanied the boggart and the rest of Hunter's hounds. Thomas's fists opened and closed in pure impotent fury as the birch girl he loved struggled within the snare.

There had been no need to capture Thomas; only his beloved. It was as effective as capturing the half-human, half-trow brute, and far simpler.

Hunter smiled, and in that moment Thomas saw him.

In a flash Thomas was upon him, big hands at his throat. Hunter gave one stiff nod to the boggart, who prodded Tess's ribs with the handle of the knife.

Tess made a grunt of discomfort, then was silent. Her eyes blazed at Hunter. At the sound, Thomas froze and his grip loosened, though he did not release Hunter, and the pressure on Hunter's windpipe made him want to cough.

But Hunter knew his point had been made. By controlling Tess, Hunter controlled Thomas. It was Thomas he most wanted. Thomas whom he suspected had the skills he needed.

Still, he had to admire her. Of all of the humans the Queen had dragged through her chamber over the centuries, only this one had managed to best her. Hunter owed Tess his freedom, perhaps even a place in his Court, but unless she was clever enough to claim that debt, he would offer nothing. Humans often had no skill at bargaining with the fae, and Hunter saw no need to change that balance. Tess had been human when she first met the Queen, but the Queen had turned her into another of her half-mades, a birch girl part of the time, barely human the rest. The difference between Tess and Thomas was that Thomas still owed the Queen allegiance as long as her band of bone and gold was around his arm. Tess had no such allegiance, but her history with Hunter was dark and brief. She would not encourage Thomas to assist Hunter. Thomas had been the prey of the Wild Hunt that Allantide. At the time, he had been an obstacle in the path of

Hunter's plans.

Yet now he sought Thomas's knowledge and skill. It galled him to need another to solve a problem he should have been able to address, but Hunter could not allow the Queen's depredations to continue. He had to find a way to stop her from picking off, one by one, the fae who had fled with him to the east side of the Willamette River.

Another glance from Hunter and the boggart prodded Tess again. This time she took a hard, stamping step backward onto the boggart's foot in reaction. But boggarts were not bogles or goblins, and their feet were hard as horn. Hunter gave her grudging approval for the attempt. Then he shifted his gaze to Thomas.

"Release me, or my hound will use the sharp edge of his knife."

Thomas Half-made glared back at him for several long moments, but Hunter did not blink or flinch. Then the trow took a step back, but only one. "I wondered which of you would try to finish me first," Thomas growled. "You or the Queen. I have my answer. Let her go." His head tipped back to indicate Tess.

Hunter eased one leg onto the arm of his throne and shifted his weight. He opened his hands to show they were empty. "I would have requested your presence, but would you have come?"

"Of course not, you murderer!" Tess spat.

"She is fiercer than you," Hunter said idly to Thomas.

"Believe it," Tess replied.

Thomas's head turned to the right, where Sharpwit had a few autumn-curled slugs on skewers above the coals of her brazier. "Are you well, Sharpwit?"

"Aye," said the hob.

"Here of your own will?"

"Aye," she repeated.

"Not a prisoner?"

"Nay."

Thomas took another step back, wary confusion painted on his face. His heavy brows drew down. "Release the birch girl."

Hunter noted Thomas's care to avoid using Tess's truename. He resolved to do the same to demonstrate his willingness to negotiate. "Let us come to an agreement first, Half-made. Then I will release her."

"Agreement? I'll see you in hell first."

"That's as may be. But hear me. I require your skill with iron and ley lines."

"Another bargain?" Tess demanded. "I for one have had more than enough of fae bargains. The answer is no."

Thomas glanced over his shoulder at Tess, then back to Hunter. "I have the skill. But my price is high."

"Freedom from the Queen for you," Hunter said, nodding slowly. "And humanity for your birch girl."

Thomas's head tilted to one side, and Tess stilled behind him.

Good. Hunter had their attention now.